I0551937

Killdozer
Book 1
By Cory Gaffner

Editing Team: Cory Gaffner, Jerome Koger
Typography: Joshua Wagner

Killdozer
Copyright ©2018 by Cory Gaffner
All rights reserved.
No part of this work may be used or reproduced in any manner
whatsoever without written permission except in the case of brief
quotations embodied in critical articles or reviews.

**This is a work of fiction. All of the characters and
events portrayed in this book are fictional, and any
resemblance to real people or incidents is purely
coincidental.**

Other Books By Cory Gaffner

Oliver's Universe

Oliver's Wishes

Striker's Universe

Bullets and Sunshine
I'll Be Back: Griffin's Tale

Short Stories

Matchstick Mechanical (forthcoming)

Arbiter Core Universe

Killdozer
Killcycle (forthcoming)

Chapter 1

"Hankey baby, there is someone at the door."

"Chill your tits woman, I'm getting up."

The sound of Hank's voice in the morning always surprised him. It normally sounded like he was gargling marbles when he spoke because his voice was such a deep and broken baritone, but in the mornings it sounded like he was gargling broken glass. At least until he got the drink in him. Hank figured this was one of the side effects of already having a deep voice and then shouting at work crews on various construction sites for over a decade. *Where did I leave that drink anyway? Ah, there it is...* thought Hank. Half a bottle of lukewarm malt liquor from the night before, he guzzles it all down in one giant gulp.

"Ew hankey, that's nasty."

"You just aren't use to being around a real man. Now get up and get out woman, unless you are making breakfast. If you are cooking you can stay awhile."

"Oh Hankey you are so funny!"

The pounding on his door resumed, **BANG BANG BANG**. He wondered if the lot-lizard knew he wasn't joking. Hank looked around for some pants or boxers in the mess of beer cans, dirty clothes, and used condoms from the night before, but gave up when he heard even more pounding at his door. Oh well, if they were going to bang on his door like that then they should be prepared for the consequences.

Hank stomped over to his front door, not because he particularly wanted to stomp, but because Hank was huge. Hank also didn't particularly care about being lithe or stealthy, it just wasn't his style, so his walking kind of always sounded and looked like someone stomping. He had solved every problem in life by being bigger than everyone else. He didn't have many problems to begin with though, he was generally polite and minded his own business. Hank didn't know it, but it was his lawyer Saul who was at the front door, coming to give him some very bad news. Hank ripped the front door open while shouting "What?" Let's be honest, whoever had come to bang on Hank's door was interrupting some potential morning nookie, and this made Hank disgruntled.

"Aw Jesus, Hank put some pants on please. For the love of all that is holy cover that thing up," said Hank's lawyer Saul.

"Saul my man, sorry for the surprise from Hank Jr. Give me some good news."

"I'm afraid I can't... They won Hank."

At the news, Hank grabbed a chair from his dining room table and lobbed it across the house while he screamed in frustration. The chair landed in the drywall sideways, legs first. The legs sank so deeply into the wall that it stayed in place, seemingly floating in the air. The woman who was in Hank's bedroom chose that time to come out and make some coffee. She was holding a sheet with one arm over the front of her body in false modesty.

"Hankey baby, you want coffee?" she asked.

"Why does no one in this house have clothes on?" asked Saul.

"Those sons of bitches, how did we lose?" asked Hank.

"It was Eugene Tillerman again, his fingers are sunk too deep into... Well everything really. I'm 90% sure he paid off the town council. My one witness clammed up all of a sudden as well. I don't know if he paid her off or threatened her, but she retracted her testimony," said Saul.

What Saul and Hank were discussing was a rare town charter that hadn't been used in over 50 years. The town council had pulled the archaic and tyrannical piece of legislation out of the town's archives and put it into play in order to claim a rare form of eminent domain which they would be using to steal Hank's land and business out from under him. Hank ran the town gravel yard which he had inherited from his father. Hank only had a few loves in his life and his gravel business was one of them. It was also his last real and tangible connection with his father who had passed away a few years earlier to "complications," which meant the Agent Orange his father had been exposed to when he was killing communists in Vietnam had finally caught up to him, God rest his soul.

Ever since he was a boy Hank had loved the gravel yard. He loved helping around the gravel yard too, hauling gravel, organizing gravel, loading gravel, showing customers the different types. He loved the striations in the rocks, the colors, the textures, the variety. Hank loved rocks and gravel because he was very much like a rock himself; big, hard, quiet, and heavy. He felt at home in the gravel yard like nowhere else in the world.

The gravel yard was where Hank had gone from being a boy to being a man. When times were tough Hank's father would do free boulder and rock removal from people's land. His father would drag the enormous rocks to the gravel yard where he would hand Hank a sledgehammer and tell him "Make gravel boy," and Hank did. Hank loved making big rocks into small rocks. Swing after swing, and year after year. As he swung the sledge his arms became larger. His body became harder. His father made sure to feed him giant hardy helpings of seasoned steak and fresh milk which caused Hank to grow even further. As Hank aged, his sledgehammer strikes hit harder, his swings became elongated and confident. He loved the feeling of going up against a seemingly immovable and unbreakable object and utterly destroying it.

Even when their business was booming and they could afford to buy their gravel from local mines and other sources, Hank still loved breaking boulders. He eventually started a side business when he was younger and got his driver license. His side business was for large rock removal. He was the cheapest rock-remover within a two hundred mile radius. He could afford to charge just small fees for the service since he was mixing business with pleasure and creating inventory for his father.

He loved the process of driving great lengths to discover what kind of unruly boulder he would have to load onto his old truck. Each new boulder was a potential battle that he knew he would win. How would he do it? Would he have to break it up a little on the spot to get it to fit into the bed of his truck? He loved the faces of the people who had called him, expecting to see a team of men arrive to haul away their rock and to their surprise only finding him. He especially loved the people that doubted he would be able to accomplish the task on his own, he loved proving them wrong.

He would take the large rocks back to the gravel yard just like his father had done for him when he was boy, and then break them apart. It was his hobby, his workout, and his job. His father would even pay him a fair price for the gravel that he created, those were good times for Hank. He only took breaks to spend time with the many young women who were throwing themselves at him in high-school. All of the work in the gravel yard, breaking rocks in the sun, had turned Hank into a muscular and bronzed Adonis. Top that off with his buzz-cut of blonde hair and shockingly blue eyes, it was enough to drive any red-blooded woman crazy.

This pissed off the local football team something fierce. Angry that Hank was spending time with half the women in the high-school they decided to come after him and "teach him a lesson." Half the football team ambushed him at the lake one weekend where he had been taking the most beautiful girl in school there on a date; Suzanne, or Suzie Q for short. The "Q" stood for cute, but she was anything but cute, she was stunning in a classic way. She was the type of woman who woke up in the morning beautiful, the type of woman who men wrote songs about and fought wars over. Hank and her had been dancing circles around each other for a long time at that point, both knowing they were beautiful and unyielding. Both not wanting to be the first one to break down and approach the other.

Hank broke first as men often do in the face of beautiful and unattainable women. He brought a giant bouquet of flowers to school one day his senior year and waited for her in front of her locker. When she saw him standing there in his in his usual blue jeans and tight yellow tank top with his father's companies name on it "Steel Gravel," her breath caught in her throat and she felt electricity in the air. Some part of her knew she was in love with Hank, even then. She couldn't let him know that though. Hank was a conqueror of regular women, if he sensed weakness he would move on. She had to maintain an air of unattainability. She slapped her best coy smile on her face and walked over to him.

"It took you long enough. Pick me up on Saturday at 8." She had told him, and then she walked away swaying her hips.

Leaving him there with a view of perfection. She couldn't resist glancing once behind her to see if he was looking. He was, with his mouth slightly opened, stunned, still holding the flowers in his hands which she hadn't even bothered to take.

That Saturday the date had been going great. They were laying in the bed of Hank's truck talking about anything and everything, stealing glances at each other often, smelling the scent of one another. They were both completely enthralled with one another as young lovers often are. Then they heard the vehicles coming. They both stood up to see over ten vehicles surrounding Hank's truck at the edge of the lake, blocking all paths of escape. There was a mixture of cars and trucks carrying randoms students from the school and most of the football team. The biggest instigator among the high-school boys, the once then captain of the football team, the one who had been getting everyone riled up and angry at Hank, stepped forward. It was none other than Eugene Tillerman, the man who was now paying off town officials to steal Hank's land and business.

Eugene shouted while hiding in a crowd of his peers from the football team, "We are tired of you Hank. You take all the prettiest girls and leave none for us. We rule this high-school. All you do is fail classes and peddle gravel. It isn't fair that some peasant like you is stealing our women. It's high time we teach you a lesson."

Hank couldn't believe it. He harbored no ill will towards these men. He always treated his dates with respect and left them happier than when they had found him, he didn't know what he had done to make these guys mad. Hank knew that despite all of the exercise that these guys did for the football team that he was much bigger and much stronger than most of them. He didn't want to accidentally hurt them in a fight.

9

"I don't want any trouble. Please leave," shouted Hank. No one had ever accused Hank of being a master of diplomacy.

"We aren't leaving until you learn to leave our women alone. Get em boys!" Shouted Eugene.

The two largest bruisers from the team stepped forward, one black, one white. Jerome Johnson and Joe Buckley. These two were notorious steroid abusers and it showed. Their Letterman jackets barely stretched over their bulging muscles and ever expanding backs. Small town football is a big deal in America, especially back when Hank was in high-school. As long as the team was winning the coaches and faculty looked the other way when it came to a little steroid abuse or switching out a failing grade for a barely passing one.

"Jerome, Joe, please don't do this," said Hank.

Jerome and Joe started approaching Hank while cracking their knuckles. Hank jumped from the bed of his truck and landed hard. Some of the young men from the football team swore they felt the ground shake a bit. Hank was very dense.

"Last chance guys, please turn around and go home. Hell, I'll even send you guys away with enough money to buy a 12 pack of beer if you leave now," said Hank.

He noticed as they got closer though that their eyes were a little glazed over, these guys were abusing more than just steroids. Hank knew then that these guys wouldn't be holding back. This had just become a fight for his life. Hank wondered if he should get the sledgehammer from the inside of his truck, or the rifle he kept in the window rack that he hunted deer with, until he looked down at his fists. They were large and callused, lined and creased from years of hard work. His hands were rock solid and heavy. Hank didn't need a weapon for this fight. Hank *is* a sledgehammer, Hank *is* a weapon. If the football team wouldn't have peace, then Hank would give them war.

Hank started walking towards the big bruisers which confused everyone. He walked towards Joe Buckley first hoping to single him out, but these two bruisers were used to working as a team. So Jerome oriented his body as well to intercept Hank. Hank picked up speed and so did the bruisers. The three men collided like the titans of old. This wasn't some back alley brawl, these were living gods smashing into each with the force of small vehicles and the confidence of known immortality that only the young and the dumb have. Between the three of them they represented about a thousand pounds of muscle and fury. At first it was an insane melee, the three tumbled to the ground trying to gain superiority on one another, raining down blows. Jerome and Joe were high on whatever was being peddled by the local drug dealers in the small town and at first didn't feel Hank's fists and knees as he rained them onto them over and over again.

Soon the divide between Hank and the two bruises became evident to everyone watching. Hank's muscles were hard earned and well honed. They had been earned over a lifetime of destroying things that man was never designed to destroy. Joe and Jerome had gained their muscle over the last few years through the use of steroids and lifting weights in a controlled environment. Even with the help of the pain reducing narcotics flowing through them, the slams of Hank's heavy fists, elbows, and knees began to feel sharper and harder as the brawl went on. Hank was able to regain his feet first as Joe and Jerome started to shift their strategy to defense. That's when Hank did something that surprised everyone that night. Before Joe Buckley could regain his footing Hank grabbed his ankle, and like Hercules himself Hank spun Joe as hard as he could and let go

11

when Joe was facing the forest. Joe bounced along the ground for at least 13 feet before finally wrapping his midsection around a tree and losing consciousness.

The smarter young men of the football team knew then and there that this wasn't a fight they could win. They were able to snap out of the spell woven upon them by the hateful words of Eugene and their inner cavemen telling them to protect their women. They were about to see this situation for what it was; they had come here to beat an innocent man and the plan was failing horribly. They couldn't beat Hank two on one, Hank knew it, Jerome knew it, and Eugene knew it.

"Everyone dogpile him!" shouted Eugene, and they sure tried. About six of them came forward, the ones that had been drinking before coming here and the ones that had the most testosterone boosted false bravado. If Hank thought they were playing for keeps before, now he knew it down to the marrow in his bones. He could see the hatred in Eugene's eyes. Suzie Q. watched the madness unfold with an elevated view since she was standing in the back of Hank's truck bed still. She saw something that even Hank couldn't see, Eugene grabbed an empty bottle of beer and broke it over the corner of a brush-guard on one of the trucks. He was aiming to stab Hank! Suzie wasn't sure if Hank would be able to fight off seven attackers plus Eugene trying to stab him. She knew she had to help.

Back at the fray, Hank was breaking arms and wrists left and right while backpedaling ever closer to the lake. If he let the angry young men surround him he knew it would be over for him. He had to keep this fight at a range. Finally he felt the ground behind him begin slope down as he retreated while throwing straight kicks and the occasional jab. He knew the lake was close behind him and dark thoughts swirled through his head of the possibility of Jerome holding his head under the water while the other young men kicked him to death. He hadn't felt fear like that since he was a child. This fear came to a dark swirling mass in his core where something new was born… Righteous anger.

Who were these men to try to attack Hank on one of the best nights of his life, and for what? Having too much fun? Hank grabbed the closest football player by the belt and tucked his chin into his chest knowing he was going to take some punches to the face to pull this move off. He yanked the man forward via his grip on the man's belt. As the man came forward he threw all kinds of jabs at Hank's chiseled face. Hank sprang up and threw his knee straight into the man's sternum, he felt it crack, one less in the fight. From that point he tried to shift the fight so that they were moving horizontally to the shore instead of back towards the lake, the thought of being held under the water still worried him. Two came at him at once, angry at what he had just done to their friend. Hank straight kicked one as hard as he could directly above the man's knee and the man went down crying, another one out of the fight.

The second one fell back on his football training and tried to lean his body low and tackle Hank, but again Hank the Rock Breaker was just too dense. The tackle only staggered Hank ever slightly, and he did not go down. He roared like a wild bear and brought both of his fists down onto the man's back who was still trying to push him over. The man let out a very undignified yelp of pain and fell down, another one down. Hank decided to pick on someone who was in a much lower weight class than him for the first time in his life. He grabbed the smallest one in the bunch, planted a fist deep in the man's stomach and then lobbed him into the lake using the back of the man's belt as a grip.

13

Suzie was jogging to catch up to the mad melee now. She could see the dark look in Eugene's eyes, she knew she didn't have long. She heard bones breaking in the middle of the crowd where she also knew that Hank was fighting for all he was worth. She saw Eugene trying to circle the crowd to try and sneak in and stab Hank like an opportunistic predator. She caught up to the group and managed to sneak up behind Eugene, her plan was to yank the bottle out of his hand, that's it. She didn't want trouble, she just didn't want anyone to die tonight. She lunged for the bottle and locked her hands around Eugene's wrist, on the arm he was carrying the bottle with. Eugene spun on her, anger flashed through him and he threw his arm outward hard. The broken bottle sliced across Suzie's face and her scream was sent out through the night.

The remaining men that were attacking Hank stopped and spun around, curious to what the noise was. They saw Eugene standing there with a bloodied bottle in his hand, and the town beauty queen at his feet clutching her face trying to staunch the blood flow. All of the fight went out of them, all of the anger they had for Hank transferred onto Eugene. The giant Jerome was the first to speak, "WHAT DID YOU DO!" he shouted. Hank barreled through the men that were standing around to get to Suzie. He picked her up and cradled her in his arms. He didn't know much about first aid, but men got hurt around the gravel yard and he knew enough to keep pressure on the wound and to wrap it. He took off his shirt and started biting strips off of it. He used the strips to wrap her face and keep pressure on the wound. Her hands slipped at one point and he saw the cut ran straight from her forehead, over one of her eyes, and finally terminated around her chin, it was bad. He prayed to whatever god was up there that she wouldn't lose the eye.

That's when he sensed motion moving behind him, it was Eugene. He was trying to sneak off of the scene. Hank lifted Suzie up cradling her like a small child against his large frame. He looked at Jerome and spoke with the authority that can only come with grief and shock.

"GET OVER HERE, TAKE HER TO THE HOSPITAL NOW!" He shouted, and he gently handed Suzie off. Then he started slowly walking towards Eugene. Eugene, who was trying to hide among the trees and other onlookers. Eugene who had instigated this whole mess.

"Where do you think you are going!" Hank shouted for all to hear. Eugene looked around knowing he was being judged by his peers. If he didn't take Hank's challenge, if he ran, he would always be thought of as the town coward. He knew Hank was much bigger than him, he knew Hank would probably beat him in a fight… well maybe not, what if he cheated?

Eugene slowly shifted the broken bottle he was still carrying until it was behind his back. He tried to make the gesture seem non-obvious so he could lure Hank into a false sense of confidence.

"Oh you actually want to fight now, you were so busy running and crying before. I thought you had learned your lesson," said Eugene. Hank didn't say anything, he just kept resolutely marching forward. Eugene waited until Hank was right in front of him and then slashed out at Hank, cutting an angry red line across Hank's chest. Hank didn't even acknowledge the wound. He grabbed the hand Eugene had the bottle in and then squeezed until he felt his hand start to break. Hank was nice enough to let him drop the shards of glass from the bottle before he continued to squeeze. Eugene futilely beat on Hank's chest with his hand that Hank wasn't crushing. Hank didn't care though.

15

All Hank could see was red and the image of Suzie holding her beautiful face as blood pooled around her hands.

Hank roughly threw Eugene on the ground like so much trash. Eugene knew then that all of his plans had gone terribly wrong. Hank began to systematically punch every inch of Eugene. He only took one break to say something that Eugene would remember for the rest of his life.

"If you ever hurt a woman again. I'll come to you, wherever you are, and I'll kill you." Then he began to beat Eugene again. Relentlessly the blows never stopped, some of the onlookers gasped in horror at the horrific beating. One of Eugene's sycophants rushed in and tried to help him, Hank effortlessly punched the man in the stomach so hard that it would cause internal bleeding. The man fell off to the side and then Hank calmly resumed his beating until Eugene stopped crying out. Only then did he stop, when he knew Eugene was completely unconscious and wouldn't be awake to feel the pain. Eugene had needed to be punished, he had needed this beating.

Eugene's friends hesitantly approached Hank who was standing over Eugene now with his fists dripping in blood. One of the women who Hank had been on a few dates with was the only one brave enough to approach Hank.

"Hank, we have to take Eugene to the hospital now, okay?" Hank didn't respond to her, he just quietly walked away and got into his truck. He drove straight to the hospital where they were keeping Suzie Q. He ran straight through the ER shouting her name. The nurses on staff tried to chase the shirtless man with the seeping chest wound, Hank noticed them but he had no care for himself at this point, he had to find her. He saw Jerome standing confused covered in mud from their scuffle and blood from Suzie.

"Where is she?" he shouted. Jerome just pointed to a curtained off section down the hall he was in. Hank kept running with the nurses still chasing him, and in his haste he almost barreled over a man of small stature, a very serious looking man. The man grabbed his arm and never let go.

"Stop right there young man."

"Excuse me sir, let me go please. My friend is hurt I'm trying to get to her."

"That friend you are talking about is my daughter. Look at me," Hank did stop to assess the man. He could see some of the same features he loved in Suzie on this man, high cheekbones, a pert nose, the hazelnut hair, etc. Before Hank could ask him where Suzie was the man began to speak.

"Hank, listen to me. You are going to stay far away from my daughter. I do not give you permission to see her. If I hear about you coming anywhere near her I will call the police. Leave this hospital right now, or I will personally see you in handcuffs before the end of the night."

Hank wasn't sure what to do. He wanted to run to Suzie to check on her and offer any support he could, but this was her father. For a split second something rushed through him, the thought of pushing Suzie's father to the floor and finding Suzie anyway, but he threw that thought away. That's not who he was, Hank Sr. had taught him better than that. Hank tried to plead with the man instead.

"Sir I--"

"LEAVE!" shouted Suzie's father with his finger pointed towards the exit.

"Yes sir." said Hank, resigned, for now…

As he walked back through the halls of the hospital the frantic nurses caught up to him and began expertly addressing his chest wounds.

The next day the police came and arrested Hank. The night before he had spilled his heart out to his father and told him everything. His father had sat quiet for a while and simply said,

"You did what you had to do junior." After that his father had told him, warned him really, that he might be arrested. Hank sat quietly in his cell for two days. He did push ups and sit ups occasionally, but mostly he just sat perfectly still. Sometimes he sat so still he scared the guards. After the second day they released him. The investigative team that checked out the lake had ruled what Hank had done self-defense. This decision wasn't made lightly by the investigators. A few investigators had even been bribed by Eugene's well-to-do parents to "find" more evidence against Hank, but so many of the onlookers from that night had come forward and stated so clearly that Hank had been the victim. When you have over 30 witnesses saying the only reason Eugene and the football team went to the lake was to beat Hank senseless, there really isn't much you can do.

Eugene escaped prosecution with more payoffs from his parents and had to finish the school year in the next county over as part of whatever plea deal his parents had made. Though he couldn't leave a hospital bed for a month after the beating Hank had given him. Hank tried to visit Suzie a couple of times at her house, but each time her father ran him off. She was in and out of reconstructive surgeries the rest of that school year, and the doctors did end up saving her eye. Hank graduated and went off for a short stint in the military, never having resolved things with Suzie. When he got back from his time in the military he actually ran into Suzie at the bank in the small town they lived in, she was

18

working there as a teller. Suzie had treated him cordially, but coldly.

A few weeks later he got a letter in the mail from the courts, it was a restraining order stating that he had to stay away from Suzie. Hank was confused and hurt at the news of the restraining order. He didn't know why Suzie would do something like that to him. He could never figure out why she had burned him so badly, broken his heart really. He had thought about her often when he was away in the military, she was kind of 'the one that got away.' It was then that Hank decided he would never really settle down. He wasn't a one woman man. People were fickle, women included and he couldn't expect people to live up the same standards he lived by, so he wouldn't. He wouldn't get emotionally invested, he wouldn't give people a chance to hurt him anymore. He would become even more like the rocks he spent so much time around.

After that time seemed to slip by. Hank worked with his father in the family business. Hank built his body. Hank bedded beautiful women from all around. His life was good, if predictable. Until now of course, now Eugene was back. Eugene had finally forgotten the lesson that Hank had beaten into him. You don't bully people, and you especially don't bully Hank. Eugene would need another lesson...

"Eugene again! I'll find him and rip him in half!" Hank shouted at his lawyer Saul.
"You can't do that Hank. He has half the cops in town on his payroll and he has heard about your... less than reputable past. The man isn't dumb... he has off duty cops protecting him; if you attacked him now it would be even easier for him to steal your land and business. The media would paint you as a criminal and

him as a martyr. Take the money the town is offering and get a fresh start somewhere else, besides your life doesn't look so bad from where I am sitting," said Saul who was openly staring at the woman who was making them coffee, still wearing nothing except a thin sheet.

Chapter 2

When Saul had referenced Hank's 'less than reputable past,' he was talking about a small time frame where Hank had worked as an *equalizer or peacekeeper,* of sorts. Shortly after Hank had come home from the Army he was approached with the offer of a lot of money if he worked for one of the loan sharks in town. At first Hank had balked at the idea until he actually sat down and talked to the loan shark, who was known simply as Jimmy around the town. You see, criminals often go by aliases or refuse to give out their last names to people to make it harder for law enforcement to chase them or eventually prosecute them. *Well there are lots of people named Jimmy, are you sure it was this Jimmy?* That kind of thing.

Hank's first blatant refusal to work for Jimmy didn't dissuade him at all. Jimmy always took the "sweet" over the "sour" approach. So one night while Hank was out hunting for women, Jimmy found him and he offered to cover Hank's bar tab if he would sit down and just listen to a more in-depth explanation of the job. Hank didn't particularly like drinking, but in his mind you don't turn down something that is free and there was no point in being rude while this guy was buying.

Jimmy had explained that what he did, while illegal, was a much needed enterprise. Men in their small town gambled their money away at the local Indian casino from time to time. Then they used Jimmy's loans to pay their bills until their next paychecks could come in, at which point they would set everything right. All the while keeping their wives in the dark about their tenuous financial situations, thanks to Jimmy of course. He didn't advertise his business, only people in real need came to him and he had a pretty low interest rate compared to any other loan shark in the area. The people he gave loans to had such terrible credit that they couldn't get a loan anywhere else. Without Jimmy these people would be completely out of options, or forced to leverage some vital piece of their lives as collateral in a traditional loan... Yea, randomly using the family car as collateral… That's the kind of thing that causes the wife to take the kids and stay at her bitch sister Linda's house. Nobody likes Bitchy Linda.

Jimmy hated violence, and he hated blood. This is where Hank would come in. All Jimmy needed was for Hank to stand around and look big and scary. Not even on a full-time basis, just on occasion or when Jimmy knew he had a particularly tough customer coming in. Jimmy also promised that he would never send Hank to collect a debt. He simply needed his presence at the "office". Hank had become somewhat of a local legend after his night at the lake where he kicked half the football teams ass, and there were whispers that Hank had done some pretty dark deeds when he was with the military. Jimmy needed Hank's folklore legend to protect his investments, and to stop the local idiots from trying something stupid.

Hank begrudgingly agreed to take Jimmy's job on a trial basis under the implication that he would leave if things weren't above board, well as above board as an illegal loan shark business could be. Jimmy and Hank were polar opposites. While Hank was tall, handsome, muscular, blonde, and quiet. Jimmy was of average height, had a very average face with a nose that you could tell had been broken one too many times. Jimmy's hair was jet black and long, tied back into a ponytail most of the time. Jimmy was also skinny as a bean pole and loved to talk, which drove an even sharper contrast between him and Hank, since Hank was a man of such few words.

Despite their differences, Hank soon found himself becoming fast friends with Jimmy. As long as Hank made sure Jimmy was safe, Jimmy didn't really care what Hank did. So Hank mostly found himself with a bar floozy or two in his lap, stroking his giant muscles or something else on occasion. Hank eventually became such a fixture in Jimmy's office that Jimmy had a top of the line weight bench installed for him. When people originally heard that Hank was Jimmy's new muscle they couldn't wait to pay their outstanding debts. The mere thought of having Hank break your legs made most debtors come running back to Jimmy, begging to pay in full. Hank was good for business. Hank didn't cause problems or get drunk, and Hank's motivations were clear: he liked beautiful women and getting bigger. These things were easy for Jimmy to provide.

Male friendship was a new concept for Hank. The same reasons that made most men hate Hank or feel uncomfortable around him, just made Jimmy like Hank more. It became more than just a business relationship for them both, a friendship was born out of trust and mutual respect. Hank respected Jimmy because of the way he ran his business. Jimmy never went out of his way to hurt people and he only hurt people who really deserved it. Much in the same way that Hank had to hurt Eugene that night at the lake. Some people don't want to learn until you give them a few bumps and bruises. Jimmy could see the dark intellect hiding behind Hanks mounds of muscles, and Hank knew it. This also made Hank like Jimmy, he enjoyed people that saw him as more than just a slab of meat.

23

All of this came to a screeching halt when Hank's dad got sick. Old Agent Orange had finally caught up with him, along with whatever other medical evils lurked in the humid jungles of Vietnam. The symptoms built up quickly in Hank's father and knocked a once thriving and tanned workhorse down to a husk of what he once was. He was moved from the hospital back to his small house that tucked neatly into the back of the gravel yard, and was quickly put on in home hospice care. Hank had to keep skipping more and more shifts at Jimmy's to take care of his father or just to spend time with him. Jimmy understood and even picked up the tab for most of the hospital bills.

One of the nights that Hank sat next to his father in the hospital bed that the hospice had moved into their house, his father had pulled him close. Hank stared deep into his father's face, noticing the sunken cheeks, the pallid skin, and the rheumy eyes. He knew his father had only days left to live. When he was close enough his father whispered something to him, something important.

"Hank, I bought this land and started this business for you. I took all of the money I earned in the military and I built this business from the ground up. So I would have something to leave behind, for you. My father, your grandfather, he didn't do this for me. You see, I swore I wouldn't repeat the same mistakes that my father made with me. I tried to raise you right Hank. In a harsh world where people are chewed up and spit out, I made a rock and a man of morals. Don't stop being who you are. Stand up for what you believe in and never let anyone push you around." His father had to stop to take a few deep breaths of pure oxygen from a mask he had tied to one of the rails on the bed. Hank patiently waited for his father to continue. When his father looks a little calmer he continued.

"Use this business that I built to finance a good life for yourself. If you run it right it can provide jobs for the people in this town who need them, and it can uplift our family for generations. Don't spoil this gift. Lastly, you should have a child. It has been my greatest honor to have you in my life, to watch you grow. To know that our family will continue on. I know that girl Suzie hurt you something fierce son, but it's time to open your heart again. If you really can't do that then there is always adoption right? Raise a good person, the world needs more good people."

Hank's father had to stop and cough into a handkerchief. When he pulled it away from his mouth Hank could see there was blood on it. Hank's father stared at him and waited, Hank got the cue.
"Yes father, I will," said Hank, his father smiled.

Hank stayed sitting at this father's bedside most of the night, just remembering all of the good things that his father had taught him and showed him through the years. Hank was staring at his father's gaunt face and remembering the wily Army combat veteran that had amazed him, inspired him, and shown him a love that other children would never know. Around 3 a.m., Hank heard a strange noise around the front door of their house. His father had heard it too in a rare moment of lucidity, they both didn't speak. Being veterans they knew to stay quiet and keep the element of surprise. Hank gave his father the hold symbol with his fist, meaning that his father should stay in bed. His father nodded. Hank's father's room was the only room in the house with a light on it so when he went into his living room it was pitch black, he backed into a corner and waited for his night vision to adjust as he listened to the strange scratching like sound at his front door.

Hank had eyes on his front door from his position. As soon as he felt his eyes adjust to a point he was comfortable with he noticed the deadbolt on his front door slowly slide into the 'open' position. Then his door handle started to jiggle and he heard the scratching noise again. Hank realized what was happening, someone was picking his locks! They had already got the deadbolt, all they had to do was pick the door handle and they would be in his home. That meant the person was likely on their knees outside with their hands full for at least a few more seconds. Hank considered for a brief second going to get one of his father's guns, but he was just too angry at that point, and he knew the lockpicker would be off guard. Hank quietly moved over to the front door and then ripped it open. Sure enough, there was a man in a full black balaclava knelt down in front of his door, with a lockpick set in his hands.

Hank quickly realized his mistake when he saw the man behind the lock-picker pointing a gun at his chest. Hank grabbed the one on his knees and held him in front of him like a shield as the gunman opened fire. Hank felt a burning in his chest and knew he hadn't been quick enough, he'd been hit. He also felt round after round smack into the man he was holding up in the air who had a very distinct look of fear and pain on his face. Hank heaved the man he was holding as hard as he could toward the gunman. Hank's massive strength sent his impromptu projectile right on target and the men collided. The one who had been shooting lost his gun during the collision and Hank saw it skitter across the gravel in the front of his house.

Hank took one look at the gun and the gunmen knew Hank could get to it first. So instead of going for it, the gunman opted instead to try and run away from Hank. Hank considered retrieving the gun from the gravel and killing the man, but he wanted answers. He quickly looked around the doorway of his house for something to use, his eyes landed on the old antique wooden coat rack that his father had picked up somewhere. He grabbed the coat rack and sprinted after the escaping shooter. The shooter was skinny and was quickly losing Hank, so Hank did the only thing he could do. He ripped the few hats and coats off the rack and then threw it like a spear. Hank's strength more than made up for the lack of aerodynamics on the coat rack and it flew true. It struck hard directly in the middle of the gunman's back and sent the man face first into the rock infused dirt of the gravel yard.

Hank caught up to the man who was holding his arm, which was bent at a very unnatural angle. The man saw Hank coming and tried to play the victim.

"You broke my arm!"

"Don't be a pussy. Besides you shot me, I think we are even," said Hank as he rubbed his hand around the new hole in his chest checking to see if it was bleeding and how bad it was.

"Now, tell me why you are here before I break a broom handle off in your ass."

"You are Jimmy's main muscle. We have to take you out so Jimmy won't have no protection. It's just a job man, it's nothing personal."

"Right, well have fun spending the rest of your life in prison. I hear they make great cock-meat sandwiches there, I bet you will love the taste."

Hank roughly grabbed the man and dragged him by the collar of his jacket back to his father's house. That man whimpered and tried to keep his broken arm from bouncing around too much.

Hank knew the man was in an extreme amount of pain, but when you play stupid games, you win stupid prizes. And attacking Hank is ALWAYS a stupid game. Once Hank was inside he yelled back to his father that the house was clear and that he was okay. His first call was to Jimmy to warn him that men were in town to kill him. Jimmy picked up on the first ring and didn't interrupt as Hank explained the situation. Jimmy thanked Hank profusely, but Hank told him he had to go. The urge to kill the man who had shot him was real, but he would honor his father's wishes and try to be a good man. So he called the police next.

Soon his house was swarming with police, and investigators were interviewing him as paramedics worked on his chest. A cute paramedic female let him know that it was a clean through and through, and she slipped her number on a piece of paper into his hand when her colleagues weren't watching. They told him he needed to go the hospital, but Hank would drive himself later. The last thing he needed was a giant bill from riding in an ambulance, especially when his truck worked just fine. When the investigators got to him, he kept his mouth shut mostly. No need to self-incriminate, even though Hank wasn't particularly sure he had even done anything illegal. One of the investigators was a pretty woman in her late 30's. She had kept a neutral face throughout Hank's explanation of events of the night. Once she had basically ruled Hank's actions as self-defense in her own mind she dropped her 'all-business' facade and asked Hank more about the part of the story that had been nagging at her.

"So let me get this straight. You killed the first guy with your bare hands, and the second one you stopped with a coat rack?"

"No ma'am, the gunman shot the first one, I was just holding him in front of me at the time. Not sure if that was on accident or on purpose on the gunman's part, but yes then I proceeded to throw the coat rack at the second one."

"How did you know that would work?"

"I didn't ma'am, but I use to throw some of the bigger rocks here in the gravel yard when I was a kid. I invented accuracy games with them to see how far and how straight I could throw some of the smaller boulders. The coat rack seemed light in comparison." The police detective shook her head, she couldn't believe how calm this hulk of a man was being after stopping two armed intruders without even being armed himself.

"Stop calling me ma'am, you are making me feel old."

"Old? You look about perfect to me." The police detective felt her cheeks flush at the compliment from the strapping younger man. She wrote her personal number on the back of one of her business cards and handed it to him.

"When the investigation is closed, call me."

"I need to get shot at more..." Hank mumbled with a smirk on his face as he pocketed the card with the one from the paramedic.

Once the police finally cleared out of his property, and the coroners drove away with the corpse, the sun was fully up in the sky. It was sometime mid-morning. He went and sat at his father's side once more, and waited for him to stir.

"Son, tell me why those men came to kill you and don't bullshit me." So Hank did, he told his father everything about Jimmy, their relationship, how Jimmy had paid a lot of his father's hospital bills, everything.

"Son, this Jimmy fellow doesn't sound like a bad guy, but *he is* a criminal. Those two things don't always run side by side if you catch my drift. I've known lots of good guys that were technically criminals. All of that is beside the point, you don't need him and being around him brings death to your door. I'll be dead soon, and the gravel yard will be yours to run. The people who work here will depend on you to keep this place open and running right. If you are mixed up with criminals... That could endanger everything. I realize the money was probably really good working for Jimmy, but it's time to hang that up now, count your blessings and run the business. Will you do that for me son?"

"Yes father."

It was an easy request really, and truth be told Hank didn't want the trouble. He respected and liked Jimmy, but getting shot in the chest hurt. Hank spent that whole day sitting by his father's side, conversing when his father was up to it, but mostly just sitting in silence trying to remember everything his father had taught him. He knew he should go to the hospital, but he felt his father's time was short. Unfortunately Hank's assumption was right and his father died later that night. Hank was stricken with grief and wasn't really sure what to do after hospice moved his father and their equipment out of his home.

Hank felt vulnerable and sad like never before in his life. This was a problem that his enormous strength couldn't get him through. Jimmy stopped by the next day and forced Hank to finally go to the hospital to get his bullet wound looked at. While Hank was being treated, Jimmy somehow managed to arrange and pay for Hank's father's funeral. Hank wasn't sure what to say to Jimmy so he just hugged him for a long time. After that Jimmy told him he had to leave town for awhile, Hank understood.

Hank took over running the gravel yard full time when things settled down following his father's funeral. He hired people who were in need, and fired people who didn't deserve the job. Hank was a fair and understanding boss and his employees loved him for that. He didn't tolerate any harassment on the job site either. He once caught an employee stealing someone else's sandwich out of the shared work fridge so he carried the thief off of the premise and literally threw him out into the road. People stopped stealing food from the work fridge after that.

When Hank had the extra cash he even hired a night watchmen to walk around the gravel yard. He didn't need the security, but it was his way of giving back to the community. He only hired people who desperately needed the cash. He also figured it wouldn't be good for his public record if he had to kill more night prowlers with his bare hands, things like that tend to piss the local constabulary off if you repeat them too often. Once Hank got over the loss of his father, things got better. His mood brightened, not that you could tell. Hank was as stoic as ever on the outside, but he had reached his own 'Hank Brand' of inner peace once again. He was the master of his domain, his employees loved him, he was right with the law and the gravel yard was doing good business. The local women loved Hank even more than before, especially now that he was a thriving businessman with the body of a professional weightlifter. They knew Hank wasn't looking for a serious relationship yet they seemed to try and take that as a challenge. To them Hank was like trying to hold fire in your hands, beautiful and bright, but eventually you would have to let it go.

All of that peace was shattered though, when Eugene had come back into his life. Eugene who had taken Suzie Q. from him. That coward, that piece of filth. Hank would make him pay. Saul had said Eugene had security at his house, that was fine. Hank wouldn't hit him at his house. Eugene had corrupted everyone, he had to have paid off half of city hall to have them overlook the shit he was pulling. That's fine, they could be punished too. Hank broke the coffee cup in his hand, he was squeezing it so hard without noticing it.

His lawyer Saul scooted back in his chair probably not wanting to get coffee on his expensive Italian suit.

"Hank I can see that look on your face. I know what you are thinking," said Saul.

"That's not your problem Saul. Do me one last favor though, make sure my will is up to date please," said Hank.

"Why would I do that Hank?" asked Saul.

"Just humor me," said Hank.

Hank had thrown together a quick and dirty last will and testament a few years back after he had been stabbed in a bar fight. The will basically said half of his assets should go to whatever employees he currently had, and the other half should go to charity. The thought of the state taking his stuff made Hank physically ill. Just in case he didn't survive what came next it would be good for him to know that he would still be helping people, even from beyond the grave. Besides dying an extremely messy death while your will is in litigation would be sure to fuck up Eugene's plans, a win-win you might say.

"Both of y'all get out!" said Hank.

"Whaaa?" said the Lot Lizard who was picking up the pieces of his broken coffee cup. She dropped her sheet she was so surprised at Hank's sudden outburst.

"Saul would you drive this woman home please?"

"But Hankey baby, what about breakfast?"

"Saul can get you breakfast. Go ahead and put it on my tab Saul, and thank you for telling me… everything."

Saul seemed to be in indecision about what to do, on one hand he wanted to stay and instruct his client to be calm and rational, on the other hand he was staring at a naked woman's tits. In the end, the boobies won out.

"Miss, I would be delighted to escort you safely home and I would be honored if we could have breakfast together," said Saul, while holding out his hand as an open offer. The Lot Lizard gave Saul a once over, taking in everything from his $500 dollars shoes and his expensive suit, to his Rolex. If she had been any more obvious in her appraisal you would have seen her pupils turn into little dollar signs.

"Sure, just let me grab my clothes and my purse," she said, as she jogged back to Hank's bedroom letting all the right parts jiggle now that she knew Saul was watching.

"I think I'm in love," said Saul. Hank could see the impending train wreck coming, but he decided to mind his own business, besides he had his own problems to worry about. The young woman came back out wearing more clothing... barely, and her and Saul left in short order, but not before Saul warned Hank one more time to play it cool and wait for the money that the town would have to pay him to make the whole eminent domain business look quasi-legal.

As soon as Saul and the Lot Lizard left Hank was making moves, he first called his second-in-command at the gravel yard, one of the old timers who had been there since his father's time, his name was Frank.

"Frank, it's Hank"

"What's up Hank?"

"Things with this whole eminent domain business have picked up. I'll need you to take over the yard for me until I get this situation settled, it could be a few days."

"Is there anything I could do to help? Your father was like a brother to me. If you need anything you tell me."

"No, it's fine. Me and my lawyer are going to be wheeling and dealing for a few days and I won't have time to come to the front. Please just keep the place running smoothly for me until I'm back."

"I can do that. Anything else you need, just call."

"Cya Frank."

"Cya Hank."

Even though Hank still lived in the back of the gravel yard he didn't want to be bothered at all. He was far enough back away from the business that there would be no reason for his men to come back here, plus his house was blocked from line of sight thanks to the towering gravel piles scattered about. He needed complete privacy to get this next part done. Hank got on some work pants and boots and one of his signature yellow tank tops with his company name on it "Steel Gravel." Then he headed out to the large prefab metal work shed that his father had put together shortly after he had bought this lot. The shed was pretty massive as far as sheds went. It was wide enough to fit five cars side by side with space between them, and about as tall as a two story house.

His father had originally built the shed as a place to keep his cars and trucks clean and dust free, since the gravel yard generated so much debris. Over the years the large metal shed had slowly turned into the family's private gym, workshop, and gun safe. Only one vehicle rested inside of it now, his father's pride and joy: the bulldozer. A fully customized Komatsu D355A that had been completely revamped and rebuilt ten times over since Hank's father had bought it upon returning home from Vietnam. You see, when Hank's father had bought the plot of land that the gravel yard sits on now back in the 70's it was little more than a sparse forest on the outskirts of town. A sparse *rocky* forest. Hank's father needed a way to make the giant square a level lot so he could start collecting gravel and selling it. So he bought the bulldozer.

He had used it to literally carve out their families livelihood, smashing away and shifting the large boulders and trees. Before he had died he had been in the process of replacing a few engine belts on the old thing, they sat nearby on a table. Hank hadn't so much as touched the bulldozer since his father had died. The giant loyal machine felt holy, like it carried part of his father's spirit in it. Hank reached out hesitantly to grab onto one of the handles that would lift him up into the cab. His hand slowed and he waited for just a second before pulling himself up and opening the door to get inside, he wasn't quite sure why he had to wait, but it was almost like he was asking his father for permission. He sat down in the operator's chair and inhaled deeply, it even smelled like his father in here. Hank sat quietly, not moving, contemplating everything he had to do and the gifts his father had given him.

In this place, his father's shed, in his father's bulldozer, it was like his father was sitting right there next to him, trying to push through the curtain of death to put a hand on Hank's shoulder and say something encouraging. Hank couldn't help it, he had to say something in this... place.

"Hey dad, I know you are listening to me now. I'm sorry about this mess with Eugene. It looks like I might lose the yard over it, and that would be a shame because I know you worked hard on this place, and you worked hard to get it. I'll never forget the things you taught me and the things you did for me, but it looks like I won't be able to fulfill my promises to you, especially the one about having kids. There is one promise I'll be able to keep though. You told me to stand up for the little guys, to not let evil reign, and I won't. Eugene is out there now and he has corrupted half the town. I don't know what he is planning, but if he is willing to attack even me, that probably means he will hurt lots of innocent people as well to finish whatever sick mission he is on. Someone has to stop him… The problem is, he is connected dad, like real connected. Police, the local government, hell even the local media... He has them all paid off, he is basically untouchable. If I try to stop him at his house I'll probably only end up killing a whole mess of people just trying to get a paycheck, before his security shoots me to death. Which is why I have to use this… This bulldozer will be the instrument of justice. You can stop a man, but you can't stop a bulldozer. Wish me luck dad, I might be seeing you soon."

Chapter 3

Hank had a plan and the plan basically boiled down to killing Eugene, therefore ending the darkness that had taken over his town. No one ever accused Hank of being a genius. Hank knew he wouldn't be able to shoot it out with Eugene's private security surely comprised of the best, but he could just run Eugene over with a bulldozer, and of course anyone else he saw along the way that had been corrupted by Eugene and convinced to hurt or bully the innocent. It wasn't a great plan, it wasn't well thought out, but Hank was pissed and it would work. Besides everyone knows if you back a dog into a corner it's going to bite. It's time Eugene gets bit… again.

The first thing Hank did was assess his supplies. He had basically all the tools he needed to repair the bulldozer but he needed to do more than repair it, he needed to upgrade it. He had only helped his father rarely with this side of the business, the technical side. Hank was more of a lift it or break it kind of guy, and less of a fix-it guy, but he had done some light welding and routine maintenance on some of the vehicles they used in the gravel business. His father had been the frugal type and that meant not sending their fleet or hauling vehicles to outside repair shops if they could avoid it. So his father had tried to pass down most of the basic knowledge Hank would need to keep the vehicles of the trade running. That same knowledge might help save his life now.

Hank didn't have enough metal in the shed to make the Bulldozer bulletproof. Most people don't realize that metal for the most part very much isn't bulletproof. Only certain types of metal are bulletproof and they are extremely expensive and heavy, this makes them unwieldy. This is also the same reason you don't see U.S. soldiers walking around in suits of metal armor, it's impossible, and if you armored a person fully with traditional metals it would weigh a thousand pounds. Hank had a pretty decent idea of what was bulletproof and what wasn't. Him and his father had been shooting recreationally for years in the woods on the outskirts of their little town. Since his father was a veteran, he held the ideal that all men should know how to properly own and use guns to keep their family safe.

All of the times they had gone out to the woods they had brought interesting things to shoot at and experiment with, plus target shooting is boring without targets. Hank had shot everything from car doors off of old junkers, to old water heaters. Shooting toilets and canned food was especially fun. Bullets flew pretty cleanly through all of it. Not much stopped a bullet unless it was specifically designed to. Hank remembered a story his dad had told him about a time he was hunkered down on a rocky hilltop in Vietnam, and how they had filled some sandbags with rocks since no sand or dirt was available. His father has come under fire, and to him and his squad's delight the loose rocks and gravel had stopped all of the incoming rounds and the sandbags had done a decent job keeping the amount of shrapnel to a somewhat-safe minimum.

Hank would use gravel to make the bulldozer bulletproof, it just felt right and a little ironic. Hank the rock, who worked at the rock business, would protect himself with rocks, ironic and right... The task ahead of him still seemed overwhelming. Hank walked a few feet back and tried to picture the Bulldozer as an armored hulk. The cab would absolutely have to be armored, the engine block as well. It wouldn't do to have one of Eugene's lackeys get a lucky shot and snap some vital piece of his engine off. The job seemed like an uphill battle for one man, almost impossible. Hank liked doing impossible things. He grabbed a welding helmet and his welding equipment and got to work.

Hours slipped by as he welded piece after piece of scrap metal just a few inches off of the hull of the bulldozer. He had to hammer the bottoms of the pieces of scrap metal onto the bulldozer and then weld them into place, it basically made a pocket for him to pour gravel into. The welds were sloppy, the pieces of scrap metal weren't uniform at all, it was ugly as sin, but it would hold. He lugged huge bags of gravel over each of his shoulders and carefully poured them into the pockets of metal he had created on the sides of the bulldozer. He had about half of one side finished, before he came to the conclusion that he should test his theory before continuing.

He went to the large safe his father kept hidden in the shed behind a shelf of tools. The shelf was on concealed casters so it easily slid out of the way. The safe was bolted into the very foundation of the floor Hank was standing on, beyond secure. Hank rolled the tumbler on the safe through the complex combination and turned the large six handled crank on the safe until the door popped open. Every gun his father had ever collected was inside, at least 11 rifles and over 20 handguns, and a few assorted shotguns. Hank wasn't sure of the exact number of firearms inside, he had never counted. He grabbed his father's prized 1911, the one he had used in Vietnam. Hank racked the slide back and inspected the chamber, it was empty. He dry fired it once after pointing the barrel safely away from himself, he felt the crisp and satisfying break of the sear as he depressed the trigger fully. The gun was in working order. Hank had always wondered how his father has smuggled this thing back to the states, but he had never had a chance to ask him. Hank grabbed a loaded magazine out of the webbing that lined the door of the safe and headed back into the main part of the large shed.

Shooting metal might mean a serious ricochet, he needed to find a way to safely do this. Hank flipped over the lone work desk that was in the warehouse and dragged it until he was at a slight angle to the bulldozer. The idea was that if it was going to ricochet then it should ricochet at an angle away from him. He worried about the sound though, he didn't want any of the gravel yard workers to come check on him if they heard shooting. So he turned on the large industrial air compressor in the room, it began to fill its tanks which was plenty loud enough to mask a gunshot or two. Hank went behind the desk and got a good aim at one of the armored portions on the bulldozer, then he lowered his head below the edge of the desk and fired one round. He jumped up and over the desk and sprinted to the impact site on the dozer, excited to see the results of his test.

There was a very clear puncture in the thin metal he had welded to the side of the bulldozer. The gravel was so tightly packed between the layers of metal, and the entrance hole was so small that none was spilling out. The round had actually landed on the bottom half of the door to the cab, so all he had to do was pop open the door and look for an exit hole inside to see if the armor had failed. Hank felt all around the inside of the door and checked every part of the interior cabin in case the bullet had traveled an irregular path. He couldn't find anything. So he went back to the exterior of the dozer where the bullet had landed. He got some pliers and started pulling out gravel until he saw the shine of copper. He dug the mangled slug right out of his impromptu armor, It had worked. He would have to test a rifle on it still, but he had a feeling that wouldn't go through either. This was going to work. Seeing the success of his new armor gave

40

him more motivation to get back to work. Hank hauled in a few more giant bags of gravel and set them on the side of the shed so he could fill the metal pockets he was making as he moved the project forward. He didn't want to have to leave the warehouse again.

Hank slapped on the welding helmet once again and refused to stop working. He could feel his stomach rumbling with hunger while the hours flew by. He welded piece after piece on ever so carefully folding them into the metal pockets on each side of them. His work became sloppier but he always made sure it was structurally sound. Soon he became dizzy and he assumed it was from being around the hot welding equipment with no water. So he chugged an old gallon of water that someone had left in the shed and kept working. His shirt was absolutely drenched in sweat and soon even his pants and socks were drenched as well, he had completely lost track of time.

At some point he woke up in the lone office chair in the large shed, he must have sat down for a second and fallen asleep. His stomach rumbled something fierce. He decided it would be worth it to head back to his house and get a snack before continuing his work. When Hank walked outside he noticed the sun was setting, what time was it? His clock read 6pm. He must have worked the entire day before, all of last night, and well into the next day with little to no food or water. No wonder he had crashed so hard, he had worked more than a 24-hour shift of hard manual labor. The first thing he did was storm inside of his house and get out of his sweat encrusted clothing. Once he was stark naked he ripped open his fridge and grabbed a fresh 2-gallon jug of milk. He chugged the entire thing without stopping. He needed more food, sleep, he needed to finish his work on the bulldozer, and he needed to refine his plan, in that order.

41

Hank didn't want to get dizzy or lightheaded from something as simple and avoidable of lack of calories or malnutrition. So he grabbed a couple of steaks from his fridge, some carrots, cucumbers, and potatoes and took them all out back to his grill. He poured beer over all of them and threw on some random seasonings that he kept in an empty cooler next to his grill to keep them out of the elements. Then he cranked his grill on high and lit it up. It wasn't going to be a culinary masterpiece but it would taste alright. Besides Hank wasn't really thinking about food right now anyway, beyond the fact that he needed it. His mind was preoccupied with the minute details of what could go wrong with his plan. So he stood there, still stark naked, on his back porch, while his meat and vegetables were seared to perfection. He was watching the sun go down, trying to plan for everything.

After he ate, he set a six-hour timer on his cell phone and crashed out hard in his bed. He slept like the dead in a deep dreamless sleep. Quicker than he would have liked his cellphone's alarm was going off and he knew it was time to get back to work. He thought about taking a quick rinse through the shower, but there would be no point since he was going right back out to work and inevitably get drenched in sweat again. It was about 1 in the morning now, the gravel yard would be completely empty, so he didn't even bother finding a shirt. He just grabbed another pair of work pants and his steel-toed boots. He also grabbed two 24-packs of a local beer that was known for having a higher than average alcohol content, one in each arm. In case he didn't make it tomorrow he wanted this to be a good night.

When Hank got back into the shed he looked up at the partially armored bulldozer, and again he felt his father's presence with him. He cracked open his first beer and poured some on the ground.

"That's for you dad!" Then once again he got to work. He basically had the concept of what he wanted finished in his mind and he had done the bulk of the work before he had rested, but that had been on the easy to armor areas. Armoring the sharp contours of the cab would be much harder. For one he needed to leave slots for himself to see through but he also didn't want to get shot in the face. So he needed to find some happy medium that would leave him enough vision to maneuver correctly, while simultaneously keeping the slots small enough that they would be hard to shoot through. He thought he might be able to rig up an old security camera on the exterior for vision but he wanted that to be a secondary option, not something that he would have to rely on.

This armor would also be ridiculously heavy and while the cab was somewhat load-bearing he didn't want to overload it and have it fall apart, or even worse have the armor be so heavy that it fell inward and crushed him. So he decided to weld on a rebar support network before he added any more armor. It was easier than he thought it was going to be since he was decently proficient at welding. Sure, an actual engineer would balk at the design, but it would still work as intended. Honestly the rebar cage he had installed looked like a mechanical crackhead spider had shot metal web all over the bulldozer's cab. That, or maybe some kind of fancy pants nonsense modern art, it could go either way. Hank noticed this as well, and because modern art offended him on a primal level he had to chug a beer to get the thought out of his head.

Once he was sure the cab would hold the weight of the armor he threw himself back into the work. Welding on the metal 'pockets' and filling them with gravel before sealing them and laying the next one on in line slightly overlapping the last, almost like a dragon's scales. He made sure to take a break every 10 minutes or so and chug a beer and a little bit of water. He didn't want to wear himself out like he had before, especially if he wanted to kick off his plan sometime tomorrow morning. As he worked he got better at the small details, the quality and speed of his work improved, and before he knew it he had finished welding on the last gravel filled plates. He jumped off the bulldozer and walked backwards once again to get a better view of his creation. It was… *monstrous*, devious and evil looking. This was the bulldozer from Wes Craven's nightmares… This was… The Killdozer.

Suddenly looking at his deadly creation, this plan seemed a little too extreme to Hank. Was he really going to go kill Eugene with his family's bulldozer in broad daylight? Even Hank knew sometimes you had to sit down and re-evaluate your choices, and one thing more than anything else always helped Hank think: exercise. Hank hit the weight bench that him and his father had welded together when he was a teenager. The padding on the weight bench was the seat from an old car laid flat. It was a real hodge-podge of parts, but it worked and it reminded him of his dad. The weights themselves were just different sized chunks of concrete on each end of a metal bar. Hank selected the biggest one which weighed in at somewhere around 250 pounds.

Hank started some really slow reps, really really focusing on the eccentric contractions. Most people skipped over this part of the exercise or tried to cheat it. Hank never understood why they did that, they were only cheating themselves. He ran the information and history between him and Eugene back through his head first. Their feud had started in high school when Eugene had randomly decided that Hank was some kind of a threat to him and needed to apparently be beaten. Instead of Eugene's sick plan coming to fruition Hank had turned the tables and beaten Eugene for causing such a ruckus and slicing up Suzie Q's face. You would think Eugene would have learned from that object lesson. Finally coming back to what was happening now. Eugene had weaseled his way into local business and government and was trying to steal Hank's livelihood and his father's land.

Hank came to the conclusion that Eugene was probably involved in some sort of get rich quick scheme involving wide scale land development. It must be extremely lucrative, especially if he was willing to anger Hank. That's beside the point though, his current actions matter more than his *why*, and his historical actions as well for that matter. Hank knew Eugene was willing to hurt people if he didn't get his way. In fact Eugene was probably a textbook sociopath, and most likely had been since high-school when he cut Suzie. He had to be stopped and this eminent domain deal was too far along and had too many moving pieces to be stopped now. Hank could go the legal route and maybe win, sure Eugene had the local government paid off but through enough litigation Hank might be able to win some kind of massive lawsuit against Eugene... Maybe, Eugene has always been slippery... greasy, he knew how to get out of trouble. He knew whose palms to grease and when. Besides Eugene most likely wasn't the only person who was going to make money out of whatever deal Eugene was cooking up. Hank would bet dollars to donuts that Eugene had some very powerful backers with a vested interest on keeping Eugene free and clear, and away from any litigation.

45

The legal way just didn't seem like it would work, and it also seemed like it would eventually hurt more people. Eugene was already putting Hank and all of his employees out of work, how far was he actually willing to go? Anyone that Eugene hurt from this point on would be on Hank's conscience. Hank had the power to stop him. Hell, he had the ultimate tool to stop Eugene just a dozen feet away. Ultimately to Hank anything short of killing Eugene felt too much like passing the buck, or even worse, running away. Hank didn't start fights, but he sure as hell didn't back down from them. Eugene had drawn first blood, it had been Eugene' choice to come after Hank's business. He was going to have to pay for that mistake. You grab a rattlesnake and you just might get bit, it was time for Eugene to learn that *again*.

With his mind made up and a fresh wave of anger roiling through him Hank hopped up from the bench more determined than ever. He drank the rest of the beer in his hand and threw the can on the floor. Time to put an escape plan in order. Sure the chance of him escaping was infinitesimally low, but it felt wrong to not have a plan in place anyway, just in case. Also Hank felt like he had to at least try to follow through on his father's promise to have kids someday, he had promised him. With an escape plan in place, even if it wasn't likely that he could follow through on it, he would still be following the heart of that promise.

It was about four in the morning now, he had time to stage some kind of getaway car. There was a small parking garage just near city hall for the government employees to use. Hank had a quick plan forming that involved that small parking garage. His father's truck was unregistered and had been sitting on cinder blocks for a few years under a tarp. Hank had poured massive amounts of a chemical called Stabil in the tank before he had

46

stored it so hypothetically it should still start up since the purpose of Stabil is to stop gasoline from expiring. Hank had the tires stored in here with him in the metal shed still. He grabbed the tires and chucked them on a small push cart with a ratchet set and headed out to his dad's old truck. Ha had to hurry if he wanted to get everything staged up before sunrise. He quickly threw on the tires and ratcheted the lug nuts into place. Then he jump started the battery and left the truck running so it would charge. He ran to his own truck and backed it up to a small trailer they used to transport service vehicles on and off the gravel yard. He attached the trailer and hauled ass over to his father's truck and pulled it onto the trailer. He was still afraid to turn it off in case the battery hadn't charged adequately so he left it running.

Hank grabbed a couple beers for the road and shot out of the gravel yard driving his truck, with his father's truck still running on the trailer behind hauled behind him. Town Hall was only about a 15-minute drive from the gravel yard, Hank made it in less than 8 minutes, while blasting Metallica and shotgunning beers. He pulled the trailer up fast and dirty alongside the parking garage and threw his truck in neutral and slammed the parking break into place. Then he backed his father's truck off of the trailer and drove it up to the parking garage. There was a small box where you inserted an access card of some type to have the security bar lift and let you in. Hank didn't have an access card, but he had tools. He unbolted the security bar and set it gently aside and then drove his dad's truck in and parked it in what he hoped was an out of the way section reserved for janitorial staff or interns or something of the sort. He made sure to bolt the security bar back into place before leaving and hauling ass back to the gravel yard.

Now if he had an option to escape he could do it in a vehicle that wasn't registered to him. As long as no one saw him get into his father's truck it would take the authorities awhile to connect the unregistered vehicle to him. That was only one part of the plan, he would have to call Jimmy as well and ask for help. Hank wasn't dumb, he knew he couldn't call Jimmy from his landline or his cell phone, if the police looked up his call history they would track him right to Jimmy. He would have to buy a burner phone to call Jimmy with if or when he escaped the scene in his father's truck. It was a lot of *if's*, but at least there was a backup plan.

It was about five in the morning now, the sun would come up in about an hour and then an hour after that Town Hall employees would start dribbling in. Hank needed to get the Bulldozer to the general area and staged up before that time. He ran through the shed looking for some tarps he could use to conceal the Bulldozer for a bit after he staged it. That's when the whole shed began to shake... At first Hank thought it was some kind of rare earthquake, but he swore the ambient temperature inside the shed actually increased a bit. The shaking seemed a little too violent and then it all abruptly stopped. Someone began to pound on his door, the door to the shed, the shed no one knew he was in. Keep in mind it was the middle of the night still technically, Hank had been drinking for hours, and the Gravel Yard was supposed to be completely empty. So Hank was surprised to say the least. The idea that maybe he was having some kind of drunken fatigue fever dream crossed his mind, but with the spike of adrenaline running through him giving him clarity, he doubted it.

Hank still had his father's large old fashion gun safe open from earlier, so he bolted over to it and grabbed what he thought would be a good gun for fighting in these close quarters. Some kind of ancient double-barreled sawed-off shotgun that his father had had before Hank was born. Hank knew this thing would give any ATF agent a boner with how many federal laws it broke, but he could never bear to get rid of anything that his dad had loved. Besides fuck the ATF. Hank ensured both of the shotgun tubes were loaded with some random shells he found in the safe, he hoped they were buckshot and not birdshot, but beggars can't be choosers and getting shot hurts no matter the caliber or type of ammunition, so fuck it. He also grabbed his father's 1911 but was really unsure where to put it since he didn't have a holster readily available for it, so he jammed it in the back of his pants. His father had called that 'Mexican Carry' and told him to never do it, but Hank was in a jam. Still in this place he couldn't help but say "Sorry dad!" out loud once before heading to the door.

Before he could get to it, the door blasted inward with an extreme beam of blue light. Hank had to jump out of the way to avoid the flying door. His combat training from his Army days kicked in and he let off a blast with one of the barrels of the shotgun directly at the beam of blue light still flooding through his doorway.

An extremely rough and gravelly voice shouted from outside the threshold somewhere "Hold your fire!"

"How about you get off my property and I won't kill you!" Hank shouted back at the unseen figure.

Then a female voice came through the doorway next "Sir, hold your fire, we are friendlies."

Something about the female voice calmed Hank down, or maybe Hank was just a sucker for women, especially ones that sounded hot.

"Alright, come in slowly. If you try something I'm going to rip your heads off with my bare hands!"

Two figures walked in through the light, their silhouettes were all wrong. The first one through was obviously feminine, in all the right places... Except there were two shadowy prongs coming off of her forehead which Hank couldn't quite make out through the insanely bright blue light. The second figure that came through was enormous, at least seven and half feet tall and the shape of his head, it just wasn't right.

"Kill the light, or I kill you!" shouted Hank.

The slim female figure touched a button at her wrist and the light died off. It took Hank a second for his vision to adjust and then he realized he had drank entirely too much and that this was just a dream. The female figure ended up having light blue skin and dark blue miniature horns coming out of her forehead. She had a mane of even darker blue hair that framed her very beautiful face. She was wearing some kind of skin tight scaled silver suit with a few raised portions here and there which Hank guessed were armor of some type. Her breasts were very large, and she had one of those 'bubble butts,' if her skin wasn't blue this would have been the type of woman Hank normally chased.

The second figure was at least partially reptilian, of some type, Hank didn't know shit about reptiles so he couldn't tell either. His head had two lizard style ridges starting at his temples and running over his head and then down his back. He was wearing the same style of uniform as the female except his was much bigger and his had a hole on his lower back which his enormous seven-foot long tail slipped through. He was built like a professional strongman and was absolutely covered in weapons. The most noticeable was a four-foot long double sided battle-axe that he held loosely in one hand that must have weighed 90 pounds, he was wielding it like it was from the Nerf line-up... The axe was covered with intricate designs and what looked like copper circuits similar to those on a motherboard.

They both spread out like pros and assessed every corner of Hank's metal shed. Once they were happy that it was safe they turned to Hank who was thoroughly flabbergasted. He was standing shirtless with the shotgun held tightly in his arms. The large reptile looking one reached down to his hip towards a cylindrical object of some type. Before he could touch it Hank lifted the shotgun and pointed it squarely at his face.

"Stop. Take your hand away from that, or you are going to lose it," said Hank who still couldn't tell if he was hallucinating or not. The lizard man's face contorted in obvious anger.

"Whoa whoa, calm down now boys," said the beautiful curvaceous blue woman. "He is just trying to show you a package, it's addressed to you."

The large lizard-man spoke up in an extremely gravelly voice again "You have been drafted to service," he said matter-of-factly while lifting the cylinder off of his belt. The lizard-man extended his hand with the cylinder outstretched towards Hank. Hank nabbed it away from the lizard and took a few steps back. Then Hank carefully tucked the butt of the shotgun in one of his armpits so he could better examine the cylinder. Hank could quickly grab the shotgun still with it tucked this way, just in case these creepy fucks tried something. He rolled the cylinder back and forth in his hands. It was extremely heavy, that was the first thing Hank noticed, and made out of a metal that Hank didn't recognize, like steel but much darker. It also had some kind of purple vein running through it in different directions. Hank couldn't tell if the purple vein was emitting a soft light or if it was just extremely refractive. As Hank continued to roll it in his hands

51

he finally stopped when he came to some small script in perfect English engraved on the side of it, it read:

"Hank Steel - Planet BG429"

"What the hell is this, and why in the sweet fuck are you a lizard?" asked Hank.

"I'm not a lizard you cretin, I'm a Noxian, from Zealos 7. You don't recognize my kind because you are from a backwater shithole. I say again, you have been drafted for service. This is normally where people who are from a species smart enough to recognize who we are, actually start asking questions. Be quick monkey man, my time is valuable."

Hank had to contain the urge to strike the… thing. He still wasn't 100% sure that this wasn't some kind of drunken lucid dream. The blue woman could see Hanks confusion, so she decided to give him the rundown.

"Let's start over," she said. "I'm Cerulean, this is Dractus. We are Arbiters, those chosen by God himself to police the universe. We are here to inform you that you have also been chosen for Arbiter service."

Chapter 4

"Stop. Let me get this straight, you two are aliens, and you are also cops chosen by God?"

"It's a lot to take in for someone like you, I understand that," said Cerulean.

This was a lot to take in... Hank threw the sawed-off shotgun that was still tucked under his armpit onto the desk in the workshop and began to pace. He still carried the strange cylinder in his offhand, it was extremely heavy for its size and it almost felt like it was putting out a low electrical current. Hank had a million questions flying around in his head, so he figured it was best to drop into his Hank-zen-mode. He relaxed his shoulders, slowed his breathing, and turned to face the two aliens in his workshop.

"Why me?"

"We don't really know, but I can take an educated guess. You are a relatively nice person and you have been willing to take a stand against evil when a lot of other people on your planet haven't. Sound familiar?" asked Cerulean.

"What do you mean you 'don't really know', you were sent here to recruit me. How could you not know why I'm being recruited?" asked Hank.

"That's not how this works Hank, that canister in your hand is delivered to us by God himself. We just take it from there and make sure it gets to you."

Hank raised one of his eyebrows insanely high before continuing, "So you are telling me that the heavens open up, the clouds part, and God walks down on a glowing staircase to hand you one of these," said Hank while holding up the canister in her direction. "That's horseshit and you know it," Hank finished.

"You are wrong and you are right monkey man," said Dractus.

"How so?" asked Hank, he was to curious now too be mad at Dractus' slight insult.

"There is a competing theory, one that I'm a subscriber of, but to understand it we are going to have to go back to the beginning," said Dractus.

"I'll get beers," said Hank. He reached into an almost empty box at his feet and retrieved three lukewarm cans. He threw one each to Cerulean and Dractus, they both caught them out of the air. Dractus examined both sides of the can before just putting the entire thing in his mouth and chomping down. The can of beer exploded down his throat, and then Dractus spit the now mostly-empty can on the floor.

"Refreshing beverage human, thank you. Amway where was I… Ah, the beginning of the Arbiters."

Hank and Cerulean shared a look of amusement over Dractus' beer consuming show. She carefully copied Hank's actions and popped her can open using the tab. They both became focused when Dractus continued his story.

"So, thousands of years ago a race of beings much similar to your race now, became spacefaring, but out of necessity. Their planet was used up, abused. They were out of natural resources, overpopulated, and large swaths of their planet had been cleansed by nuclear fire, leaving it uninhabitable for life. Something had to change, the last of the reasonable governments on this planet assembled a team of their best scientists, warriors, and explorers. They also shared funding and all of their own independent research to build a coalition ship. A ship the likes of which had never been seen before, to send on a mission of great importance. Their goal was to find a Goldilocks planet. Am I saying that right Goldilockssss?" Dractus made sure to drag out the extra 'S' sound at the end of 'Goldilocks' using the lizard architecture of his mouth.

"I have no idea, I don't know shit about Astronomy," said Hank before taking another slug off of his beer. Dractus mumbled something that sounded like "backwards monkey planet," before continuing.

"Well, a Goldilocks planet is a planet that is in a perfect alignment with the nearest sun and stars. It's just warm enough to support life, yet not too warm to be a charred piece of trash. There are obviously planets in the other direction as well, giant frozen balls of useless shit, I'm getting off point though. The point is, there are a lot of planets, but only a few that you can live on without massive amounts of terraforming or oxygen filled infrastructure. Goldilocks planets are highly sought after prizes because of their rarity, civilizations rise and fall over wars fought for them.

So this mega ship built by the best scientists from all over their world, using the technology of over 20 different cultures, set off to find a habitable planet in the hopes of saving their race from destruction. Their ship was swift, their scientists were bright, and their warriors and explorers were eager to navigate the unknown. Within sixteen solar months of this planet's time they had found two Goldilocks planets! That may seem like a long time to you, but the speed of their ship was unheard of at the time, and their ship despite being state of the art was somewhat of an experimental mess. They had left relay satellites as they traveled to ferry messages back to the coalition of governments that was supporting them.

The people of their planet were elated to hear the news of their discovery, yet there was rumor among the population that a religious fanatic had snuck aboard the expedition and was looking to sabotage the ship and their mission. Surely this rumor had no merit, for only the best representatives from each country had been chosen, avatars of virtue and accomplishment. The expedition couldn't return conquering heroes until they set foot on the ground of each of the planets they had discovered. Readings from space are one thing, but they had to know without a doubt that each planet was safe for habitation. There was too much riding on this mission to send future settlers out into space on speculation alone.

So after a tenuous atmospheric entry the expedition landed on the first planet which was named BG-1. If you haven't figured it out yet BG is a common designation for planets that have a good ratio of land to water with vegetation of a certain type on them. The BG in particular stands for blue-green the blue being water and the green being foliage. Of course there are habitable planets that aren't colored blue-green from space but they get a different designation. Anyway, continuing the story. BG-1 was a dangerous world, but beautiful. The wildlife there was extremely violent and was constantly at war with itself and when the aliens arrived they quickly became part of the local ecosystem.

The warriors and explorers they had brought with them were stalwart and experienced, though they balked at the dangerous creatures and gunned them down. Still tensions ran high and everyone was constantly on alert. They had to make many scientific expedition into the depths of this planet's jungles, rivers, caves, and other environments to ensure that it was safe for a colony. Yes the creatures on the planet were dangerous, but walls could be built, and soldiers could be deployed. It would be worth it for a fresh start for their home planet's best and brightest. They just had to ensure that the creatures were the full extent of the danger.

As they explored they discovered evidence of a stone age civilization. They found things like bowls, stone knives, mud-based pottery, simple arrowheads. They knew they weren't alone, but they also knew whatever civilization lived here had to be insanely fierce to have survived alongside the vicious creatures of the planet. They knew at this point they would have to find this civilization. Morally they couldn't uproot the people that already lived on this planet, but the planet's landmass was huge and they hadn't run into any settlements yet. There was more than enough space for everyone to share, and the explorers were willing to share technological advancements with the stone age civilization in exchange for a peaceful coexistence.

They followed the breadcrumbs of the primitive civilization. They moved through the trees searching day in and day out, all the while the animals of the planet attacked them with ever more veracity. Almost like they were trying to stop them from moving forward. Finally the brave expedition came to a fort tucked so neatly among the thick forest that they didn't see it until they were practically stumbling through the front gates. Inside the fort walls there were signs of a small town, maybe of a population of 1000. Except there was no town folk running about, and the air was just a little too still. The expedition walked down what looked like the main road through the town. This town rested among the forest you see, and the people who had cultivated and built the town had left many live trees inside the town walls so it was hard to make out its boundaries and landmarks because it was so cleanly blended with the forest. The exterior town wall was even tied into live trees here and there which hid the existences of the small town even further, the whole thing was *organic* in nature… There was an aura in the air as the expedition moved deeper into the town, something felt *off.*

The expedition continued until they saw a large structure in the distance and began to hear humming or chanting of some sort. The found the source of the haunting humming. It seemed the entire population of the town was knelt in prostration in an enormous semi-circle like shape around a large building that resembled some kind of open air town hall. Whatever they were humming had a slow sing-song motion to it, rhythmic but terrifying, somehow you could feel that It was dark and represented something unnatural. The situation was so insane that the explorers hardly even thought about the fact that they were walking among aliens. 'Alien' is a stranger term though, and a lot of what is 'alien' is in the eye of the beholder. The aliens had two arms, two legs, two eyes, two ears, sure they weren't exactly the same, but your mind can recognize the pattern and quickly normalize aliens. They lived in a town, they had families, they had walls, this was very much a civilization, these were people.

The expedition had some of the best linguists and universal translators that their planet could offer with them. They moved among the people with armed escorts trying to communicate with hand symbols and different basic forms of language, but none of the townsfolk would leave their trance or stop their humming. The captain of the ship, a burly man known for his command prowess soon tired of the locals ignoring him and against the wishes of the cultural experts with him he lifted one of the aliens to their feet and shook them a little bit. There was no reactions so he poured some water on the alien's head.

The alien stopped chanting and his eyes snapped open, alert and confused like he had just left a dream. He looked around at all of the town folk chanting and then at the large structure that everyone was facing. He said three words and then before anyone could stop him he grabbed a stone knife he had concealed somewhere in his loincloth and slit his own throat. None of the people praying or humming or whatever they were doing even seemed to mind that one of their own had just killed himself. The captain was appalled, angry, and sickened by the behavior of the alien and his fellow townsfolk. He demanded his interpreters tell him what the man had said. The interpreters were mostly stymied except for one, he came forward and told the captain what his best theory of the translated version of the three words were: God Help Us.

Let's just say at that point the mood darkened even further after hearing the ominous translation. The only obvious moves left was to run screaming back to their ship or to explore the large structure and see what all the fuss was about. With the weight of a world on their shoulders the expedition knew what they had to do. They all moved directly to the front of the large structure, they noticed then the intricacies of it. It was tied into four or five living trees and had live branches beautifully braided through the wood that made up the walls and roof of it. This must have taken generations to build and nurture the trees into this formation, this was clearly a holy site. The captain decided to split the party for the safety of all. He would enter with the interpreter who had been able to translate the three words along with a four-man fireteam. The plan was to find the shaman or mayor or whatever person lead this village and establish diplomatic communications with him or her.

The six-man crew entered the structure and all was quiet for twenty minutes or so, the townsfolk' humming remained the same, but as I said before it was almost rhythmic and it was easy to drown out. That spooky feeling never quite went away though and as time went on the remaining party began to worry. As they were debating whether to send more people in or return to the ship the translator they had sent into the temple came out alone. He looked happy, or perhaps a better word is manic. He was humming the same thing as the townsfolk as he walked through the threshold of the structure. He looked at the remaining members of this expedition party, he raised his voice loud and clear before shouting: 'I'd like to introduce you to our new dark lord and savior!'

Then something *else* came out of the structure. It was one of the aliens from the town, but it was bigger than the others, by a large margin… It would be about 9 feet tall by your earth measurements. It was wearing ceremonial armor made from the trees of the region. The armor was stained with something and leaked sap in a hundred different places. The branches that made up the armor had been expertly bent into a functioning suit. On his head he wore a crown of the branches. Some of the branches were piercing his skin in places and blood leaked down his face, he didn't seem to care. Around his neck he wore a necklace made of ears. On his back a cape rested, when the explorers examined it they found that it was made up of the alien's scalps… Unlike the rest of the aliens, this larger one had fingers that came to distinct points, each one looked as sharp as the finest knife.

The giant alien placed his hands on his hips and laughs loudly and then barks out a few rough sentences. The translator's eyes fill with absolute glee upon hearing whatever the large alien said. The rest of the expedition stares and waits for the translator.

'He said bow before him, and he introduced himself with a name that I am not fit to say."

At this point the executive officer of the expedition had heard enough. It was clear the captain was either dead or being held captive and that the translator was the traitor they had been warned might be hiding among the expedition. It was time for him to take charge and stop this madness. That man's name was Magnus Jesus Supreme..."

"Wait a minute I'm calling bullshit, time out!" shouted Hank.

"You dare interrupt the greatest story ever told?" asked Dractus.

"How in the sweet fuck is this dudes name Magnus Jesus Supreme? That sounds like a wrestler's stage name," said Hank.

"STUPID HUMAN! It's a translation to your mud language! Magnus is the closest possible name according to the etymology of your planet. Same with Jesus which probably means son of God in your mud tongue, and Supreme obviously because he was the best!"

"Alright alright, don't get your lizard panties in a twist, I had to ask," said Hank with his hands in the air in a placating manner. "So you just buy these universal translators somewhere like at the alien mall?" asked Hank.

"No initiate! My universal translator is my body!" said Dractus while slamming his hands on his chest. "It's a perk bestowed upon the Arbiters, no mere translator could make me speak your mud language so perfectly like this. Now let me finish the story!"

"Where was I, yes Magnus Jesus Supreme had taken charge of the expedition. He had tired of the madness. He yelled at the feeble translator and asked for the whereabouts of the captain, since he would happily rescue the captain if he was still alive. Instead of answering him the translator went on a manic tirade about how some things were meant to end and how the fate of their planet had been doomed by God, and that it was their duty to die and be judged in God's eyes. The translator also thought that the large evil alien parading around as a religious leader to this village was some kind of an emissary from the heavens. His ranting had gone on long enough. Magnus Jesus Supreme pulled his battle rifle into position and shot the translator in the face.

Everyone was shocked, the giant evil alien demon, every member of the expedition, even Magnus himself, but he knew it had needed to be done. The townsfolk never stopped their chanting or humming or whatever it was. It wasn't Magnus' place to do what he had done, and he had broken every rule of universal law pertaining to contact with civilizations in their infancy. Next he yelled the words that would inevitably shape the future for every being in existence: "KILL THE DEMON!" Magnus turned his battle rifle on the giant evil alien demon and fired, the other armed members of his party followed suit and fired as well. The rounds impacted hard on the demon's wooden armor sending wooden shards and black alien blood everywhere. The giant alien tumbled backwards and fell over in the face of the unexpected barrage from the expedition party. All around the townsfolk were coming to their senses and running for the hills.

'BACK TO THE SHIP!' Magnus shouted, while shoving his people in the direction of the entrance to the village. Behind their party a mighty laugh burst forth from the downed evil alien demon and in Magnus' own language he shouted "That tickled!" The alien rose from the ground and brushed off shards of his armor and flaps of loose flesh, then he turned on the men and women of the expedition. Magnus knew he had to stand and fight. He ordered his remaining people to run while he would stay and buy them time. He squared off against the mighty alien and dumped his entire magazine in the demon's direction. The demon moved almost faster than Magnus thought possible and closed in on him. The demon ripped away Magnus' rifle and threw it off into the distance.

Magnus drew his two favorite combat knives, he was not afraid because he knew that his sacrifice would ensure that his people could get to the ship, and that the expedition could carry on. They would head to the next Goldilocks planet and survey it, his planet would be safe. He prepared to die an honorable death as he rushed the demon. The demon and Magnus exchanged blows. Black squirming alien blood full of evil, bacteria, and foreign maggot-analogs sprayed into Magnus's face as he cut at the monster. The demon struck back and dug his wickedly sharp claws into Magnus' chest, piercing his technologically enhanced armor. Their melee went on, Magnus slashed and hacked and the demon scratched and sunk his claws into Magnus when he could.

When Magnus was sure he could go on no longer and he was preparing for his final charge that would surely mean his death. A lone alien from the village stepped forward, armed with only a spear. The alien rushed the demon and came to Magnus' aid. Together Magnus and the allied alien from the village battled the giant evil demon to a standstill. A few more villagers came back and threw spears at the giant evil alien demon. Magnus took the opportunity to leave with his life while he could, he dragged the alien ally who was now cut to shreds with him. With their arms over each other's shoulders they stumbled and retreated away from the fight. When they got to the edge of the town Magnus tried to apply the best first aid he could to his own wounds and then his alien partners.

He wasn't sure if the alien's biology was even similar enough to his own for the first aid to help, but he had to try, this person has risked their life in an honorable pursuit. The alien ally was dying, that was clear to Magnus. He knew this planet didn't have the medical technology to help his new ally, his only chance at life was if Magnus could get him to the ship before they took off and left this godforsaken place. Magnus lifted his injured ally onto his mighty shoulders and did his best to stagger all the way back to the ship. Along the way his wounds began to fester and leak black ichor. For the evil of the demon had seeped into his very body. A few times he fell over and uncontrollably retched, to his sickening surprise only more black ichor came out as he expelled the contents of his stomach. His body was trying to expel the evil, but it was killing him in the process.

When he came out of the dense woods near his ship's landing site he was pleasantly surprised to see it was still there. They were making final takeoff preparations. He approached the ship and they quickly lowered a ramp for him to climb. A full complement of the ship's finest security came down and helped him and his ally up the ramp. Magnus refused to go to sick-bay and instead he insisted that he be treated at the helm of the ship as they flew to the next Goldilocks planet which was only 3 days away. Magnus ordered the ship on its way and the medical professionals on board did there best to keep Magnus and his new ally alive.

During the three day trip as Magnus sat in the captain's chair the rumors of his braveness spread through the ship and everyone prayed for his recovery. Unfortunately his health only declined, he couldn't eat or drink without throwing up more black ichor and his wounds refused to close as they continually seeped liquid evil onto the deck of the ship. Meanwhile his alien ally was moved to the med-bay as he went into a coma and his pulse slowed down.

They arrived at the next planet shortly after. This new planet had very moderate temperatures, unfortunately it only had a few water sources on it which left most of the planet as a wasteland devoid of life. They dubbed this planet T-1, you could probably guess why. Their ship's scanners quickly picked up a large structure that looked engineered. At Magnus' orders they ignored all security and ship protocols and landed the ship directly in front of the structure. The structure ended up being a temple of impossible architecture. Spiraling towers that defied gravity, archaic yet futuristic looking overhangs, large transparent glass windows struck through into geometric designs. The whole structure was made of an alien metal, the same alien metal that makes up the canister in your hand now Hank. It might look similar to what you call a large decorative church.

Security teams rushed off the ship loaded to bear with the most deadly ordinance available. After the mishap on the last planet they weren't taking any chances. At this point Magnus was overwhelmed with a feeling that this was where he was supposed to be. The security teams reported the temple was empty and that there was no movement or thermal readings for any living creatures on the planet. Magnus exited the ship while being held aloft by two of the ship's officers. A team of medics had the allied alien on a stretcher trailing behind Magnus since that was what

Magnus had ordered them to do. They argued that the alien should not be moved, but somehow Magnus knew he had to bring him.

They entered the ancient yet somehow futuristic temple to find it completely empty, not a chair, not a person, not an insect. Just a large open area with natural light being let in through the many large decorative windows. At the back of the temple sat a large cube covered in more of the geometric designs and also made up of the strange metal. Magnus knew this was where he had to go. He limped forward, the black ichor still falling out of his wounds and dripping all over the floor leaving a trail behind him. Two streams of the liquid evil leaked from his nose and soaked his shirt. As he coughed flecks of it stained his teeth.

His people set him down in front of the cube. They noticed then the dead center of the cube had a circular hole on it heading deep inside of the cube. The hole spit out two cylinders. One of the security officers hesitantly picked up the first one and noticed it had Magnus' name on it. He handed it to him. At this point Magnus was so tired and close to death he could barely open his eyes. Somehow though on instinct alone he opened the canister with no seams. Two things fell out, two small metal effigies. One of the small metal sculptures was a set of scales, they are the representation of the Scales of Justice. I believe you use this same symbol on your planet. The second small sculpture was that of a sword.

Magnus ripped off the remainder of his shirt and slapped the small sculpture of the scales to his chest just where his heart lay under his skin. The sculpture melded into his skin and his eyes shot open, all weariness gone from him. All of his wounds sprayed black ichor almost comically in small jet streams soaking those around him and spraying the floor. He threw up one more time, more evil spilled out of his mouth. Then he stood, stronger than before, smarter, cleaner, he knew the way. He ran over to the other cylinder and brought it to the alien ally he had brought with him. He struck the alien in the face a few times to rouse him. The alien sat up from the stretcher he was laying down on, he opened the second canister and repeated the process.

Magnus' people came to him with many questions 'Captain, Captain, what happened, what is this new development, what was in those canisters?' They all became silent as he jumped on top of the cube. He stared at the expedition and his alien ally, and then he spoke.

"I am no longer the captain" he shouted. "I am Arbiter Magnus, the first of my line." The people of the expedition were stunned, they thought he had gone raving mad or been infected by this alien technology, but they couldn't deny what they had seen... the technology had healed him. That's not the real kicker though, the members of the expedition with the most doubt immediately had it put out of their mind when the alien Magnus had healed miraculously started speaking their language and backed up everything Magnus had said.

So that's the story of the first two Arbiters. Also this is where the conflicting theories come into play. Some believe the sacred Arbiter temple was put there by God himself as a way to balance out the evils of the universe. Then there are others like me who believe that an ancient alien race left it there, and of course that theory just opens up an entire can of worms about the reasons they put it there. Either way it seems more plausible to me at least than the man in the sky theory. What do you think Hank?"

"I think you left out a lot of details. What was the second Arbiters name? What did both of these Arbiters look like? What kind of ship were they driving? What happened to the demon on BG-1?"

"Let me stop you there, I left those details out on purpose for many reasons. We have a saying on my planet and I find this saying very universal, we say "You must walk before you can run." If you are interested in the histories of the Arbiters you must first finish whatever conflict you have going on here and then come to the temple of the Arbiter. I also now think you know enough to ask questions, we must leave soon so please ask important ones."

"You said there was two small sculptures in the canister, one was the Scales of Justice which he used to heal himself or something, the other was a sword. What does the sword do?" asked Hank.

"Good question, there are different types of Arbiters, some are hard chargers and some are closer to calm and analytical detectives. I thought I had you pegged as a hard charger, but you might have skills in both categories. You are incorrect though in your assumption that the scales healed him. The Scales of justice prepare your body to be an Arbiter. Despite thousands of years of research from the more scientifically inclined Arbiters, we haven't figured out the full capabilities of the Scales yet or even what mechanism drives them. I can tell you what we do know about them before I move on to your question about the sword.

To be an Arbiter you have to be able to go to any civilization and blend in, hit the streets, be one with the people. You can't very well do this if you can't understand them or even eat the same food as them. So one thing we do know for a fact is that the Scales alter the Arbiter's body so he or she can metabolize things that would otherwise kill them. Now it wouldn't make sense to go through all this trouble to get a message and a job from God to simply be killed by some foreign bacteria a week into the job now would it? That was rhetorical, so the scales didn't heal Magnus so much as enable his own body to heal itself and for it to adapt and be able to metabolize and/or expel the liquid evil that he had been infected with by the demon. Also I mentioned at the end of Magnus' story that his alien companion began to speak the same language as everyone else, this is also a function that the Scales enable. You can not gain intelligence on the enemy if you can not speak the language of his cohorts.

There is a third function of the Scales, some say this is the most important. You see the symbology of the Scales is something that transcends all peoples, all races, all planets. Almost every species uses the symbol of the scales in some way to represent justice or balance. Though the definition of justice varies from planet to planet the scales never lie. Once you have taken the Scales into your body you get a sense of right and wrong, let's call it 'intuition on steroids'. Some Arbiters can push further than that intuition and actually see the evil of the world. We only have a few among our ranks who are that in tune with their Arbiter skills. That is beside the point though, some of the best Arbiters rely on their intuition the least

Oh I almost forgot about the least important aspect of the Scales, they either double or triple your lifespan," Dractus finished.

"WHAT! That's the least important? I'm going to live two to three times longer?" shouted Hank.

"I just told you that you will be able to literally sense evil, speak any language as fluently as a local, be immune to almost any poison including Demon essence, and be able to eat almost any food in the known universe. Yes being able to live a little longer **IS** the least important. We are running low on time we must move on to the Sword!" Dractus shouted with one finger in the air.

Hank let out a little laugh which made Dractus frown disapprovingly. Hank threw another round of beers to everyone. Cerulean and Hank waited patiently for the Dractus-chomp-town-extravaganza-beer-show to begin, but he noticed them watching and opened the can normally with the tab.

"AWWWWW," said Cerulean, who apparently had also really wanted to see Dractus chomp on another can.

"The Sword!" Dractus said once again with his finger in the air, Hank tried to keep a serious face but he lost it when he saw Cerulean's face take on an even deeper shade of blue, her very own brand of blushing, as she slapped a hand over her mouth to stifle her laughs. Dractus took notice of them both laughing at his showmanship.

"You both are ruining the flare of this story! Anyway, the Sword is simple, you apply it to your weapon of choice and it enables the weapon to become more."

"What do you mean by *more*?" asked Hank.

70

"More than it already is, but there is a stipulation. For your weapon to become stronger and grow, you must fuel it with the souls of evil-doers," said Dractus just a little too matter-of-factly.

"What? I have to kill people to become a better Arbiter?" asked Hank.

"No, not exactly, some of the best Arbiters kill no one. You have to destroy evil to make your weapon of choice more powerful, there is a distinction. Think of the sword effigy as a software install."

"I don't speak nerd."

"BAH! You are obstinate. You'll figure it out, just touch the sword to your weapon of justice, it will do the rest."

Chapter 5

Dractus stood up, Cerulean took his cue, killed the beer in her hand, and joined him.

"Whoa, wait you are leaving?" asked Hank.

"Yes, we are here on mission, we must make haste," said Cerulean.

"I thought I was the mission?"

"No, you were just on the way, but it was nice to meet you, and thank you for the beers. We will come find you when we are done with our mission. We'll give you a ride to the Hall of Arbiters if you want one, it is strongly encouraged that you head there as soon as possible to turn in your canister and get your stipend."

"Turn it in? I haven't even opened it yet."

"Well obviously you open it first, then you come turn in the empty canister to us. I forget you are so new to this. Most species we deal with have been living with the knowledge of Arbiters for centuries. Long story short, if you die your canister melts. So we can use your canister to keep track of you in a way, or at least use it to be able to tell if you are dead or alive." When she was finished speaking she held her fist out, Hank instinctively bumped it with his own fist.

"I'm going to be honest here Cerulean, I'm still not even sure if this is some kind of drunken dream or not, but on the off chance that this isn't a dream I would love to spend some time with you. Maybe you could show me around the Arbiter Hall?" asked Hank with a sly grin on his face.

"Stop attempting coitus pre-rituals with my partner!" shouted Dractus. "I need her to be focused on this mission! Now, Hank Steel you never told me which theory you believe in regarding the origins of the Hall of Arbiters and the canisters. Before I leave I would like to know which one you favor, if you would honor me with an answer."

"I don't think it matters, we use the tools we are given and do the best we can," said Hank.

"Ah, now you sound like an Arbiter!" said Dractus as he slapped hank on the back so hard that even Hank moved a little bit. "Hank, I would love to show you the farewell ceremony of my people, it involves an open mouthed kiss between brothers."

"You've got to be fucking kidding me," said Hank.

"You would insult me by not bestowing the traditional farewell meeting of tongues upon my most glorious mouth?"

"If you bring that tongue anywhere near me, I'll rip it off and shove it up your ass," said Hank while crossing his arms over his chest.

"HA! I'm just kidding initiate! I always scare new recruits with that one. See you soon noob." Then Dractus turned and left the shed.

Cerulean was left standing alone with her hands behind her back fidgeting her feet back and forth. "Hank I might take you up on your personal tour, in the meantime open your canister and stay alive. Our mission on this planet is a dangerous one, we were called here because there may be a demon about. Do your best to stay clear of us and stay out of trouble until we can take you to the Hall of Arbiters."

Hank couldn't help but think of all the dangerous stuff he was literally right about to do, and how staying safe was virtually impossible considering his planned morning activities.

"I can't make any promises on that front, but I can promise to only hurt evil people."

"Ah, the Gods above are wise, you will make an excellent Arbiter. Goodbye Hank," said Cerulean. As she tried to turn and leave Hank shouted "Wait! Hey, Cerulean, you wouldn't happen to have that goodbye lashing of tongues ceremony on your planet would you?"

"Nice try Hank!" she shouted as she walked out the door making sure to sway her hips just the right way. How do women always know when you are looking at their backsides?

Hank ran to the door of the shed and watched them both head towards a giant yellow ship. It was almost like a donut with the middle filled in. It had two stubby little wings on each side, two small tail fins on the top of it near the back, two small tail wings, and a small pointy cockpit sticking off of the front of it. It was god damn ugly is what it was. Hank had been expecting to see some kind of sleek and dark sci-fi ship, but not this. This spaceship looked more like a workhorse than anything. Ugly but obviously tough, it had a weird kind of beauty in its simplicity and lack of flair. Dractus' words came through Hank's head about how some things just aren't that alien, even if they are… well alien. The ship reminded him of a working man's vehicle. Whoever drove a ship like that was obviously his kind of person.

Dractus and Cerulean boarded the ship via some kind of lift under it and quickly took off into the early morning light. Hank realized standing there covered in three days worth of filth, that he really wished he would have showered before meeting Cerulean, and that he was pretty stinky. Also seeing the light coming over the horizon reminded him that he was on the clock. He sprinted into his house and started the coffee machine and then jumped in the shower to wash off days of funk. He quickly completed his morning grooming ritual. Then he stuffed all of his clean yellow tank tops, work pants, and socks into a backpack, except for one pair of each which he put on of course.

Hank grabbed his favorite thermos, a steel job with the words "Steel Gravel" on the side of it and topped it off with coffee. A last thought occurred to him about his small cigar collection, he grabbed about twenty of the most expensive ones and put them in a steel lunchbox and threw them in his backpack as well. As he was leaving his house he considered locking his door, but decided against it. He would never be coming back to this place anyway. He made his way over to the shed and threw his backpack up into the cab of the bulldozer. The last thing he had to do was rig up a few security cameras on the outside of the vehicle. He had upgraded the gravel yard cameras a few years back and he still had the old ones in storage here in the shed, good thing he didn't throw them out.

It's didn't take him long to get three wired up to the dozer. He had two aiming forward and one aiming back. Hank had an old 13-inch TV in the shed that he uprooted and bolted inside the cab of the dozer as well, this would get a direct feed from the security cameras. He had some small metal viewing slots on the front and sides of the cab that he hoped he wouldn't have to use. Putting his eyeballs near the tiny little slots while people shot at him didn't really seem appealing, but beggars can't be choosers.

"SHIT!" Hank yelled into the air, he had almost forgotten about the cylinder. The whole alien encounter thing still seemed like a drunken dream. Part of him expected the cylinder to not be where he had left it at the desk in his workshop. Surely all of the stress caused by this Killdozer mission had caused him to snap and there was no way the cylinder or aliens were real, right? Hank hopped out of the cab after testing the cameras and turned towards the desk. he was nervous to see the cylinder, and even more nervous to hypothetically not see it. It was there, sitting on the desk, aliens are real. Hank let out a heavy breath he didn't realize he was holding in.

Now what did Dractus say about opening this thing? Hank grabbed up the cylinder and double checked that it truly had no seems, it didn't. OPEN, thought Hank. The cylinder snapped in half, well that was easier than he thought it would be. Hank shook out the contents onto the workshop desk. Sure enough a minute Scales of Justice, and a miniature sword rolled out. Scales first, Hank grabbed them up, yanked his tank top to the side and pressed them to the flesh above his heart. An intense pain flared in his heart and radiated outward. He watched in grotesque shock as the Scales continued to sink into his skin until they were just below the surface. He wanted to drop to his knees in pain, but he refused to fall.

The pain suddenly stopped, the relief was so sudden it kind of left Hank stunned. He shook it off and grabbed up the miniature sword. What should he attach this bad boy to? Hank looked around the workshop before his eyes landed on his father's gun safe. A rifle would make a lot of sense, he kept browsing. His eyes landed on one of the bigger industrial sledgehammers, he did love to break stuff with sledgehammers, strong contender. He kept browsing, until his duh moment hit him, THE KILLDOZER. Not really sure how to apply the sword or what the sword even did, he pressed it to the door of the cab. Just like the scales it slowly sunk into the metal until it disappeared. Hank had no idea what kind of super science let a metal statue sink into an armored and metal door, but he knew the whole idea of it gave him the strong urge to crack a beer open.

76

Last minute preparation time, Hank tried to do a mental inventory of everything he might need to bring with him. He filled up a few jugs of water and threw those in the cab. He ran back to his house and grabbed some beef jerky and some cans of beans. He took the giant sledgehammer that he had been eyeballing earlier. Lastly he decided he better grab some firearms in case things went south and he needed to reach out and touch someone. He took his father's 1911 with an ammo can full of loose .45 ammunition and a few spare magazines. He found a nice leather pistol holster to accompany it in the safe. He also grabbed two shotguns, the unbranded and very illegal sawed-off from earlier, and a Remington 870. They were both chambered in 12 gauge which would make things easier. His father had birdshot, buckshot, and slug rounds stocked so he took a few boxes of each type. He figured he needed something that was going to be able to shoot accurately past 100 meters as well, so he would need a rifle to compliment the pistol and shotguns. Potentially he could be taking this rifle to space, so he needed something hardy versus overly accurate. He decided on an AK-47 variant he found at the back of the safe, Hank didn't recognize the exact model, but if he had to guess he would say it was a Hungarian. It had some nice dark stained wood furniture on it. He didn't even remember when his father had picked this one up, but it was nice. He grabbed a few of something that gun enthusiasts call "spam cans" as well, basically it's canned ammo similar to canned food, but better in every way. These particular spam cans contained 7.62x39, the ammunition he would need to feed the AK.

He tried to put his military training to use to make sure he was fully inventoried, and the Army had a saying on that front to help keep soldiers on task: 'Make sure you have your bullets, beans, and band-aids.' Hank needed the band-aids still since he was fully stocked on bullets and beans. Unfortunately all of the good med-kits were at the front of the gravel yard around the work site and he was running dangerously low on time. There was an old med-kit his father had installed in here over a decade ago mounted on the back wall of the shed, but Hank had no idea of the contents. It would have to do for now. He walked over to the steel medical box and ripped it off the wall, then chucked it into the cab of the dozer. Okay that's it, fully inventoried. Loaded up and ready for war.

Hank hopped up into the cab and started up the Killdozer. The familiar rumble shook his body in a pleasant way that filled his mind with memories of better times. He revved the engine once and the throaty growl the destructive machine made almost sounded alive and happy. Hank could smell the exhaust filling the shed and it smelled good. He could imagine it pouring out of the smokestack above him dark and billowy, but he couldn't see it because of the armor obstructing his view. He remembered he hadn't opened the larger garage door that let the Bulldozer in and out of the shed, but he decided he didn't care. He flipped the dozer into gear and drove right through it hoping he didn't accidentally rip his cameras off. The noise of metal crunching and tearing as his dozer ripped the thin garage door apart and shred it under its treads was simply fantastic. Hank could tell this was going to be a good day.

Hank didn't have a trailer on site that was rated to carry something as heavy as the dozer so unfortunately he would have to drive it to town hall which would triple the length of time it normally took to get there, but he didn't really have another choice at this point. This was around the time the local police department switched shifts so hopefully there would be no cops out on the road or they might have questions for the man in the up-armored bulldozer…

Normally Bulldozers could get up to about 15 mph, this one was customized thanks to the work Hank's father had put into it so he could push it to about 22mph. It was loud as hell and sounded like it was going to snap in half or explode at top speed, which only added to how exhilarating the experience was of driving it that fast. Hank hopped on the main road into town and saw something awesome off to his left, the east. The sun was rising, it was impossible to really enjoy it through the haphazardly mounted cameras, and there wasn't even one aiming in that direction, so he popped the cab door so he could enjoy the view unmolested. The roads were empty so he wasn't too worried about watching ahead of him so much. His father had installed a cassette player in this thing back when they were popular. Hank hit the play button to see what his father had inside. It ended up being a little AC/DC, the song Back in Black to be specific, his dad had good tastes.

For how serious the mission he was on was, Hank was in a surprisingly good mood. He took a large gulp off of his coffee, grabbed one of his favorite cigars from his backpack, cranked the music louder, and redlined the motor all the way into town. Most people would be damn near having an anxiety attack in this situation, but not Hank. He was just happy to finally have his path laid out for him, no more indecision, no more worrying. When he got to the town hall the sun was fully up and people were due to start rolling in at any minute, he had to get the Killdozer out of sight. Hank backed it into an alley across the street from the town hall and threw a tarp loosely over the top to conceal the bulk of it. Within ten minutes some security guards arrived to start their shift. Hank got a strange feeling in his stomach while looking at them. He wondered if the combination of too many beers and hot coffee with minimal food was making him sick. Then the first city employees started showing up.

A young Latina woman drove into the two-story parking garage. Hank lost sight of her while she was parking in the enclosed garage, but she soon came out of side corridor for foot traffic and headed towards the large decorative front steps of town hall. Hank couldn't explain it, but his stomach settled a bit upon getting a better look at her, she seemed like a good person. He couldn't explain why he felt that way about her, a total stranger. This process repeated itself with every person he saw. Hank left the Killdozer and came to stand just at the mouth of the alley so he could get a better look at the comings and goings of the employees of town hall. Each person that parked and walked inside gave Hank a very distinct feeling. Sometimes his body relaxed upon seeing a new person, and he had a good feeling about them. Other times he looked at someone and simply nothing happened. Then there was the last option, every once in a while he looked at someone that made his stomach try to rip itself out of his body and made bile rise in this throat. He had an undeniable urge to rip those people's faces off. Hank wondered if this was the Arbiter Intuition that Dractus and Cerulean had mentioned. In retrospect it had to be.

Hank was hesitant to trust this new power. He spent another twenty minutes watching employees enter the town hall. Most of them gave him some kind of inclination of what he assumed was good or evil. Some of them he got no feeling from whatsoever. He wasn't sure if that meant they were neutral morality wise or if they were immune to his new found power. How was this power judging who was good and who was evil? Was it using Hank's own sense or morals or something else? The person's thoughts, was he somehow reading their mind? Or was this intention based? Would someone who wants to kill the person their spouse is having an affair with be considered evil? Because Hank didn't really have a problem with that. Actions matter more than intent, wanting to do something doesn't make someone evil, you SHOULD want to kill the person your spouse is cheating on you with. You aren't evil until you actually commit an evil deed. These are some of the thoughts that were running through Hank's head. So to say he didn't completely trust his new power would be an understatement of epic proportions.

Lost in his own thoughts, Hank was following the implications of his new ability down the rabbit hole. His musings were so consuming that Hank almost missed the small convoy of five black SUV's coming down the road. The only thing that alerted him to the presence of the convoy was the strongest feeling of evil he had encountered yet. It was overwhelming and it actually made all of the muscles in his body involuntarily strain. There was something seriously sick in one of those cars. And the rest of the cars were filled with evil as well to a much lesser degree. They didn't bother heading to the parking garage, they pulled up right on the fire lane directly in front of City Hall. Who do these clowns think they are?

A small army of private security stepped out of the SUV's followed by an overweight man in an extremely expensive suit, with fingers covered in gold rings. That was the one putting off the biggest evil aura, it felt like an invisible evil rope on fire was pulling him straight at that man. Hank took a few more steps closer to the street but stayed on his side of the road, he was trying to get a better a look. *Wait a minute, is that Eugene?* Hank had to get closer and make sure. The man just looked so different than the Eugene he remembered who was an athletic young teen in a Letterman's jacket. Hank started crossing the road, it was a small town and the traffic was light so no one really minded they just gently swerved around the crazy person who hated crosswalks and muttered obscenities, it was that kind of town.

The private security noticed Hank's hulking demeanor and large frame immediately and clocked him as a threat. They spread out around Eugene and two moved forward to intercept him. One of the two that came to intercept him was calm. "Sir, you are going to have to turn back around and go to the crosswalk down the road a bit." said the calmer of the two. The second one, the hot head, couldn't wait to get his hands on Hank. He reached out to grab Hank's shoulder, and when he did Hank felt an aura flare from his evil intent. Hank grabbed the man's hand before it could touch him and he snapped the wrist. The man fell over in a clump cradling his injury. The second guy knew Hank was a serious issue at that point and reached into his coat to draw his firearm. Hank pinned his arm to his chest and then gave him the headbutt from hell, all without stopping or saying a word. He didn't even wait to see if the man would fall over, he did of course.

The rest of the security team lost all pretense of calm and drew out an assortment of sub-machine guns and pistols. They formed a protective perimeter around Eugene and backed up to the lawn of the Town Hall. Hank kept coming, he walked between their parked SUV's and only stopped when he was about ten feet out from them.

"I need a word with the man you are protecting, I'm unarmed," said Hank so calmly that it started to freak out some of the security team. Who was this brute who had just taken down two of their own like he was knocking down dominoes. Hank heard of series of bolts being pulled and actions being worked on the small myriad of guns. Why do bad guys insist on walking around without their weapon being ready to fire… amateurs.

"Open up a small hole, I think I recognize this one," said a nasally voice from somewhere inside the circle of security. The two men in front both wielding sub-machine guns squarely pointed at Hank's chest each peeled off to one side so Hank could see inside of the circle. Sure enough it was Eugene, and he had gained a ton of weight and lost a lot of hair. All of the hair on the top of his head was gone. He had one of those pedophile haircuts where the hair just rings the outside of the head leaving a shiny bald spot on top. He also had a visible gut that his expensive suit couldn't contain.

"WOW, you did not age well. You truly look like shit Eugene."

"Oh Hankey boy that's no way to talk to your betters, besides if you don't play nice I might have one of my men here accidentally shoot you."

"On the front lawn of town hall? Even you don't have that kind of clout you beady-eyed little shrimp boat bastard. I fucking dare you," said Hank with his arms held wide.

"Oh I don't *need* to shoot you, I could if I wanted to of course. I'm pretty sure I do actually have that kind of clout. No, I mean to make you a desolate vagabond. First I'll take your business and your land. I'll fire every employee you have and make sure they never get a job in this town again. Then I'll pay off some corrupt cops to plant drugs or a gun on you and I'll throw you behind bars. I don't have to lift a finger to ruin you. If you had any semblance of a brain you would have ran away screaming or begged me for mercy by now. I have my hands in everything here. The people in that building behind me are my puppets and there isn't a damn thing you can do about it."

Hank couldn't help but laugh at the short fat man lobbing empty threats at him. Hank was either going to be dead or he would be off this planet within the week. Besides Hank had never been afraid of Eugene, before this Hank knew Eugene as the young man who was too cowardly to fight on his own merits. Now Eugene was the fat balding man with a lot of money who was still so cowardly he couldn't fight on his own merits. Eugene was absolutely livid that Hank was laughing at him. Eugene's face had turned the most interesting shade of red, and he had a vein in his forehead pulsing so fast that it was liable to explode. Hank casually wondered if he could get Eugene angry enough to have a heart attack and then he could avoid this whole Killdozer business and hop on the yellow donut spaceship and try and find out if his genitals were compatible with Cerulean's.

"Hey Eugene, do you like rare vehicles? I see you came here like a coward today in those SUV's, but I mean when you aren't being a rat-coward. Do you like rare vehicles?"

"What are you blathering about moron?" Eugene said condescendingly.

"Just stay here, I've got a vehicle that you would absolutely love to see. I promise you have never seen anything like this. I've got it parked just over yonder."

Before Eugene could respond Hank turned his back on him and started jogging back across the street. He could hear Eugene yelling behind him.

"Hank goddamnit! You don't walk away from me! I don't care about whatever small town hick-mobile you are restoring!"

Eugene's frantic insults only made Hanks smile grow bigger and wider. Hank rounded the corner into the alley with giddy

84

excitement. He ripped the tarp off of the Killdozer and hopped up into the cab. He didn't want Eugene to walk away or enter town hall so he had to hurry. Hank fired up the old engine and was surprised to feel it come to a smooth idle so quickly, was that the Sword at work? He gunned it forward into the street and aimed it straight at Eugene and his men. Hank had to give Eugene's security team credit, they didn't waste any time in opening fire. Hundreds of rounds were landing on the armor of the bulldozer. The slugs were being dispensed amongst the gravel inside the armor pockets. The sound it was making was a very satisfying *ding-crunch*.

Eugene's men quickly realized the bullets weren't working and started retreating. They were scrambling in all directions, some were haphazardly firing over one shoulder as they ran. Hank knew it was now or never. He slapped the bulldozer into a higher gear and gunned it into the crowd of them. He had the blade about half a foot off of the ground and a few of them got sucked under the dozer while the blade broke their shoulders and cut into them. After the trouncing by the blade the lucky ones were quickly silenced under the treads as they were squashed into shithead pancakes. The unlucky ones were only partially squashed, an arm here, a leg there. Only to be left for dead behind the dozer with injuries sure to kill them. Hank noticed the ones being left for dead and decide to drop the ripper a few times hoping to catch a few of them with a piercing attack. A Ripper is a large spike kept on the rear end of some bulldozers, there are many types of rippers. Hank had a single point ripper installed, imagine a giant scorpion tail except aiming downwards. Normally it is used to till soil or tear up old roads, but it works pretty good on criminal's faces as well.

The screams of Eugene's security team filled Hank with an almost childlike glee, these men weren't ignorant about who they worked for. These guys knew Eugene was evil and they helped him and protected him anyway, enabling him to hurt more people. These shitheads needed to die. That was what Hank's logical mind was telling him anyway. His Arbiter intuition was screaming that he needed to rip these men to pieces and eat their souls. Hank's knuckles were white on the controls of the bulldozer as he fought to keep his rational mind in charge of his body. Hank didn't like this feeling of having to fight against himself. In fact it distracted him and caused him to lose track of Eugene's whereabouts.

Hank tried to recall through his blood-thirsty haze if Eugene had been in the crowd that he had smooshed as he scanned the remaining fleeing security men who had been quick enough on their feet to avoid the initial onslaught. It was hard to get a good view of everything through the security camera footage on the little 13-inch TV. Hank stopped the dozer and grabbed the Remington 870, a long-barreled shotgun. It was loaded with alternating rounds of buck and birdshot. He checked the feed on his rear camera to make sure there was no one behind him who would shoot him in the back, and then he cracked his armored door open. He gripped the top of the door and pulled himself over the edge of it, he braced his shotgun on the ledge and looked down the sights. He scanned the town hall grounds and saw all the dead and dying he had left behind. He could still see security men running everywhere and civilians were trying to evacuate the town hall as well. Some of them were still confused and were just trying to get a good view of what was going on. Hank could hear sirens in the distance.

There, Hank spotted Eugene climbing the steps of town hall. He was cowering behind two members of his security team. Hank took aim and let off a few shots at them with the shotgun. The Remington 870 is a pump action so you can fire it as fast as you can work the action. Some people like to get flashy and rack it so fast their hand becomes a blur. Hank was the opposite, slow and methodical, he took careful aim for center mass before firing his rounds. One of the security men went down and he swore he saw Eugene get clipped on his side somewhere as well because he had visibly staggered, hopefully from a hit rather than fear. The last security man with Eugene turned around and fired on Hank as Eugene ran inside the building. Hank had to take cover. He closed the door to his cab and revved his engine. He aimed the bulldozer at the front steps of town hall where Eugene had entered the building and where one of his security men was still taking pot shots at him, and he gunned it forward. Hank hoped the man shooting at him would be dumb enough to stay still. He pulled his blade up high so it wouldn't get caught on the steps and he began to climb them. Once the bulldozer leveled out on the landing he could see his hopes were for not because the last security man and Eugene were gone, they had escaped somewhere inside the depths of town hall.

He had a decision to make, it didn't take him long. This was the same building where the town council unanimously decided to steal his land. Hank never really understood the logic of legislatively stealing shit. Whether you are holding someone at gunpoint to rob someone, or voting for it on a ballot alone in your home, stealing is still stealing. Hank never understood how that was morally or legally allowed in the modern world. Oh well, this was the building the thieves operated out of, fuck em, and fuck this building. Hank gunned the Killdozer forward into town hall crushing everything in his path. The long standing walls of the building crumbled to the might of the dozer. Someone in a white shirt and tie tried to dart out of a side room to get away from the collapsing area of the building. Hank got a strong feeling of evil from him so he gunned it forward and made sure the man was swallowed by rubble.

He kept pushing through the building, concrete and debris were piling up on top of the bulldozer and it sounded like he was unleashing hell. Drywall dust started drifting in through his peephole slots and he could hear people screaming in other parts of the building as he continually knocked down wall after wall. Hank occasionally rolled up a bureaucrat or two, crushing them with the insane amount of rubble he was pushing. Hank couldn't help but feel elated and accomplished at how many evil souls he had destroyed.

Chapter 6

He pushed through a final wall and hit sunlight. He slammed on his breaks hard using his forward momentum to get the bulk of the debris stuck all over his dozer to fly forward. Hank heard a scream from somewhere behind him in the slowly collapsing building. His rational mind thought *good another corrupt bureaucrat bites the dust*, but his Arbiter intuition had other ideas. His whole body screamed that he needed to go back. Against his better judgment he decided to give this Arbiter Intuition thing a solid try. He grabbed his sledgehammer and hopped out of the dozer. He felt a different pull in the direction of the road that ran behind the Townhall, the road his bulldozer was now pointed at. His body was pulling him back the way he had come and forward at the same time. The feeling behind him felt cool and calming, the feeling ahead of him felt hot and angry. Those descriptions weren't exactly accurate, but there were the closest things Hank could come up with to describe the feelings.

He scanned the street ahead of him until he saw what his body was directing him towards. It was Eugene and his last security man getting into a police car. He started walking toward Eugene and began to draw the 1911 from the holster at his waist, then the feeling behind him flared up again and he heard a woman scream "HELP!" very clearly. He had to choose between helping an innocent or killing Eugene. Hank stood there and stared as Eugene got into the police car and drove away "FUCK!" he couldn't leave someone behind. He spun around and darted into the building. The screams were coming from somewhere above him, the woman was on the second story.

She screamed again and Hank heard the building groan in protest, he must have taken out way too many load-bearing walls. This thing was coming down. There was too much rubble, he couldn't find a way to get to where he was guessing the stairwell was. He ran back outside and looked for a way to climb up the ornamental bricks and he just didn't see one. There was a small decorative ledge that would be a great handhold but it was at least 13 feet up. His bulldozer was still parked just outside the building though, he thought he might be able to jump from the top of his bulldozer into one of the windows on the second floor. The building groaned again, he was out of time. He scaled the dozer with his sledgehammer in tow. He didn't see a way he could jump across with it so he threw it through the large window closest to his parked dozer. The glass shattered and left sharp edges everywhere. Hank didn't have any gloves, the woman screamed again…

He made the jump knowing it was going to hurt. The glass cut into his hands as he pulled himself through the window. He picked up his sledgehammer and headed toward the door that he thought his Intuition was pointing him towards. He saw the problem right away, it was some kind of security door and the frame was warped because the building was collapsing. The door was probably jammed in there impossibly tight.

"HEY IF YOU CAN HEAR ME IN THERE, STAND BACK!" he shouted.

He reared back and used all of his strength to swing the sledge at the top part of the door where it looked like it was lodged into the frame the most. The door shifted and screeched, Hank could see he had gotten that particular piece unstuck and it was even bent backwards into the room a bit. He swung again this time directly at the door handle. His hit landed true, the door handle and the deadbolt exploded into the room and the door popped open. He ran inside and noticed the floor was at a slant, that's not good. There was a woman crying in the corner, it was the Latina woman from the parking garage earlier. He ran over to her and crouched near her, he waited for her to meet his eyes.

"Ma'am, listen closely to me, we have to leave. Is there any other *good* people in the building?" The woman started babbling nonsense and then switched to Spanish.

"MA';AM!" she got quiet. "Listen carefully, is there any other *GOOD* people in the building?" That time something clicked and she understood, though she looked slightly confused while answering.

"Si, uh yes, Tim next door." she pointed at the wall that Hank assumed went to the next office over. Hank stood up and hefted his sledgehammer over one shoulder. He ran at the wall and took a long downward swipe through the drywall careful not to overextend his swing. He didn't want to hit someone who might be standing just on the other side of the wall. He peeked in through the new opening and he did see a man slumped over on his carpet just behind his desk. Hank pushed himself through the drywall and went to the man. He pulled him up by his shirt and the man's eyes snapped open.

"Where am I? What's happening?" the man was confused.

"It's okay, we are leaving, this building has to be evacuated. Can you walk?" asked Hank.

"Yes, I think so. I'm embarrassed to admit I have narcolepsy I was just taking a small nap. What's going on?"

"It's not safe here, just follow me."

Hank walked back through the hole he had made in the drywall and helped the Latina woman get to her feet. She was favoring one leg and it seemed like she may have twisted an ankle. She kept her arm around one of his shoulders and they walked back the way Hank had come in as the building continued to groan.

"Sir, your hands are bleeding quite profusely," said Tim.

"It's okay, I'll take care of it when we are safe."

They got to the window and both of the people with Hank looked stunned and worried. "Sorry to tell you guys this but the stairway is destroyed. This is the safest way out. Jump to the bulldozer down there, it's only about a three foot jump across, the rest is just falling down. It's not hard." The male town hall employee who the Latina woman had referred to as Tim looked confused and put his hands on his head with his hands interlocked and took a few paces around the hallway then seemed to come to the realization that this was the only way as he looked around and heard the building groan and shift some more.

"Okay, I'll go first, and then I'll stay in place to help you two," said Tim. Hank was glad he saved him, this was a good guy.

"Wait!" The woman shouted. "A madman was driving that bulldozer and attacking the building, that's why this place is crumbling. We can't jump onto his roof he might be down there waiting to kill us." Hank knew he couldn't tell these people that he was the madman.

"Oh he is gone, he fled the scene. We have to move!" Hank's point was taken seriously as the building groaned once more. Apparently that was Tim needed to hear because jumped out the window narrowly avoiding the broken glass. Despite being in his forties with salt and pepper hair he made it to the roof of the bulldozer with ease. The Latina woman with Hank looked out the window and turned back to him with fear on her face.

92

"Mister, I can't jump that and you can't throw me that far."
Hank decided to check as well. He COULD throw her that far, but
not without injuring her.

"I've got an idea to get you safely across," said Hank.

He took his sledgehammer and scraped all of the remaining
shards of glass out of the frame of the window. It was a skinny
and tall window, and it started only about a foot off the ground.
Hank looked out the window again and threw his sledgehammer
near the driver's side area of the bulldozer's cab on the ground.
He didn't want to lose that one, it felt lucky for some reason. He
picked up the Latina woman in a cradle carry and before she
could protest he jumped out of the window and landed on top of
the bulldozer. He almost lost his footing, but Tim had stood by his
word and waited for them. Tim was able to stabilize Hank before
he slipped. Tim helped Hank get the woman safely to the ground.

Right about this time two police cruisers pulled around the
back of Town Hall, there was probably two or three times as
many out front. Officers jumped out of the vehicles with pistols
braced over door frames aimed at Hank.

"What the hell are they aiming guns at us for?" shouted Tim.

"Well Tim, I hate to be the one to tell you this, but I'm the one
they are looking for. Anyway thank you for helping me, and would
you please stand back away from the vehicle. It looks like I have
to leave now and I would hate for the police to shoot you nice
folks on accident."

Tim looked confused and hurt as he partially realized what as
going on, and Hank felt a pang of guilt he couldn't quite explain
at Tim's betrayed expression. He felt he had to say something. "I
promise I had a good reason for this, you may not understand it

93

now, but I was protecting people today." Tim didn't respond, he just stared at Hank as if he couldn't trust him and helped the Latina woman get a safe distance away from the bulldozer. Hank took a step towards his Bulldozer and a round landed at his feet. One of the officers reached into the patrol car and quickly pulled out a megaphone.

"SIR IF YOU TAKE ONE MORE STEP TOWARDS THAT VEHICLE WE WILL KILL YOU!"

Hank couldn't get caught up here. Eugene was still out there and Hank knew Eugene had the money to drive the narrative of the story of what had happened today. People wouldn't know that Hank was destroying evil and protecting a small town under siege from a megalomaniac sociopath. Hank would get painted as some kind of anti-government nut and locked in a cell to rot. Fuck that, he would rather die. Sure, maybe Dractus and Cerulean would come for him, but he couldn't count on them. For all he knew they had some kind of rule about not interfering with the local constabulary. Besides they were busy dealing with a demon, whatever the hell that meant. Hank was on his own.

He bolted, pushing his legs like never before. Hank hated cardio, in his opinion cardio was for weirdos and women having a midlife crisis. He had entertained the idea of laying down his own covering fire during the run but he couldn't bring himself to shoot at police, especially when his Arbiter intuition was telling him that both of them were pretty nice guys. The sound of the incoming gunfire definitely gave Hank the motivation to move faster, but it wasn't enough. He felt searing pain fly through his left calf, and then another line of pain across his back. He jumped, pushing off on his right leg aiming for the cab. He pulled himself in like his life depended on it, because it did. He yanked the cab door shut and threw the rudimentary crossbar he had installed to keep it locked.

94

He could feel blood filling his left shoe, *that's not good*. He yanked his work boot off and rolled up his pant leg. He had absolutely taken a round to his leg. A clean through and through, he could touch the exit wound and tell it was serious. He broke open the old med-kit and found some gauze that was so thin it had to be over two decades old. He would just have to wrap a few more layers on. He pressure wrapped the wound as best as he could for now, knowing that if it kept bleeding he would have to tourniquet the leg. That would not be good. Once he had tended to his leg he pulled off his yellow tank top that was now partially drenched in his blood. He reached behind himself and used the tips of his fingers to assess the wound on his back. He couldn't tell exactly what was going on but it felt like a long superficial gash, the kind that bleeds a lot but isn't too serious, he hoped... His hands were still torn up and weeping blood as well, but that was small fries compared to the hole in his leg. He used a knife to cut off the parts of his shirt that weren't already covered in blood. Then he cut that same blood free section in half. He wrapped each half around his hands. Best he could do for now.

He had been so consumed with his first aid activities he hadn't realized he was surrounded. He saw in his monitor that there was cops everywhere. Multiple teams of cops had riot shields in front of each group of raiders that were approaching his vehicle on all sides, and one particular brave cop had even started tugging on the door of his cab. *SHIT,* he thought as he slammed the bulldozer into the lowest gear and started a slow roll to throw them off a bit and buy himself some more time. His Arbiter Intuition was going crazy, half of these cops were genuinely good people and the other half were throwing all kinds of strong evil vibes. Those must be the ones that were on Eugene's payroll.

Hank couldn't afford to hurt the good ones, he didn't know what to do.

It was then that he noticed a little blinking yellow icon on the bottom right hand corner of the television he was using to run the security camera feed into the dozer. The little icon was shaped like a sword. *What the fuck is that!* thought Hank as he tried to rub it off with his finger. As soon as his hand touched it though, some words appeared above the view of the cameras, filling the length and width of basically the entire screen. They said:

"You have four upgrades available, please choose where to invest your souls:

Speed +

Armor +

Offense +

Defense +

U.I. +

Efficiency +

Advanced Upgrades (Click for more options)"

"What the fuck, this isn't even a touchscreen!" Hank shouted. *Well whatever, when in Rome…* He quickly pressed the plus signs next to Speed, Armor, and Defense. At that point a gray bar at the bottom of the screen popped up with the words "Confirm Choices?" on it. He pressed it, and the button disappeared. The whole Killdozer started to shudder. The most noticeable thing from Hank's perspective that was changing was the small forward facing slot that he had cut as a backup viewing measure. It was normally six inches across and two inches tall, except it had just started expanding...

"NO NO NO!" Hank shouted at the impossible thing happening in front of him.

Hank got lower in his seat and moved his body to the side in the hopes of avoiding incoming bullets as he shifted into a higher gear and tried to speed up. He didn't understand why the slot was enlarging, but if it got too much bigger he was surely going to get shot in the face. As it expanded he got a better view of what was going on in front of the dozer. There was cops crawling all over it who had been just out of the view of the cameras. One of them had just finished crawling on to the top of the engine compartment and was only a few feet away from Hank. The cop shakily stood on the moving vehicle and grabbed the smokestack for leverage. He had gloves on or he would have just lost some skin. The cop lifted his gun and pointed it at the slot that was still expanding, directly at Hank's chest. Hank's Arbiter Intuition was telling him that this was a really bad dude. The cop grinned and fired.

Hank exhaled hard wondering why he wasn't dead. He looked at the police officer who was equally confused. In between them seemingly floating in the air in the middle of the once-was slot was the police officer's deformed slug that he had fired. Hank stared closer and noticed a small spider web stretching out in all directions from it. He tried to touch the slug but found he couldn't, his finger hit a transparent resistance. Somehow a thin layer of extremely strong glass had grown in the slot, the slot that was now about two feet by two feet in size. Hank wouldn't call it a windshield since it was so small, but it was definitely a window or view port of sorts and it was easier to use than the forward facing view from the security camera. The new glass was bullet proof or at least bullet resistant. The slug had damaged it somewhat, Hank could see that, so enough sustained damage probably would bring it down. The police officer fired again and another slug lodged itself into the glass and more spiderwebs appeared.

Shit, he had to get that guy off of there. He cranked the Killdozer from side to side and tried to dislodge him but the fucker was holding on tight...

Hank's Killdozer left the rear lawn of the Town Hall now that he was picking up speed so he aimed it down a residential alley nearby. He could see in the rear camera that almost every squadcar in town was chasing him and he still had cops climbing all over his bulldozer trying to find a way inside. His screen was blinking again, this time it read 'Deploy defensive electric blast?' Hank didn't think twice, he tapped it. Cops went flying in all directions except for the evil one on his hood who was still holding on. The electrical current only made his grip stronger it appeared as the cops muscles involuntarily spasmed. Hank could tell when the electrical current stopped because the cop looked up at him again, but this time groggily. The cop slowly started raising his gun back toward Hank's new windshield. The button to deploy the electric blast was still on the screen. Hank hit it again, and again, and again. The third time he noticed something weird... He swore he saw a red ethereal version of the evil-cop rise a few inches out of the cop's body before it's face put on a grimace of pure terror. Then the ethereal red version of the cop started stretching and elongating towards the engine compartment of the bulldozer. This continued until the whole thing had passed through his hood. "What the shit was that!" Hank shouted. To his surprise a quick reply was displayed on the screen "1 evil soul consumed."

Hank hit the next major thoroughfare and hooked a right, not really sure where he was going. It was only about 9 a.m. on a weekday, so luckily traffic was light. Otherwise the giant Killdozer and the 20 squad cars chasing it would probably have caused quite a commotion. He started shifting through his gears to get to max speed. He wanted to see what this thing could do now with the new speed upgrade. There was no speedometer in here so he couldn't get the exact number but it felt like he was moving at least twice as fast as before so maybe somewhere just over 40 mph, which is insanely fast for a bulldozer. He knew whatever he did he was going to have to get these cops off of his tail, especially the evil ones. He was too far away from them to be able to use his Arbiter Intuition to separate which were which so he couldn't risk hurting them unless they got close so he could verify that he wouldn't be hurting innocents. He could still hear rounds dinging as they hit his vehicle so someone somewhere was taking potshots.

Hesitantly he reached up to the side slot he had cut to see to his left. He had one on his right as well and one aiming backwards. He had to test this theory, he pushed his hand at the slot and hit resistance, just like he had when he tried the front. When he pulled his hand away there was a bloody fingerprint on the glass filling the left slot. It was so new and clean it appeared almost invisible. So, he was completely sealed in now by bullet proof material, good. If he wasn't slowly bleeding to death he would probably be pretty elated about this situation. Hank had to get medical attention quick, find some way to meet up with Dractus and Cerulean, and find some way to ditch the authorities. Lastly he had to find and kill Eugene.

None of the squad cars had dared pull ahead of him yet. Hank didn't blame them for being hesitant after seeing the Killdozer in action with its many unknown capabilities. Hank decided he was going to use their position to his advantage. He was a little afraid to try this at the speed he was going but he didn't have much of a choice if he wanted to lose these clowns. He pulled to the far right side of the road still going a little over 40mph and dropped his ripper. He fought hard to maintain control of the dozer, the ripper was tearing the street to shreds and bleeding off his momentum quickly. He yanked the controls hard and aimed the dozer sharply left. He cut a jagged diagonal line all the way across the road and jumped the dozer up onto the sidewalk before lifting the ripper back up. He had created a foot wide crater all the way across the road with jagged razor-sharp asphalt edges. Some of the police officers were smart enough to hit their brakes but some tried to drive over the new ditch and lost axles or blew tires on the sharp edges. One swerved into it and began to roll. Others were hit by flying asphalt that the ripper had thrown up into the air at terrible speeds, it was pure pandemonium. Hank couldn't help but smile.

Hank's cellphone began to ring, shit he should have turned this thing off. The caller ID was saying the number was unknown. He wondered if Cerulean was calling him. His blood soaked finger couldn't get the touch screen to work for a second but the third attempt went through and the call connected.

"Hello?"

"Hank, It's Jimmy."

"Hey Jimmy, good to hear from you. I'm a bit busy right now."

"I know, I'm guessing you are the crazy fucker in the armored bulldozer?"

"Yeah that's me, you can't talk me out of this. I mean to kill Eugene."

"I'm not trying to talk you out of anything. Listen to me, some local movers and shakers saw what you were doing on the news, look above you and see the news helicopter. Anyway they are using you as a distraction to rob the bank."

"So? It's insured, let them rob it."

"Hank, you aren't thinking straight right now. The bank in your town Hank, where Suzie works. The gal you would never stop talking about whenever you got drunk enough. The robbery isn't going well, they have hostages. I've got a few guys in the area and I'm on my way myself, but you are the closest. If you still care about this lady, she is in danger... Listen the choice is yours I just thought you should know. I still keep an ear to the ground in your neck of the woods and check up on you. You know, I just felt I owed you. You were the only person I ever felt I could really trust... You get it."

"Thanks for calling me Jimmy but you really shouldn't have called me. The police are surely going to check my phone records."

"Hank, this aint my first rodeo. This is a burner and there about 10,000 'Jimmys' in this state... Are you going after her?"

"Yeah."

"I'll try to meet you there, I might be able to help you out of that situation you are in."

"Don't come anywhere near me Jimmy. These cops are shooting to kill and half of them are on Eugene's payroll."

The line went dead. Hank tried to call the number back but all he got was an automated message saying the line was out of service. *SHIT, Jimmy is liable to get himself killed or arrested.* Now two people Hank cared about were going to be in danger. Hank decided to make a beeline for the bank. Eventually more cops caught up to him but he would just drop the ripper here and there to throw asphalt at them and create potholes that they would have to dodge. Eventually they decided to back off and let the helicopters track Hank.

Hank arrived at the bank in short order. There was only two squad cars in front of it, both had cops huddled behind them. Hank heard automatic gun fire and could see a muzzle flash coming from just inside the bank which was obscured in shadow. Soon rounds traced their way up the side of one of the police cars. The cops were pinned down and couldn't enter. They were also extremely out-manned thanks to Hank. Hank had disabled half the police cars in town and slowed the other ones down miles back. Hank had a mini-flashback of all those years ago of not being able to defend Suzie as Eugene slashed her face. He couldn't fail her again.

If he got out of the Killdozer and tried to enter the bank on foot the cops were liable to gun him down, so were the bank robbers inside for that matter. He couldn't help anyone if he was dead. He couldn't really see another option for a safe entry other than just crashing into the side of the bank with the Killdozer, but he also didn't want to accidentally kill a bunch of innocent people in the process so he couldn't go in blind. He was still losing blood from his leg, and he was getting lightheaded. He was running out of time, blood, and people he cared about. His mind came back around to his new Arbiter Intuition. How did it work exactly, what was the range? He tried to get a feel for the cops taking cover in front of the bank, they were about 100 feet away from his position. He couldn't get a reading off of them. So he figured there must be a range on the ability or he wasn't trying hard enough.

He pulled the bulldozer up in line with the police cars in front of the bank and looked out one of his side slots to see the comical surprised expressions on their faces. He tried his Intuition again now that they were only about thirty feet away from him. He immediately got a reading off of both of them. One was a shining

102

beacon of positive light, the other one was more of a muted gray and dull type of energy. Keep in mind Hank wasn't seeing any actual colors, these were just some of the things his mind used to make understanding the Arbiter Intuition a little easier. He was obviously getting a read on the police officers through the heavy armor on the Killdozer. So it seemed like solid objects didn't interrupt his ability, it could be reducing the efficiency but there was no way Hank could figure that out short of getting out of the dozer and standing in the line of fire.

He remembered outside the town hall when he was on foot at the mouth of the alley that he was getting reads on people clear across the street. There was too many factors to consider here. Was he getting better reads before because there was no material between him and the people or was it because he was more energetic and awake, or because he had more blood in his body? *Stick to the facts you are going on a tangent*, thought Hank. He knew the Arbiter Intuition worked through solid matter, it was the only real edge he had. The bulldozer wouldn't be much help in a hostage situation… Realizing that made Hank have his first real whiff of regret for choosing the Killdozer as his Arbiter weapon... He pulled the Killdozer closer to the bank, he angled it around the side of it so those inside wouldn't see him. He parked with his vehicle facing the side wall. He started trying to use his Arbiter Intuition on the wall of the bank.

At first all he got was vague impressions of what might be inside, but he couldn't be sure if that was his guess based off of his memories or if it was his actual Arbiter Intuition working. It reminded him of the hearing tests he used to take for school and the military. Some of the beeps the testing machine would make were so faint that he couldn't tell if he was actually hearing them or if his mind was generating them, this whole situation was just

103

like that. The Arbiter Intuition isn't like hearing though, it's some kind of metaphysical power. Hank wondered if it had any limitations at all or if the only limitations on it were the ones his mind was making up as he went. Maybe he was trying to relate it to the wrong thing. He decided to think of the Intuition like a strong muscle and using the power as lifting a heavy weight. He focused again on the wall and pushed with his new imaginary muscle. Then he tried to imagine a beam of light coming from his body and going through the wall.

He actually felt physical resistance when he did particular exercise. It felt like his attempt had been physically bounced off of the wall, it was so surprising he stopped. He realized he had been clenching his eyes closed while trying it. When he opened them he actually felt dizzy. He felt wetness on his upper lip as well. He reached up and touched it, fresh blood… He was pushing so hard he had somehow injured himself. *Well fuck it, a little blood never killed anyone and she still needs me.* He closed his eyes and pushed again. This time his imaginary tentacle of light burst right through the wall. He could *see* everyone inside of the bank. A smattering of cool blue figures on an ocean of black. Spaced among them evenly was a half dozen red and burning individuals with angry looking auras marching back and forth nervously. One of them was leaned forward, his body was vibrating as he pulled the trigger on an invisible gun. Hank could even see his body move with the recoil of the weapon that Hank couldn't see. His Intuition must not work on inanimate objects.

Near the back of the bank was a woman who had a red figure's arm wrapped around her neck. One of his hands hovered about six inches away. He was holding an invisible gun and pointing it right at her head. Somehow Hank knew that was Suzie. He started looking for an area that was clear of "blues." In

104

the back portion of the bank there was a giant black box he couldn't pierce with his power it was about the size of a small bedroom. Hank guessed that was the vault. Just next to it was a space where only one red figure stood with no blue or Grey figures around him. Hank could use that as his entry point. He pulled his power back to his body and immediately felt like he was drowning. His eyes snapped open and he gasped for air, he couldn't breath. He couldn't catch his breath, he was dizzy beyond belief and his naked torso was covered in blood that had been dripping from his eyes and nose. He slumped backwards and couldn't move, his whole body felt tingly.

He didn't have time for this nonsense. He fought to move his limbs and they slowly responded with needles of pain coming from every direction. He made a mental note to never use his Arbiter Intuition like that again. He felt like dying would be a nice reprieve from the pain he was in now, but he still had people who needed his help. He started revving the engine of the bulldozer. As he was about to shift it into gear a familiar face peeked around the back corner of the bank. Jimmy?

Chapter 7

Eugene was busy stuffing loose valuables and bundles full of cash from his safe into a large duffel bag as fast as he could. He knew when it was time to get out of dodge and that time was now. Even with all of his security and the cops he had paid off he still wasn't safe from Hank's ire. With so much attention drawn on their small town his PR team would be busy for weeks putting out fires and trying to clear his name of any wrongdoing in this mess. Might as well sit somewhere on a warm beach like Cabo San Lucas sipping margaritas with hookers and wait out the madness.

Eugene wondered if Cabo San Lucas had any of those underage ladyboys like Thailand had, he sure did love him some ladyboys. He went to Thailand as often as he could to sample their specific *flavor*... Even that wouldn't make him fully happy though, he knew that. He wouldn't be content until that rat bastard Hank was dead and in the ground. He was finally on the verge of getting his revenge from what Hank had done to him all those years ago at the lake. Then Hank had to go and rig up some infernal redneck machine to spoil all of Eugene's plans. Hank the thief, Hank the brute, Hank the peasant. He was disturbing the natural order of things. People like Eugene were meant to lead, people like Hank were meant to sweep floors. *That giant oaf needs to die.*

Eugene could always arrange an untimely demise for Hankey boy from the safety of a private beach. Eventually law enforcement would stop Hank, Eugene knew that, and then it would just be a few phone calls to the right people and old Hank would be swinging from some shoelaces in a jail cell. Eugene would personally piss on his grave at that point. Hell, he might even pay some desperate poor people to kick his corpse and light it on fire, or even start up some rotating shifts for hobos to come piss on it daily. He would cross that bridge when he came to it, either way the world could rest assured that Eugene Tillerman was going to fuck up Hank's entire existence.

Eugene finished packing, he was a little light on clothes but he could always buy more suits when he arrived. He only had one member of his security team left, Joe Buckley. The rest of his security had either been murdered or ran off by Hank, but not Joe. Joe Buckley had been a true acolyte in the Church of Eugene. Truly a zealot by every meaning of the word, fanatical and beyond loyal, just the way Eugene liked them. Eugene often had some kind of half baked excuse whenever he had to have his men muscle someone into submission or when he needed a little evidence hidden or destroyed. Joe Buckley never questioned these easily seen through lies, he accepted them, got paid, and moved on. For these reasons Joe Buckley quickly moved up in Eugene's inner-circle of confidants.

Any particularly nasty task Eugene needed completed he would always send Joe. Like the time he had gotten a little overzealous with that hooker. You know they say a choking fetish can be fun. Well whoever 'they' are couldn't be more wrong. Nothing is fun about having to roll up a corpse in plastic at four in the morning with your head of security, talk about awkward. Luckily Joe took care of her quietly and quickly. Joe owns a dozen acres of backwood land *gifted* to him by Eugene. Said land happens to have an industrial grade wood chipper on it that can really make unwanted things disappear quickly. Besides you wouldn't believe how good a human body is for compost. You can grow the most amazing lilacs on ground soaked with human blood.

"Joe, carry this out to the Lincoln please," said Eugene.

"Yes sir," replied Joe, diligently as ever.

The Lincoln, Eugene's only great love. The Lincoln was a 1970's model Lincoln Limousine, not in the traditional sense of the word limousine of course. When you hear the word limousine you think of a giant stretch-mobile full of horny kids getting picked up for prom. Or maybe even captains of industry courting a new client. This was a limousine in the traditional sense, being that it was only ever slightly longer than your average car. Just long enough for some of Eugene's night guests to be able to get on their knees with room to spare in the back...

The entire vehicle had been refurnished, refurbished, and rebuilt from the ground up. It now sported an engine powerful enough to drive something twice its size that could go from 0 to 60 in six seconds. Kevlar layers had been added to the interior of the doors and the trunk lining making the vehicle mostly bulletproof, but not completely. You can't retrofit armored glass into these older models it would have made the weight of the vehicle too cumbersome. That didn't bother Eugene though. If he did his job right and eliminated problems ahead of time he wouldn't be getting shot at anyway, worst case scenario he would just have to get lower in his seat for a bit until his security whisked him to safety. Of course it also had a top of the line sound system, a mini-fridge, a mini-bar, and a full sized television in the back. Some people would have balked at updating an older model like this, but there was just something about the hard lines of 70's automobiles that Eugene loved.

Lastly Eugene had the entire car painted in a dark royal green that was borderline black. There was just something regal about the color and it was unique enough that no one else would have it which sent the message that Eugene wasn't like the peasants that surrounded him on a daily basis. Eugene loved to use any excuse he could to let people know he was better than them. Even something as subtle as a custom color on a collector's car.

Eugene took one last glance at his large estate as he got into the Lincoln wondering when he would be able to come back here and how long it would take to shake the political headhunters looking for a scapegoat off of his tail. In the end he decided it didn't really matter, he could always relocate and start his game somewhere else. He had enough seed money packed away in his bag and located in untouchable tax free overseas accounts to guarantee that.

Eugene had to really maneuver to get his sizable girth through the car door. The rear doors weren't small by any means, but Eugene had some well paid for size on him. He had considered getting back into shape a few times, but with money like his he could always pay beautiful people to be with him. And isn't that what self-vanity is really about, wanting to attract other attractive people to you. The whole concept was irrelevant for Eugene since there would always be someone as desperate as he was disgusting and rich.

Joe Buckley hopped in the driver's seat and they were on their way. Eugene was heading to a small airport nearby where he had chartered a private jet. *Only peasants fly commercial,* thought Eugene. He also decided that this was a good time to mix himself a drink and get the party started. Other people in his situation would have been extremely upset right now after seeing most of the men who had been protecting him over the last few years brutally murdered, but not Eugene. He could always hire more. Besides their whole job was to keep people alive including

109

themselves and it wasn't Eugene's fault that they sucked at their job. Or at least that was the way Eugene figured it as he mixed himself a Manhattan from the mini-bar in the back of the limousine.

"Sir I recommend we head through the warehouse district. Downtown is still a mess with local and federal-level authorities," said Joe.

"Do what you have to do Joe, I trust you," said Eugene. After saying that he realized he did trust Joe. It was a strange feeling. He would even go so far as to say he actually liked Joe. He was glad Joe had been the one to make it out of that mess earlier with him. Eugene relaxed his considerable girth even further back into the seat cushions and decided to ponder on his relationship with Joe and whether or not it actually might be a liability. He lost track of time going down this line of thought before he finally landed on the conclusion that he should give Joe a raise. That was the last thought Eugene had before a giant black tentacle smashed through the front window and ripped Joe's head off.

Eugene didn't even have time to scream or take in his surroundings before he was thrown around the back seat and then shrouded into darkness. It almost felt like an earthquake and he wondered idly as he was further tossed around if he had fallen into a sinkhole of some sort, but that line of thought didn't explain the removal of Joe's head. The car was jerked around a few more times and then everything got really still. Eugene scrambled in the backseat for the hidden gun safe he had back here with a small .38 revolver resting inside of it. It was just under the driver's side seat aimed facing him behind some wood paneling that was part of the mini-bar. It was almost impossible to get to in the dark, but Eugene wasn't a complete moron he had practiced this maneuver many times and he quickly found the trap-door in the wood and had his fingers pressed onto the fingerprint authentication area of the micro-safe. The safe made the best sound in the world that Eugene could've heard in this situation, a soft buzz meaning it had accepted his prints and the door popped open. Eugene quickly grabbed the gun, not sure where to aim it. He always kept it loaded. There was more ammo in the safe, but he wasn't worried about that right now.

He heard a heavy clack from somewhere far off and the sound echoed, the echo told him that he was inside. A distant set of lights appeared. Then another clack, and another. Lights were coming on far above him, he could tell he was in a large warehouse. He was still on the dark end of the warehouse but the lights were quickly turning on in sequence and heading his direction. Soon the area he was in would be illuminated. He could see the dark silhouette of Joe Buckley's decapitated corpse ahead of him in the driver's seat. He knew it was time make a run for it while he still had the cover of darkness. He also surely knew he needed to get out of whatever fucked up situation he was in.

He had to get his bag from the trunk, it had most of his cash and his passports in it, his real one and his forgeries. He kept an extra set of Lincoln keys on him for situations like this, well not just like this... He trusted Joe, but he trusted himself more and kings always have contingencies. He quietly stepped out of the back of the car and snuck around to the trunk of the vehicle. He had to hurry, the lights were getting closer and whoever dragged him in here would surely see him as soon as this end of the warehouse lit up. He popped the trunk, grabbed the bag, and prepared to run. His heart was beating so fast he could barely breathe. He was too late, the lights above him flicked on.

Standing just off to the side of him were two creatures straight out of a nightmare. One was a man entirely composed of a shiny black stone with red glowing eyes. The stone was joined in hundreds of places, almost like irregular shaped scales. The stone man was a summer dream compared to the thing standing next to him. If the stone man was scary, this thing was horrifying. It was at least 13 feet tall, maybe more, it was hard to tell because it was slumped over. It's arms were so long that it's fists rested on the ground much like a gorilla. Though it's limbs were twice as thick as any guerrilla Eugene had ever seen, and they were lined with rock hard muscle. It's skin was wet, dark, and slimy looking. The skin seemed out of place on a bipedal creature land creature. This was the kind of skin Eugene had only seen on octopuses and deep sea creatures during nature documentaries. Jutting off of it's back were four long tentacles flailing in different directions seemingly of their own accord.

One of the tentacles shot outwards and stretched into the driver's side window of the Lincoln. It wrapped around Joe Buckley's body and lifted it high into the air. The thing tilted its head back and opened its maw wide. From Eugene's angle he could just see that it had layers and layers of teeth, far too many teeth. The tentacle dropped Joe head first, well if he had a head left, Joe fell a few feet until he landed in the creature's mouth. Apparently the creature had a limit on how much he could fit in there at once because poor old Joe only sunk in up to his waist. His legs still dangled out the thing's mouth. Eugene watched in horror as it gulped a few times and it's mouth seemed to enlarge. Joe Buckley's corpse slowly slid the rest of the way into the thing's mouth and Eugene could see the shape of Joe's shoulders under the skin of the thing's throat.

Eugene couldn't contain his fear any longer, he let out a guttural scream and opened fire with his .38 revolver. Shot after shot landed on the creature until he was pulling the trigger on empty cylinders. The rock man calmly walked over and took the gun from Eugene and then crushed it in his rocky hands.

"Please don't shoot my associate. I assure you we mean you no harm." Eugene was too terrified to even speak. He tried to stutter out a response but instead his throat let out a loud hiss like whine and he pissed his pants.

"I can hear your heart rate is extremely elevated. I don't know what the norm is for your species but that doesn't sound healthy. Is it supposed to be that fast?"

Eugene still couldn't form a response, he kept trying but he was just entirely too scared. His vision blackened and he felt his feet go out from under him. A strange dizziness hit him next as he laid on the floor of the nightmare warehouse, he wasn't used to being afraid, this was a new experience for Eugene. The face of the rock man appeared above him with his strange red eyes. Then the face of the living nightmare appeared next, still chewing Joe's corpse. Eugene couldn't handle the situation, not even a little bit. Fear seized him anew and he felt himself losing consciousness, Eugene welcomed the darkness. Anything was better than being stuck with these two.

Eugene slowly came to consciousness and quickly realizes that he couldn't see or breath in whatever environment he was stuck in. These two driving factors stop him from studying his surroundings more. He inhales sharply and his lungs and mouth fill with some kind of vile fluid. It tastes like death, swamp, and darkness if a flavor could be attributed to such a primal thing. He panics and starts kicking and scraping. His foot hits something that feels vaguely flesh like... A membrane of sorts. This little bit of contact is enough to get Eugene to start using his rational mind. He is underwater or something like water, the taste of it doesn't remind him of any water he knows. Whatever he had kicked was holding him in, that was the wall, the door to his salvation, the exit.

He knew he had to fight to survive, so he pushes himself harder. Scratching and kicking more and more in all directions. Finally his foot pierces whatever slimy wall he had been kicking and he feels cool air on his ankle. He tries to back up through the new exit, but can't get enough traction, whatever liquid he is trapped in is much too viscous. He spins his body around in the thick fluid hoping that in this orientation he will have more leverage. He claws and scrapes his way towards the tear he knows his foot has made. The membrane exists all around just out of his reach, he can feel it from time to time in his frantic scrabbling. Soon he feels the pull of the liquid that is draining out of the hole he had made and it partially yanks him along for the ride. His lungs felt like they were about to burst so he pulls himself along as well hoping for salvation.

Soon his hands find purchase on the ragged hole he has made and pulls for all he is worth. Apparently the other side of the membrane is a few feet above ground level because he falls a short distance before his chin hits something hard and the bubble-like thing he was kept in pushes him the rest of the way out. He immediately tries to breathe in as much of the beautiful air as he can but his chest spasms painfully. Something horrible is happening inside of him. He realizes he is choking, his lungs and throat are still full of whatever the evil liquid was. He rolls over and coughs and coughs as the fluid leaves his lungs, sucking in as much air as he can in between retching. The fluid is a truly disgusting shade of dark green and it is congealed like old blood. Once he feels the bulk of it is out of his lungs he allows himself to fall flat on the floor and rest, still taking deep heaving breaths. The floor below him is cold and hard his fingers run along a dry spot and he realizes its smooth concrete. He knows he is laying in a pile of the filth that was inside the bubble, but he is too tired to care. He continues to take deep heaving breaths trying to reoxygenate his body.

After a short time he shakily sits up. *SHIT!* He is still in the warehouse, but it is dark again. Upon further inspection he realizes it is only dark on this side of the warehouse, there is a section far away from him that is lit, leaving just enough light on this side for him to barely make out his surroundings. His eyes follow the trail of fluid he had been laying in back to a now deflated dark green sack sitting in what could only be described as some kind of over sized reptilian nest of sorts. There are many other sacks full of something dark and alive at roughly the shape and size of a man. Eugene can see whatever they are moving around inside the sacks that are semi-translucent. The light is bad here but their silhouettes look like children swimming or spinning in circles or flips. In between the sacks there are thick organic pipes lining the floor pumping the fluid that Eugene had choked on, maybe it would be more accurate to call them *veins*. Under the bed of veins there is a bed of what feels like dead flesh. He was back in the nightmare.

The sack closest to him seems to be especially active, the dark silhouette inside of it is convulsing hard causing the whole sack that is about five feet tall to jiggle like an oversized dark green water balloon. Eugene inches closer to get a better look. The sack shakes more violently than even before when he is about an arm's length out and for a second he is afraid it is going

115

to burst. A webbed hand appears on the inside of the membrane that makes up the outer layer of the sack and it shoves until the sack stretches thin. Eugene reaches his hand out to touch the hand still pressed against the membrane, right before he touches it though he hears a deep voice.

"I wouldn't."

Eugene spins around, it was the man made of the shiny black rock.

"Bertha is very protective of her brood. Please, no touching."

"Who are you, what have you done to me!" Eugene shouts as he trembles in fear. The creature inches forward and hands him a hand mirror.

"We had to fix you up, it appears you had several minor heart attacks and you were quite close to death. "

Eugene was hesitant to take his eyes off of the creature, but his curiosity got the best of him and he looks in the mirror. It was hard to make out because this side of the warehouse was still pretty dark but Eugene saw taunt fresh muscle under his slime covered torso. He angles the mirror up to his face, he looked younger and he could swear his cheekbones even looked a little higher. His double chin and jowls were gone along with the remainder of his hair, no big loss there. He looked just like he had in high school except minus his normally thick dark brown hair that he had been losing since then.

"I don't understand, how is this possible?" Asked Eugene as he continued to rub his head and his body as he looked into the mirror.

"Let's retire to your vehicle. I understand you might have refreshments and clothing inside," says the Rock Man.

"Uh, okay…" Eugene was hesitant to go anywhere with this creature, but so far he hadn't shown any aggression at all and it wasn't like he had much of a choice. He didn't see any obvious doors out of this place and he knew if he ran they might just kill him, he had watched the rock man break a gun with this bare hands. So it wouldn't be a stretch to say he could kill Eugene easily. He had to switch into negotiation mode before he got to the vehicle, if these monsters wanted him dead they would have killed him not healed him. They needed him.

They got to the vehicle and the monster calmly held a hand out signaling that Eugene should enter first. As Eugene entered he noticed the Lincoln was running and when he opened the door the dome light flicked on. Even the television in the back was playing a movie which he instinctively pauses. He saw the Stone Man was coming in behind him so he quickly scoots over. The monster crawled in after him and casually sit insides a measured distance away from Eugene, a professional distance. Eugene feels the shocks of the vehicle strain under the intense weight of the newest passenger. Everything about the rock mans current demeanor screams business casual and formal business deal. Despite the fact that Eugene was stuck naked and covered in slime in a confined space with a deadly alien, he couldn't help but feel that he was in his element.

"This is a nice vehicle, very comfortable. I explored it a bit while you were convalescing. I hope you don't mind."

"That uh… No, that is fine. Make yourself at home," said Eugene who was extremely nervous, but still trying to put on a brave yet welcoming face.

"You are probably curious about who I am and why I am here. For simplicity sake you may call me Obsidian, my associate you met earlier is Bertha. Why don't you prepare us some of your native drinks while we discuss these matters." Eugene nods and began grabbing two tumblers to mix up some Manhattans.

"I have a job to do, a very important job. I did a bit of cultural research on your planet over the last few hours while you were indisposed and I was happy to find out that your people have a religion that mirrors the philosophy of my very important job. Tell me, have you ever heard of Taoism?"

"No," says Eugene as he hands Obsidian a Manhattan in a glass tumbler. Eugene is surprised to see how delicately Obsidian grabs the glass before taking a tentative sip.

"Delicious, anyway even if you haven't heard of the religion I am sure you have seen their symbol. I found it in all forms of media and pop culture in almost every country on your earth. It is called the Yin and Yang," said Obsidian.

"Yes, I'm very familiar with the Yin-Yang," says Eugene. What he doesn't say is that a lot of the cheaper whores he has *perused* often get this symbol tattooed on themselves with a myriad of other nonsensical bullshit. Everyone wants to seem worldly.

"So the Yin and Yang speak of balance by recognizing the need for predators and prey, a very evolved concept and symbol. Those who are short-sighted would only focus on the light side of the symbol, yet this will surely lead to disaster. Let me run an example by you. Let's say a good Samaritan wants to honor nature by planting trees everywhere as often as possible. So he does this, he spends his entire life planting trees and protecting the ones that already exist. A hundred years after his death all of the trees he dutifully nurtured have grown tall and wide and spread even more saplings on their own. These trees now surround and grow into every major town for a thousand miles. Until a dry season comes, the trees become extremely parched and continue to grow dry and brittle. A lightning strike hits, one of the trees catches on fire.

Out of this never ending dry forest a wildfire arises, the likes of which have never been seen before. The fire consumes thousands of people, it destroys lives, millions of animals, the local ecosystem is decimated.

The moral of my story here is that this tree planting gentleman focused too much on the light side of the balance. In his rush to do good he inadvertently ruined thousands of lives. What if instead of planting so many new trees he instead explored the forests and established places that needed fire breaks. You see from a simpleton's perspective all you would see is this gentleman traveling the woods and destroying the trees, but in reality he is killing for a purpose. He destroys wide swaths of trees in the most dense parts of the forest. Then again in a hundred years the dry season comes just like before, lightning hits, the fire starts. The wildfire spreads and is immediately stopped at the first firebreak. A large swath has been cut through the woods, the fire can't bridge the gap and it slowly extinguishes itself and no one is harmed.

You see that man, the second man who established the firebreaks, he will see no glory. He will be seen as evil, he will be seen as a destroyer, yet he is the one who saved lives. Most people are too short sighted to understand this. It takes a special kind of person who is willing to destroy for the greater good. I am here now because I think you are the right kind of person for this duty. You can be the dark side of the Yin and Yang. You have the foresight to understand that the universe needs balance, and of course we can have some fun along the way," Obsidian finished and took a long drink.

"So this is a job offer?" asked Eugene.
"More than an offer, unfortunately this is kind of more of a draft. The universe picked you for this duty. I was just polite enough to explain it. No reason to be worried though, the job

119

comes with lots of perks as you have already seen in your new enhanced body. You will live for an extremely long time, a full life of beauty and health. You can have whatever you want now, and grow as strong as you wish," said Obsidian.

"I wasn't born yesterday, what's the catch?" asked Eugene.

"Ah, a smart man you truly are. There are lots of downsides. First of all, this is a thankless job and you will be looked down upon and sometimes hunted. For the most part those are non-issues, you will be so rich and happy that you won't care who looks down on you," said Obsidian.

"I'm already in a situation like that," said Eugene.

"Good, then nothing will change on that front. As far as being hunted this also won't be an issue for you. You will be so strong that with a simple slap you will dent your enemies skulls in. Gaining that strength can be problematic and difficult. You see there is a mostly untapped source of power we can utilize. When the universe decided that we would be the balance it also unlocked an ability in us. The ability to harness this latent power. On your planet you would call it the soul," said Obsidian.

"Are you saying I have to kill people to become stronger?" Asked Eugene.

"Those terms are simple. I am saying like the second man in the story you have to destroy a few trees to prevent a massive disaster. I need you to have the foresight and the ambivalence to look deeper than surface actions. Is killing a homeless vagabond that bad if that same homeless vagabond was going to murder a child in the future. Or let's say a hundred people are stricken with a terrible disease that leaves them with no ability to move their limbs. Their loved ones and family would spend the rest of their lives caring for them, never able to move on or live their own lives. What if you were to kill those hundred people. At first their families would be sad yet within a year or two they would move on, their lives would blossom like a beautiful flower, they would form new relationships and ultimately flourish.

We can not let the system strangle itself. We have to be the balance, the ones who set the world right. We are the reaper, we pull the weeds so that the flowers may grow. As a reward for this the universe lets us feed on the souls of the weeds we have to prune. Our bodies and minds are strengthened and we can perform our duties to a higher standard."

"So if we are the dark side of the Yin-Yang, who is on the light side?" Asked Eugene.

"Once again Eugene, for one so young your perception amazes me." Eugene couldn't help but smile a little at the compliment. Normally people complimented him out of fear or because they wanted his money, he could tell Obsidian's compliments were genuine. It was a ridiculous situation, sitting in the back of his limousine with an alien recruiting him for some kind of Angel of Death service. Yet he couldn't help but feel honored. It wasn't often in life that he was chosen for things. He normally had to pay his way into positions or scare people so much that they gave him what he wanted. If what Obsidian was telling him was true then he had been chosen for this based on his merits and his intelligence. Eugene had never had a purpose before, this could be his.

"Yes, the light side of the Yin-Yang exists in reality and they have grown out of control. They lack the foresight we have. They call themselves Arbiters and they have been doing their darndest to kill members of my faction for the crime of existing. We call ourselves The Balance, yet they call us Demons or Chaos-

121

Makers. Doesn't sound very enlightened does it, damning an entire group of people for simply being different. I'm not saying the Arbiters are bad, they are needed just like we are. I just wish they would stay in their own lane so to speak and let us do our job, but we are way past that point. The Arbiters have established a major foothold on a prime planet used for trade and commerce and they have arbitrarily announced themselves as rulers of the system that governs the universe, above reproach or questioning as it were. They have grown fat and lazy in their short term success, and I am afraid like the first man in the story if they aren't stopped soon they too will cause a great disaster. That conversation is for another day though.

For now we need to focus on you. We got some actionable intel that a new Arbiter was going to be awakened on this planet. Sometimes they send an older Arbiter to help the new guy along. There are a lot of pieces in play here, but with me, you, and Bertha on this planet there are three members of the Balance and only one or two Arbiters depending on if the older Arbiter left yet. It is well past time we prune some of their population in order to fix the balance. And on this planet we outnumber them and we have more resources. Soon Bertha's brood will be born and we will have a small army of foot soldiers at our disposal. Bertha's brood will surely tip the already tipped scales in this conflict. In the meantime we have to get your power level up. Also I have a gift for you," Obsidian paused his speech and reaches into a very small crack on his leg, he comes up with a metal vial with a black stopper on the top. He carefully hands the vial to Eugene.

"Apply this to your weapon of choice and it will share in your soul harvesting. It will grow with you and become a powerful utility for the Balance," says Obsidian.

"I can put this on anything and it will enhance it? Anything at all?" asks Eugene.

"Yes, but chose wisely whatever you pour this on will be with you forever. It should be something you hold dear," said Obsidian. Eugene didn't think twice or hesitate. He opens the cap to the vial and threw the contents on the dash of the Lincoln. Eugene is surprised to see it's an iridescent bright green fluid. At first it harmlessly splashes across the dash, but very quickly it forms into complex patterns and then begins to squirm around the vehicle sinking into key positions and disappearing.

"Wise choice," says Obsidian as he claps Eugene on the shoulder.

Chapter 8

"You've got to be fucking kidding me, what are you doing here Jimmy?" shouts Hank with his door open as Jimmy runs over to him.

"Hank, you are literally covered in blood, it looks like even your eyes are bleeding. What the fuck is going on?" asks Jimmy.

"Shit happens when you party naked. Quit changing the subject, why are you here?" asks Hank.

"Because you needed my help you crazy fuck. Why are you destroying the town in a Bulldozer?" asks Jimmy.

"Jimmy, I promise you on my father's grave..." Hank's face falls into his hands because he is so overwhelmed, but he only ends up smearing some blood around so he stops that quickly. "I'm not crazy Jimmy. I only killed really bad guys. I have an exit strategy of sorts for all of this, but we don't have time for any of that right now. We have to stop these shit heads. I know the other side of this wall is clear. I can doze through and kill the ones on the other said," said Hank.

"I'm not even going to ask how you think you know the way is clear. I don't know how clearly you are thinking…. Hank do you know that most of your blood is on the outside of your body right now? Why don't you smash through and then let me lead the charge. I've got two guys around the corner who can help me," says Jimmy. Hank wants to argue with him, but he realizes how much energy it is taking just to stay awake, so he nods his head in agreement. Jimmy whistles and two overly muscular bald men come around the corner sporting FBI windbreakers.

"Nice costumes Jimmy, where did you pick those up?"

"Heh, costumes… yeah. Let's do this thing, hit that wall and we will rush in and clear the bank." Jimmy hops off of the ledge of the cabin and runs over to meet his guys. One of them throws him an M-4 variant and another FBI windbreaker which he hastily puts on. He spins back around to Hank and gives him the thumbs up. Hank can't help but grin as he slams the door shut and revs the engine a few times, before finally popping it into gear. The Killdozer lurches forward faster than it ever has before, the upgrades have clearly been working their magic. He smashes entirely through the outer wall of the bank and slams on the breaks as fast as he can so he doesn't run over any hostages.

His Arbiter Intuition is going crazy, screaming that he needs to help these poor souls. Jimmy and his two men fly in guns blazing. There is sporadic gunfire from each side and some of the hostages start to run. One woman is clipped in the arm and spins around once before falling. Hank can't sit this one out, if he does more innocent people might be hurt. He grabs the AK47 and hops out of his Killdozer into the smoke and dust still floating in the air and immediately rolls his ankle in the rubble he created from crashing through the wall. He falls onto his back into a pile of rebar, sharp concrete chunks, and brick shards that were once the decorative outer-wall. Hank isn't a quitter though so he gets up and glances at the cab of the Killdozer just long enough to see the puddle of blood leaking over the seat where he had just been. *How much blood did I lose?*

The gun is slippery in his bloody hands and trying to manipulate it at all brings about great bouts of pain from his shredded palms. He works his way through the smoke, shirtless and covered in blood. Still drowsy as hell from the fatigue of his injuries. He takes one more glance back because he feels something weird tugging on his Intuition. One of the bank robbers is half crushed below the treads of his Killdozer. He is dying as Hank watches him. Again Hank watches a man's soul get sucked up into the engine. He can hear Jimmy and his men yelling at the remaining bank robbers to put their guns down. Hank only has eyes for Suzie, or rather Arbiter Intuition for Suzie. He has been passively using it to track her position, barely even cognizant of the fact that he is doing it. Hank spots the man who is holding her at the back of the bank. He sees the bloody apparition that is Hank staring at him and immediately begins pulling her back further into a hallway that Hank can only assume leads to the manager's office. He has to follow, he won't let her get hurt again.

Hank can hear Jimmy yelling somewhere behind him. He is yelling for Hank telling him to wait, but Hank is too tired to pay attention and too desperate to protect Suzie. He heads down the hallway, a door at the end slams shut. The employee bathrooms are on the left side of the hall, as he walks past them a man lunges out behind him and tries to put Hank in a choke hold. Hank is too slippery though and years of muscle memory had his chin pinned to his chest before the man could fully constrict his arm. So instead of a choke hold the man ends up on the piggy back ride from hell. Hank loses the AK47 in the fight so he just throws his back against what he thinks is the outer wall of the bank. The bank robber is crushed behind him. Hank picks up his AK and calmly shoots the man in the face and then watches in sick detail as the man's soul leaves his body. Instead of going towards the bulldozer it flies directly into Hank's chest. "Well that's new," Hank says to no one in particular.

He gets to the doorway at the end of the hall where he knows an armed gunman has a weapon pointed at Suzie's head inside, *Arbiter Intuition is awesome*. He steels himself, he only has one shot at this. Hank spins the door handle as quietly as he can with

126

his off-hand and then spins around the corner and begins to raise his rifle. That's when the bank robber holding Suzie shoots Hank in the chest. Hank falls backwards and loses his weapon as his bare and bloody back hits the shitty industrial too-thin carpet.

He hears the bank robber shout something like "Take that you fuckin idiot!" but he is too tired to make out exactly what it was. Jimmy comes through a second later. He steps over Hank and puts a round right through the remaining bank robber's head.

"Hank what in the fuck were you thinking!" Jimmy screams. "You, get over here," he yells at Suzie. She runs over and he takes off his windbreaker and t-shirt and hands her the t-shirt before putting his windbreaker back on. "Hold that t-shirt over his wound, don't let up. I have to finish securing the bank!" he yells before running off. Then it's just Hank and Suzie.

"Hey mister, keep your eyes open. I don't think you are supposed to close your eyes in these kinds of situations," said Suzie. Hank cracks open one of his eyes, the other one doesn't want to work it feels like glue is holding it together but it might just be dried blood.

"Suzie, how you been?" asks Hank. Suzie Q. looks very confused for a second before recognition shows on her face.

"Hank?"

"In the flesh."

"Hank, oh my God! What are you doing here?"

"I couldn't let you get hurt, not again," he says with a smile on his face. This time Hank can't help but to close his eye. He is just too tired to do anything else.

"Don't go to sleep Hank, don't do it!" she screams.

A short while later Hank comes to laying in a ridiculously comfortable form-fitted bed of some type. The ceiling above him is purple, it's the first thing he notices as he glances around.

"Hank are you awake?" asks a female voice, he can't see who it is because he is still laying down staring up.

"Am I dead?" Hank asks no one in particular. Before Hank even has a chance to sit up Suzie is wrapping her arms around his prone form. "Well hello to you too."

"I thought you were dead, it was a shitty feeling," she says before sobbing a bit into Hank's chest.

"Yeah, but why am I not dead, or in handcuffs for that matter?"

"Because the aliens came..." before Suzie can finish telling her story a door opens with the slightest of noises at the end of the room and Hank sits up to investigate. Cerulean and Dractus walk in wearing their futuristic silver onesies trailed by Jimmy. Hank looks town and sees his torso is almost entirely wrapped in something that looks like thick plastic with blue wires running horizontally through it. His hands are also wrapped in it, along with the leg he got shot in earlier. He is also surprised that he is in a pretty minimal amount of pain overall. Jimmy is standing side by side with Cerulean and Dractus, which is also a confusing sight for Hank.

"I have just so many questions," said Hank.

Cerulean is the one who answers him "Blame me. I was able to sneak a tracker on you earlier that also monitored your vitals. I saw you were close to dying and we came running. It was a real shit show when we arrived. Let me tell you, your local authorities do not like aliens in giant flying ships. Anyway when Dractus threw you over his shoulder this one here about shot him in the face," she says as she points at Jimmy who only smiles.

128

Sometimes shooting people in the face is an average day for Jimmy.

"Anyway this woman comes running out," she says while gesturing towards Suzie. "We had to move quickly and these two refused to leave your side so we just took them with us."

Hank tries to parse the story he just got told quickly and piece it all together, but he did just get shot twice earlier this day so he is still a bit sluggish. Finally he comes to a terrible conclusion and his heart starts pounding in his chest.

"WAIT, WE HAVE TO GO BACK! MY BULLDOZER!"

Again it is Cerulean who answers him "No worries Hank, this baby is a galactic tug, Leviathan Class." she says while stomping her foot on the floor of the ship. "I'm hauling your bulldozer below us, it's safe and sound."

Hank feels like a weight has just been lifted off of him. "Thank you, fuck that had me worried. Where are we going now, and why is this place purple?"

"We are headed to the general area of where the demon was last spotted. The purple around you is an all-purpose spray to protect the steel components of the ship. It stops rust, it's bacteria resistant, it's a great insulator, and it is surprisingly hardy. We can talk more about that later though. For now we will give you some time alone with your friends."

Dractus and Cerulean turn to leave "Wait!" shouts Hank. They both turn around "Thanks for saving me, both of you. Dractus I guess you can have that tongue thing whenever you want it now since I owe you one." Cerulean giggles at the comment and keeps walking. Dractus turns his head slightly without turning around and flips his lizard tongue in the air a few times before walking out and laughing softly. After their departure the room suddenly feels a little awkward. Jimmy catches on quickly.

129

"Hey I'm going to go see where a guy can take a piss in this tub. I'll be back in five minutes."

Once he leaves the room Hank can't wait to blurt the question out that's been bothering him for years. "Why did you do it? The cold shoulder, the restraining order, everything?"

Hank realizes Suzie is holding one of his hands with both of hers. She looks down at the floor before responding.

"It was Eugene. He sent men to my house, they threatened my family. Eugene said if I ever talked to you again in a friendly manner he would have my father killed..."

"So why didn't you call the police, or come to me? We could have dealt with it together. We had something, I know you felt it. All of the wasted years because that little weasel lobs one threat. You should have come to me!" Hank lays back down when he realizes he has shouted his last sentence. Suzie doesn't say anything, she just keeps staring at the floor.

"That was a bullshit answer Suzie."

Hank can tell he has devastated her. He doesn't care though. What they went through together was a lot and he could have used her support. He can't help but notice how viciously beautiful she still is, even with one side of her face marked with a long jagged scar. If anything the scar only increases her natural beauty by drawing attention to the soft curves of her face.

"I don't know what to tell you Hank. I was young and scared. I knew Eugene's family was powerful, and I knew he was insane. I love my father and I didn't want to potentially throw his life away over some high school relationship. Can't you understand that?"

"Why didn't you come to me Suzie, I would have helped you."

"Hank you don't understand. Back then, yeah you were big and a skilled fighter, but beyond that you were just a yokel local,

130

a boy with a pretty face and big muscles. Eugene is connected to some very bad people, even back then he was."

They are at an impasse and they both know it. Hank can never forgive Suzie. He also wonders if maybe the spark he felt with her all those years ago was just teenage hormones. As if she can read his mind she speaks up again "That's all in the past Hank. We are here together now, we can try again. I heard you ran Eugene out of town. The police were looking for him for questioning but apparently he loaded up a suitcase and disappeared. I know now what I should have known then. That you would have never let me or my family get hurt."

Hank sees her expectant eyes and doesn't really know how to respond. She left him when he needed her. Now that he had saved her from harm he feels his karma has been reset. He didn't fail this time, he no longer owes her anything. Before he can tell her as much Jimmy comes back into the room. He rests one of his hands on Hank's shoulder.

"Hank, you son of a bitch. You should have called me. I could have had Eugene whacked on the down low. That whole bulldozer mess was nonsense."

"No, it was my problem Jimmy, I had to deal with it. I appreciate everything you have done for me... and my father. I really do, but it was my problem." Jimmy just nods, he understands.

"So your new friends tell me you are some kind of a space cop now. This should make this next bomb I'm going to drop a little easier for you. It seems especially trivial to keep it a secret now with aliens flying around and what not... Hank I'm a federal agent, I work for the FBI."

Hank just raises an eyebrow questioningly. Hank and Jimmy know each other well enough to know that the raised eyebrow carries some serious meanings and implications. Like for example if Jimmy is a cop why is he working as a loan shark in small towns and beating up deadbeats. Why didn't he arrest Hank in some kind of a Rico case. Why didn't he try to arrest Hank when he was destroying town hall with a bulldozer. Jimmy being a cop just doesn't add up. These were all the things Hank had implied with the lift of that brow. Best friends can do that kind of thing, exchange messages via eyebrows.

"I'm telling you the truth Hank. I'm a federal agent. I've been deep undercover for years. I don't have any close family and I love the work. So I just keep volunteering to stay under longer. I have one of the most notorious covers in FBI history."

"I'm not really sure what to say Jimmy... Congrats? I dislike criminals as much as the next person, but I worked for you as a criminal for a long time. Why didn't you turn me in?"

"Because you aren't a criminal Hank. Standing around and looking scary isn't against the law. Besides I only chase kingpins and syndicates. And as you know... I really did count you as one of the best friends I have ever had. In the world of shit that I call home you were a ray of sunshine. I've kept track of you since then, just to make sure that none of my world spilled into yours. You've become a pillar of your community. I've seen you help people. How could I lock someone like that up. I kept your name out of the paperwork bud."

"Yeah, until I became the maniac killing people with a bulldozer."

"Well, you're a space cop now. I'm pretty sure Galactic law supersedes federal jurisdiction."

"Is that the same logic you use to justify the crazy shit you do?"

"YEP!" Jimmy says with a grin.

"You haven't changed at all Jimmy."

"Look who's talking."

***

Jimmy and Hank had a good time catching up. Suzie sat by Hank's side patiently just holding one of his hands while they talked. They filled each other in on the last few years of their lives and what they had been up to. Hank couldn't help but think that Jimmy should have been the one chosen to be an Arbiter after hearing just some of his exploits. Apparently Jimmy had really moved up in the criminal world. The reason he had to flee Hank's small town was because a mid-level kingpin decided that he didn't like that Jimmy wasn't paying him a cut of his loan sharking business. Jimmy systematically ripped the kingpin's organization apart by killing or incarcerating everyone in his way. He also survived multiple assassination attempts during the dispute. This gave him enough street cred to connect to some national level crime syndicates. Since then he had been planting moles among their ranks, some of which were other FBI agents, and some of which were criminals who thought they were spying for Jimmy, but really they were spying for the U.S. government.

Altogether Jimmy has fed enough information to the FBI for them to make over 3000 arrests once the warrants come through. They hadn't made any yet, but they were just finalizing the deal with prosecutors now and within the next few years they would be dismantling more than half of the organized crime in the country. At which point Jimmy would have to disappear forever since he would surely be hunted for the rest of his life. Jimmy also admitted that the whole situation made him nervous as hell.

Not the being hunted part, but the quitting and laying low part. He had become accustomed to the lifestyle and he loved it. He didn't want to quit. It scared him more than the idea of dying.

"I'll tell you Hank, there was a couple times I really could have used your help. It was hard not to call."

"You could have called. I would have showed up in a heartbeat."

"That's why I didn't call."

"Well you got me now. I'm done at the Gravel Yard forever. I'll get with Cerulean and Dractus to see if I can leave you some way to call me once I head out with them. If you ever need my help I'll be there."

Hank, Jimmy, and Suzie all turn towards the door as they hear it start to open. Cerulean and Dractus are back.

"We just came to tell you guys and gals that we are landing in an empty lot and heading out. We are close to the last sighting of the demon. We are going to go see if they are still around and if they are Dractus will cut the things head off," said Cerulean. Dractus runs his hand over his own neck to emphasize her point. Apparently that gesture really is universal, in the most literal sense of the word universal.

"Well you are going to need my help, this is my planet, my turf..." says Hank as he starts to sit up, but Cerulean puts a hand up.

"Nope, you are bedridden until that fancy-pants machine you are hooked up to says you are ready. Don't worry it shouldn't be long, Arbiters get the best tech," she says with a coy smile.

Jimmy can tell Hank is going to protest further, but he knows his friend is severely injured. "Don't even think about it Hank. I'll go in your place, this is my planet too. They can give me the rundown of what we are chasing in route, this is my purview. Besides I have law enforcement databases I can access and criminal alliances I can use. You stay here with Suzie, I'll help them find what they need.

Hank still wants to go, but he knows he has already lost the argument. "Be safe Jimmy."

"Ha, I'm not worried about me. Whatever this *demon* thing is should be worried. Have you seen that dude's battle axe?" says Jimmy while pointing at Dractus.

"Hey wait a minute," says Hank while looking at Cerulean. "If Dractus' Arbiter weapon is his axe, what is yours?"

"We are all standing in it. The Tug is my weapon. Haven't you wondered how a glorified space tow truck is able to go stealth and have warp capabilities?"

"I don't know shit about space or spaceships," says Hank in a deadpan tone.

"Okay well, let's just say this old tug is one of the most dangerous ships in the known universe," said Cerulean.

"Well that is just badass. Are you going to be safe out there? If the ship is your weapon how do you kill a demon?" asks Hank.

"In all honesty I just plan on letting Dractus cut its head off like I mentioned before. if that doesn't work I'll just use the ship to bombard it safely from a few hundred feet in the air. The biggest badasses in the world will still die from a missile to the face. Alright we have to go. Come along Jimmy."

"Yes Ma'am!" says Jimmy sarcastically. He winks at Hank before heading out with Cerulean and Dractus.

When the door slides shut behind them it's just Hank and Suzie. Suzie has a very devious look in her eye. "Hank I think it's far past time that we catch up and make up for some of the time we missed."

"Isn't that what we have been doing?"

"I meant on a more intimate level. Me and you never really got to the next level."

"I think I'm supposed to be resting Suzie, and I was going to tell you..." before he can finish the sentence Suzie puts a finger over his lips.

"Shhh, you just keep resting. I'll do all the work," she says as she starts unbuttoning the white blouse she is wearing. Hank knows he should stop her and tell her that he doesn't have feelings for her, but Hank Jr. is having different ideas especially as he sees the light blue bra she is wearing below the blouse.

***

"You can't ride those through the city," said Jimmy. He is standing with Cerulean and Dractus in a tiny garage near the back of Cerulean's ship. Jimmy is looking at the motorcycle from hell with tires that would look more at home on a monster truck. Every inch of it is coated in additional armor and storage compartments. It's at least twice as long as a normal motorcycle and it has what looks like two auto-cannons on the front of it. Next to it is a slimmed down version that is basically the same that presumably belongs to Cerulean.

"I'll do what I want Human!" says Dractus in a gruff and loud tone.

"No seriously, the police will be all over you. Then the military. We are going to have to steal a car or rent a moving truck or something," says Jimmy.

"We should trust him Dractus, feel him out," says Cerulean. Dractus walks over to Jimmy and rests one hand on his shoulder and closes his eyes.

"Uhhh, what the fuck is he doing?" asks Jimmy."

"It's called Intuition. He is reading you. Every Arbiter uses it differently, we aren't sure why. At first we thought it had to do with what species you were, but we got to a point where we had two Arbiters from the same species and even they tapped into it in different ways and at different levels of proficiency."

"An Arbiter is what you call space cops right?" asks Jimmy.

"Right," says Cerulean.

"I think Hank used this earlier to check through the wall of the Bank to make sure it was clear before he crashed through," says Jimmy. This makes Cerulean raise an eyebrow.

"You must be mistaken. Arbiter Intuition doesn't work through solid walls like that." says Cerulean.

"Uhh, you might want to tell Hank that then," says Jimmy. Dractus finishes what he is doing.

"Wow, your aura is all over the place, but overall you seem like a good man. You are my kind of people puny human," said Dractus.

"Wow a compliment followed only by one insult, that means he likes you," says Cerulean.

"Right, well I'm going to see if I can grab a truck off of my ride-sharing app," says Jimmy as he grabs his cellphone. He looks at Dractus one more time measuring him up. "It's going to have to have a big bed."

They exit the ship and walk to the nearest street and wait for the vehicle to arrive. While they are waiting Jimmy flips his FBI windbreaker inside out. An older model Dodge Ram with an extended bed rolls up. The owner obviously cares for it because the paint and rims are brand new. It comes to a complete stop in front of Jimmy with the windows down. The driver is scrolling through his phone instead of paying attention to his surroundings and starts automatically saying his usual spiel for customers.

"Alright bros and/or dudettes, no drinks in my ride. If you throw up you are going to pay a 200 dollar cleaning fee. I pick the music, but if you don't like it we can..." he looks up and notices Dractus and Cerulean. "WHOA, wicked cosplay costumes! Is there a convention in town?" Jimmy answers quickly before either of the aliens says something crazy.

"Kind of, we are getting paid for some special appearances. I'm their security and agent. His new costume won't fit in my tiny car which is why we needed a truck. Listen, we have to make a few stops, but if you play it cool I'll give you an extra 100 now and then another 100 when we are done. Deal?"

"That works great for me. I'm Chad by the way."

"Nice to meet you Chad," says Jimmy as he jumps in and hands Chad his first hundred dollar bill.

There is no center console, the front seat is just one giant bench seat so Jimmy sits in the middle hoping to stop Chad from staring at Cerulean too intently and noticing just how real her "cosplay costume" really is. Dractus takes a leap straight from the ground and lands in the back of Chad's truck which shakes the whole vehicle.

"Whoa bro, go easy on the shocks!" shouts Chad out of his opened window. Cerulean taps Jimmy's shoulder and shows him a small tablet with a map and a blinking address on it so Jimmy relays the address to Chad like it was his idea and they are on their way. The first stop is a convenience store and gas station. All of the windows are boarded up, but it's still open with the lights on inside. Though there are no customers in sight.

"We'll be right back Chad. Please wait here and remember our deal."

"Yep, no problem bro."

This time Dractus gets out of the truck a little more carefully. As they get closer to the store they stop at the side of the front door and inspect the door frame, just out of view of the owner. It once held a glass lined door like the front of all convenience stores but the whole frame is skewed and bent like the door was ripped away.

"What did this, what are we looking for here guys?" asks Jimmy. Dractus ignores him and stalks off around the side of the store sniffing the air loudly so Cerulean is the one who responds.

"We are looking for a particularly nasty demon that goes by the designation Bertha. It is large, much larger than this establishment is tall. Its skin is black and wet. It is bipedal yet it relies mostly on four large uber-strong tentacle-like appendages that extend from its back."

"What are its crimes?"

"It's a demon." Jimmy doesn't like that answer and Cerulean can see it on his face.

"Okay fine, it eats sentient beings and stuffs its body with calories until it can produce a nest made with raw materials it makes again from its own body's stores. This is why it constantly has to eat. The nest can produce thirty or more younglings which aren't true demons but they are still nasty little things that go about murdering and destroying the area around their nesting ground in an ever expanding radius as they mature. We believe Bertha is on this planet because she thought the Arbiters wouldn't find her here and that this would be a good place to start a new hoard."

"So that's what she was doing in this store, eating people?

"Probably."

"Have you checked the camera footage?"

"Yes, we pulled the footage from traffic cameras which showed her heading this way."

"No the camera footage..." says Jimmy as he points to a camera dangling from some wires at the edge of the building. Cerulean pulls her tablet out and scans through it for a bit.

"I have no data that this camera exists," she says skeptically as she continues manipulating her tablet.

"That's because it's old school, analog, it's hardwired. Stay here."

Before she can respond Jimmy heads into the store. An older man dressed humbly in his late 60's stands behind the counter, he has thinning gray hair and looks happy to see a customer.

"Hello sir, can I ask you some questions?"

"You can ask me anything if you are a paying customer. If you aren't a customer then I don't have any time for you. There is a vanity display of Zippos emblazoned with different designs, emblems, and sayings on the counter. Jimmy grabs the entire display that holds around 30 Zippos and moves it into the center of the counter. Then he puts two one-hundred dollar bills down.

"I bought these. I'm a paying customer now. What caused all the damage?" says Jimmy as he points at the storefront.

"A car drove through the front of the store," says the old man. Then he swipes the money off the counter so fast that even a magician would be impressed.

"We both know that isn't true."

"Truth be told, I don't know. I don't normally work the storefront here. The employee who was on staff disappeared that night and all of my other employees quit. As you can see this place has been a ghost town since then, the locals are afraid to come near."

"What about the cameras?" says Jimmy as he points at a glass bauble in the ceiling that clearly holds a camera.

"The police confiscated the footage from those. Why you asking around about this anyway?"

"I run an internet blog about strange encounters, it's very lucrative. If you hypothetically had an extra copy of that tape and if you accidentally let me film it with my cellphone. Then I might accidentally drop five hundred dollars on your counter here and never speak of how I came upon the footage."

The store clerk looks around warily before looking back to Jimmy. He uses his finger to make a "come here" motion and Jimmy follows. There is a door behind the counter that goes into a tiny office. There is a poster on the wall of a cat with the caption "Hang in there!" on the bottom of it. The man lifts the poster which exposes a crushed part of drywall that has a VHS tape lodged in it. He pulls the tape out and puts it into a small television and VCR combo. Jimmy quickly pulls out his cellphone and starts filming as the man hits play.

It's the view from outside of the store, where Jimmy had seen the broken camera. The store looks like it is having a slow, but average night. Jimmy has an extremely wide view so the camera must have a fisheye style lens. His suspicions are confirmed when he sees slight distortions at all corners of the screen. There is a single car at the pumps being filled up by an obese woman driving a minivan with her hair in curlers. She finishes up and leaves, then something huge comes into the corner of the frame. It's definitely a hulking alien walking on its feet and its knuckles like an overgrown gorilla. Except its head reminds Jimmy of the comic book villain Venom.

141

Jimmy has to stop his hand from shaking that he is filming with. The creature turns towards the storefront and bends over slightly exposing all of the slithering tentacles on its back. The tentacles shoot forward and elongate bursting into the store through the glass and metal frame that is holding it in place. A young black man with dreads gets pulled out through the front of the store. The creature lifts its tentacle carrying the black man high above its head and then tilts its head upwards and unhinges its jaw somehow. There is no sound but it is clear that the young man is absolutely terrified and screaming at the top of his lungs. The creature drops the man into its mouth and then starts chewing. It turns to leave while it's still chewing. The young man's feet are still sticking out of its mouth. The alien being drags its tentacles along the exterior wall in an extremely hard swiping motion smashing everything in its path before finally hitting the camera, at which point the footage stops.

"HOLY SHIT!"

"That's what I said the first time I saw it."

Chapter 9

Jimmy left the small manager's office as soon as the tape ended. He wrapped around the counter and grabbed his case of over priced Zippos and headed for the door.

"HEY!" shouts the old store owner.

"What?"

"You said you were going to leave five-hundred dollars on the counter."

"Oh yeah. Well I'm actually an officer of the law and I'm not paying you to view subpoenaed evidence in an ongoing investigation. I will however not report you as a way to honor the spirit of our bargain."

Jimmy didn't wait for another response, he just burst out of the store.

"Get Dractus over here, he should see this too." Cerulean nods and taps a button on her tablet. Dractus comes sprinting around the corner. Jimmy gives her the phone and shows her the play button.

"Yep that's our Demon," she says as Bertha comes into the frame. They watch the rest of the video until the point where Bertha eats the store clerk.

"Ouu, you can't put medi-foam on that," said Dractus. Cerulean rolls her eyes at his comment.

"I caught her scent, I know her general heading," said Dractus.

"I have her on a few more traffic cams before she disappears. Look at this map Dractus what do you think?" says Cerulean as she hands the tablet to him.

"This area here," he says as he drags his sharp lizard fingernail in a circle around some warehouses.

"Looks like we have our next stop."

They all hop back in the truck, but Chad looks really confused. "I thought this was a special appearance. Where are all the people?" he asks.

"Oh it was just one person, special request. They paid in advance so I didn't ask questions," said Jimmy.

Chad just shrugs his shoulders "Where to next?" Jimmy gives him the cross streets nearest the center of the circle of warehouses that Dractus pointed out on the map. Chad's music mix is an eclectic combination of classic rock and dubstep, and it's not helping Jimmy's mood after seeing the video of the giant creature eating a store clerk. In short order they are in the warehouse district. They all hop out and Dractus sniffs the air.

"We don't need him anymore, we are here," said Dractus.

Jimmy turns around and gives Chad the extra hundred dollar bill he promised. "That's all for the day, thanks for the ride."

"No, thank you bro! Call me anytime it was a pleasure!" says Chad before taking off.

"I'm setting an auto-pilot timer for 5 minutes for the ship to head this way. I don't want it to come too soon and spook Bertha," said Cerulean.

Dractus lifts his battleaxe off of his back and sniffs the air again and then points at a warehouse down the street "That one," he says. Jimmy lifts a Glock 17 out of a concealed holster he has and ensures he has a round in the chamber. He wonders again if he knows what he is getting himself into. They all start walking in the direction of the indicated warehouse.

"So why do you call them demons? I mean they are just different types of aliens just like you guys right? Why not call them criminals?" asks Jimmy.

"We have criminals as well. Demons are a different breed entirely. They normally start out as criminals. Generally speaking they are really evil people. Then they are augmented in some way, they become stronger and their evil grows. We call them demons because it's the best word to describe them," says Cerulean.

"But you don't really believe they come from hell do you?" asks Jimmy.

"No we don't, but I do believe whatever chose them to become demons came from hell," says Cerulean before burying her face back into her tablet.

Some of the other warehouses in the area have noises coming from them of men at work and machines whirring. They have cars in the lot or on the street near them. The one Dractus has led them to doesn't. And even Jimmy can feel the foreboding aura coming from it. Something bad happened here. Dractus stomps up the front lawn of the warehouse almost like he isn't aware of the sidewalk. Jimmy can hear Catholic nuns yelling in his memories every time he thinks about ditching the sidewalk so he sticks to the path. When they get to the door Jimmy figures they are going to convene and make a plan of action but Dractus just gently shoulders the front door which flys inwards as if a truck just hit it. Which technically with the size and power of Dractus it might as well have just been hit by a truck. Cerulean follows him inside and draws a small sliver of silver from her waist. Jimmy doesn't get to see what it is before she heads in.

Jimmy quickly follows them in. The inside of the warehouse is unlit, the only light they have is coming in from the doorway they came through. Cerulean activates some kind of flashlight app on her tablet which is surprisingly bright but still doesn't work that well in a large warehouse. Jimmy realizes he is still holding the case full of Zippos so he sets it down in an out of the way spot. Then he draws his sidearm and starts scanning the areas he can see, the corners nearest him and even the ceiling beams. He knows underestimating a giant gorilla-octopus alien that eats people is probably a bad idea.

"It's too dark in here. COME OUT COWARD, FACE ME!" shouts Dractus.

"Subtle," says Cerulean.

Jimmy starts scanning the walls, he recognizes the layout of this place. His uncles and fathers had worked in places like this his whole childhood and he remembers the many times he visited. He sees what he is looking for, the breaker box. He pops the lids and flips all the breakers and some of the lights start coming on. The lights are starting in sequence at the end of the warehouse and turning on in rows heading their direction. A few seconds before the lights hit their side of the warehouse the trio hears a most terrible sound. It's like a car horn mixed with a high pitched version of a lion's roar. At first it's just one set, but then more sounds just like it start up.

Before anyone can respond a squirming pile of black fury lands on Dractus at top speed and knocks him over. Jimmy aims his weapon intent on shooting it and Cerulean flips out the piece of silver in her hand which folds out rapidly into a full length katana. Before Jimmy can get a clean shot on the creature attacking Dractus something lands on him as well, hard. Something tries the same with Cerulean but she simply flicks her katana before the thing hits her and sunders it in half. Jimmy is on the floor wrestling with whatever is attacking him when the lights pop on in their area. *Oh God it's a nightmare from hell.* It's a miniature version of Bertha. Jimmy can see now its tentacles are wrapping around his back and pinning one of his arms down. He tries to punch it and the thing screeches in his face while leaking spittle all over him.

It uses another one of its tentacles and holds his other arm down and then it slowly lowers its face closer to Jimmy's. Its eyes are blood red and angry with vertical pupils. Everything about this thing is wrong. Jimmy is fighting as hard as he can to push it off of himself but its arms and tentacles have the resistance of steel bars. The thing continues to lower its face and then it bites Jimmy's neck. Jimmy's blood starts pumping down the things throat and it lets out a groan of pleasure. Then Cerulean is there. She swipes her katana once in a flash, too fast for Jimmy to accurately track its path except for a vague silver blur. The thing leans back off of Jimmy and its grip eases. It turns to see what new threat is near, but that's when the top half of its head falls off. Cerulean's cut had been so clean it took a second for gravity to catch up.

Jimmy throws the thing off of him and grabs his firearm which is laying on the floor nearby before quickly hopping to his feet. He aims it everywhere and nowhere, he realizes he is in shock. His blood is soaking his shirt around his neck wound. Dractus saunters over covered in bites all over his face and exposed neck. His fancy armor has protected his body.

"Wow those suckers hurt. Jimmy why didn't you just rip it in half? That's what I did with mine," says Dractus. Jimmy can't focus on Dractus's poorly timed humor though, he is still scanning for more threats. Cerulean walks over and gently puts her hand on his firearm and pushes downwards very slowly.

147

"It's over Jimmy, we're safe. There is no more. Look at me. It is safe," says Cerulean.

Something about her demeanor does calm Jimmy down. "Thanks," he says with a nod. Cerulean grabs his neck gently and inspects his wound.

"You are going to need antivenom for that," she says and begins digging in her belt. She pulls out a small syringe and gently takes Jimmy's wrist in her hands. Then she turns his hand over gently again and pushes his windbreaker up to his elbow and injects it into his forearm. Her calm and slow demeanor and just the general way she is taking this situation in stride is really helping Jimmy calm down further.

"Okay, you are good to go Jimmy. Your neck wound is superficial and I neutralized the venom. Though there will be mild side effects," says Cerulean.

"Side effects!?" says Jimmy who is feeling his heart rate increase again.

"Yes, nothing major. Just numb-tongue and shrinking penis," says Cerulean matter of factly as she slides the empty syringe back into her belt.

"Shrinking what?" Jimmy exclaims.

"Don't worry Jimmy," says Dractus. "I can help with that, there is an easy cure for shrinking penis."

"WELL, WHAT IS IT?" Jimmy shouts.

"The saliva of my people cures most common maladies. You are going to have to kiss me," says Dractus in a most serious manner.

Jimmy is staring at Cerulean and Dractus waiting for any other solution to present itself. How did it come to this?

"Hurry Jimmy, time is short!" says Dractus who then flicks his thin lizard tongue through the air a few times to emphasize his point. Jimmy's face is a mask of pure horror. That's when Cerulean giggles, she tries to stifle it by covering her mouth but she can't help it. Then Dractus starts laughing too.

"Oh, you motherfuckers!" shouts Jimmy.

"You should have seen your face!" says Cerulean.

"Was I ever even poisoned?" asks Jimmy.

"Yes, big time. Those things are highly toxic. No worries though the shot really did cure you. No side effects. It also had a multipurpose immunity booster for bipedal mammals from an oxygen based planet and a mild pain reliever. The kissing Dractus thing is a joke we play on people. We did it to Hank too."

"Assholes," Jimmy mutters as he walks slightly away from them rubbing his neck.

"Whoa jackpot, look over here," says Cerulean who has walked around a corner of the warehouse. Jimmy and Dractus follow, when they crest the corner they see something truly disgusting.

"What. The. Fuck." said Jimmy.

"Ah Bertha's nesting grounds. This isn't the first time I've seen this. I got close to her once on RS-22," said Dractus. Jimmy pulls his shirt up over his nose to mask some of the scent. He is standing in a miniature forest of something… The ground looks like extremely expired spinach stacked 4 inches deep. Spaced among the black and green shit on the ground are lumpy things that look like giant deflated eggs. There are thick organic hoses running from egg to egg that seemingly dip into the base layer of slimy nastiness at random. Spread among the whole mess are human bones of all shapes and sizes covered in the slime of the nest.

"What's your count?" asks Dractus.

149

"Forty eight," says Cerulean.

Jimmy does a quick count of the egg like structures and sees there are roughly around 48 of them. "Wait, you mean there are forty-eight of those monsters out there?" he asks.

"No, only forty-five, we killed the three they left behind."

"So what now?" asks Jimmy.

"I can't track them anymore. If Cerulean doesn't have any more leads we are done until she resurfaces," said Dractus.

"I'm also out of leads. No more hits on the traffic cams," she says as she double checks her tablet. "I've got something else weird though. Someone attacked a school for blind children nearby here. They drove an automobile through a crowd of them as they were getting out of school and killed over a dozen just earlier today. This is too much of a coincidence for it to be so close to Bertha's nesting ground. She might have corrupted someone," said Cerulean.

"What does that mean?" asks Jimmy."

"Hard to say with what little evidence I have. It may be something simple like she is controlling him somehow or it could be something more sinister. Worst case scenario she is grooming someone to become a demon," Cerulean says calmly.

"Does none of this bother you?" asks Jimmy who is upset at how calm they both are.

"It all bothers me, but this is my job and I've been doing it for a long time," said Cerulean.

"Really, you look about twenty-two years old. I mean it's hard to tell since you are blue, and the horns and all, but you look young," said Jimmy.

"I just turned one-hundred last week, and my planet's years are longer than yours. Longevity is another perk of being an Arbiter."

"Damn, you guys are kind of making my FBI benefits look like shit," says Jimmy.

"I'm hungry, let's secure rare and exotic local food," says Dractus.

"Cheeseburgers and fries it is!" shouts Jimmy.

As they leave the warehouse Jimmy looks up the closest fast food joint from their location, but not before grabbing the case of Zippos. One of the Zippos in the case is lucky, Jimmy can tell.

"Got a restaurant about 5 minutes that way at walking speed," says Jimmy as he points down the road.

"Good the ship is in an empty lot in that direction as well in camouflage mode," says Cerulean. From that point on it's a pretty somber walk that Jimmy uses to mentally rewind his insane day. He looks over at his co-conspirators who are casually walking down the side of the road with him. A giant lizard man in silver space armor carrying a battleaxe, and a beautiful blue woman with horns who is also wearing silver space armor. *What a day.* Despite having just been attacked and bitten by a venomous space monkey Jimmy realizes he is actually having a great day. He hasn't had this much fun in ages.

"Hey Cerulean, Dractus, thanks for bringing me," says Jimmy

"He has that look in his eyes, he has heard the call," said Dractus.

"The what?" asks Jimmy. Dractus walks over and stops Jimmy, and then puts one of his enormous hands on one of Jimmy's skinny shoulders.

"The call to hunt. The greatest calling."

"Dractus, I've been in law enforcement for 16 years."

"It's not the same as hunting demons. It's not as visceral, as real. Once you hunt a demon everything else just feels like black

151

and white. Not to say your profession isn't honorable because it is and I respect what you do. There are those of us out there that need more. We need to raise the stakes because if we don't the good guys lose. It's also a lot of fun. Less bullshit as well, I was in law enforcement as well before I was an Arbiter. I remember the mountains of paperwork and bureaucratic nonsense. I have to assume it's the same way here?"

"It is."

"You won't find any of that when hunting demons. Try writing a form about how you had to shoot missiles into a residential area to stop a multidimensional brain-sucking cephalopod. There is no box to check for that one. There are just some things that can't be quantified, justified, or judged from an office chair. Hunting Demons falls into that category 99 out of 100 times. I could tell back there, even though you let that demon get the jump on you, I could see the fire in your eyes. You wanted its blood. You wanted to fight and to show your worth. That's why you are fired up now. Let me guess you are normally the big bad and you aren't used to being a victim or being on the defense?"

"That's more than correct. If people here think I am angry they generally piss their pants."

"It will never be like that with demons. They will always be ready to suck your soul out and eat your eyeballs for dessert. For some people that means running and finding a hole to hunker down in until the trouble is over. There is a rarer breed of person who runs towards demons though, because they know it's in their blood to scare those who would scare others. You are one of those people Jimmy."

"Well thanks for the compliment, and I would be happy to help you two catch this Bertha thing."

"What about after that?"

"What about it? You are going to fly off and the earth will be demon-free."

"So come with us, keep hunting demons."

"I'm not an Arbiter, Hank told me you have to be chosen by some kind of ancient aliens or maybe even God."

"Lots of people work for the Arbiter Core who were never chosen. Sure, we got lots of Arbiters who are lone ranger types who like to ignore all the politics and the Arbiter home planet and just stay in their own neighborhood killing problems as they pop up all by themselves. We also have just as many on the opposite side of the spectrum though. Those that like to work as a team and they always need good people. If you come with us I can guarantee you a spot on a demon hunting team. I'll vouch for you, I know your mettle."

"Give me some time to think about it?"

"Of course, but I already know your answer." Dractus winks as they continue to walk towards the restaurant.

***

"You should have seen the look on the kid working the register. Dractus was yelling in his face "Give me sustenance human!" Half the time I can't tell if he is serious or if he is purposefully fucking with people," said Jimmy.

"Oh he's fucking with people," said Cerulean.

"Damn that sounds like a good time. I'm sad I missed out," says Hank who is still laid up in his med-bay bed. Hank is happily munching on a triple cheeseburger and coke while he listens to the adventure that Dractus, Jimmy, and Cerulean went on without him. Suzie is still next to him, she hasn't left his side.

"Oh I forgot, I got presents for everyone!" shouts Jimmy. He digs around at his feet in the bags of food and pulls out the Zippo display. He hands one to Hank that says *Kill Them All and Let God Sort Them Out*. He hands one to Cerulean that has an image of a mermaid on it with long flowing blue hair. He hands one to Dractus that has an extremely stylized dragon on the side of it. Lastly he hands one to Suzie that has a rose on it.

"Cool, what is it?" asks Cerulean.

Jimmy flips open the one he decided to keep and shows them how it produces a flame.

"Oh wow, very thoughtful gift Jimmy. Is that why you bought them?" asks Cerulean.

"Honestly I bought them as an initial payoff to get that old man to show me the security footage, but earth has a saying I am fond of: 'Don't look a gift horse in the mouth.'

"So what does yours say?" asks Suzie. Jimmy holds his lighter up for all to see, it reads: F.B.I. Federal Booty Inspector. This elicits a round of chuckles from everyone.

"So what's next?" asks Hank.

"We are going to wait for Bertha to surface. I've also got a digital BOLO out on the vehicle that was used to kill the kids at the blind school. The windows were tinted so no ID on the driver and the license plate had been removed. In the meantime we were thinking we could squeeze in some training for you two," says Cerulean who is referencing Jimmy and Hank.

"I thought I was bedridden for a while?" asks Hank.

"You are, but some of an Arbiter's finest training can take place during convalescence. Arbiters get hurt a lot, we devised ways to use the downtime productively a LONG time ago," said Cerulean.

"You've peaked my curiosity. What about Suzie?" asks Hank.

"She should probably head home. Things are only going to get more dangerous from here," said Cerulean.

"I've been thinking about that..." says Suzie who is looking very concerned. "What would I even say, I mysteriously disappeared in the middle of a bank robbery in which authorities saw an unidentified airship. Even if they don't know it's a spaceship or if they were sworn to secrecy or whatever, how could I ever go back?"

"I've got that covered," says Cerulean as she pulls out her tablet. "Normally I would just take you to whatever authority that recognizes the Arbiter Core on your planet, but this planet doesn't have one. Also the digital infrastructure of your planet is relatively weak compared to what I am used to working with and I've been setting up Root Kits in important databases since we landed on your planet. I've got you a new identity. Your new name is Suzanne Smith and you have a bank account with two million dollars in it. Your new drivers license and bank card are printing off in my office right now. I'll bring them to you soon," says Cerulean.

Hank, Jimmy, and Suzie's eyes are wide open as they all sit in surprise. Suzie is the first to reply. "Wow, I umm... I don't know what to say. Thank you. Does this mean I shouldn't go home?"

"That's more of a question for Jimmy. I'm not intimately familiar with how law enforcement works on this planet. As a general rule of thumb though, yes, don't go home. I calculated the two million amount based on the average price of homes and vehicles in this area. Was that not enough?"

"Cerulean I only clear about 60,000 a year. If you spent it right and invested you could live off 2 million dollars forever. Well I could at least," says Hank.

Jimmy jumps into the conversation next "Yeah Suzie, just don't call your parents for at least 2 weeks and tell them to keep your re-arrival on the down-low and you should be fine. I don't know the quality of this fake identity, but don't apply for public office or a security clearance or anything like that and you should be fine."

"Well again, all I can say is wow. I'd like to stick around for a bit longer if that is okay with everyone," says Suzie.

"It's going to be boring around here, and we can't take you with us when we get a line on Bertha," says Cerulean.

"If it's all the same, I'd still like to stay for a bit."

"You're welcome here."

They ate the rest of their meal in silence. Each of them lost in their own thoughts. Jimmy was a light eater, just something he picked up always being in someone's crosshairs over the years. So he opted instead to watch Dractus eat at least twenty cheeseburgers in the span that it took everyone else to finish their meals. In fact, Dractus was the one who broke the silence.

"What animal was that from?"

"Cows," replies Jimmy.

"Cerulean, we should get some of these cows before we leave." Cerulean shakes her head and laughs as if she is used to Dractus' antics by now. Cerulean jumps up and claps her hands together.

"So who is ready to start training?" she asks.

"Shouldn't we wait for our food to digest?" asks Jimmy.

"Where we're going, we don't need digestion..." says Cerulean. Jimmy and Hank exchange a confused glance.

"Unfortunately Hank, I'll have to ask you to get up. This is a small ship, it's not a far walk. We are just going across the hall and the monitoring machines work remotely and there is another set where we are going anyway. I wouldn't risk your health."

Jimmy, and Suzie help Hank get to his feet and he winces a bit when his leg with the gunshot wound lands on the ground. They can't get a good view of it because it's still wrapped in the transparent bandage with the horizontal blue lines through it, but Cerulean assures them it is not infected and healing at an extremely rapid rate. They limp him out of the room holding him up and take him down the hall about ten feet to another futuristic looking bulkhead door. Like the room they were just in the entire hallway is purple including the floor which is just a slightly different shade of purple. Once they go through the door they find themselves in a room with ten different chairs, a few are vastly different than the rest. They all have strange looking helmets connected to the head portion that remind the humans in the room of salon style blow dryers.

"Wait a minute," says Jimmy. "I would recognize this set up anywhere. Is this the fucking Matrix?"

"I'm unfamiliar with the term," says Cerulean.

"Like a computer world where you teach us Kung Fu?" asks Jimmy. Hank just looks confused. "Hank don't tell me you didn't see the Matrix?"

"I didn't buddy, sorry," Hank replies.

"This is my standalone version of the MetaSpace," says Cerulean. "We are using Arbiter software not available to the general public. Remember when I told you that Arbiters get the best tech? You are about to experience some of it first hand. Jimmy and Hank you take those first two chairs."

Jimmy and Suzie help Hank into his chair which promptly reclines just a bit which makes Hank let out a sigh of relief. Sitting upright was agitating his wounds. Jimmy sits in the chair next to him and his chair also reclines.

157

"Suzie you can come up here with me, we can watch the show from here. Or if you get bored, hungry, or sleepy let me know and I can help you out with any of those things," says Cerulean as she gets behind a slew of monitors on a raised pedestal. Dractus walks to the middle of the room and grins menacingly.

"Why does he look so happy?" asks Jimmy.

"He has the same look a few of my drill sergeants had at my first day of basic," says Hank. "I may not have seen this Matrix movie, but I know what happens next. Bring it on," he says with a smile.

"Alright, this standalone version of the MetaSpace will be running at four times normal speed. Meaning four hours in there is only one hour out here. So if you feel like you have been in for a long time, don't worry. All Arbiter training sims have pain immersion set to 100% so if you get hit in there you will feel it. Your profiles will be created using the biometrics of your actual bodies. So whatever limitations you have now will still apply in there, minus your current injuries of course Hank. I've taken those out so you can get the most out of this training. That's the general disclaimer I give all initiates. For the record, I have to get verbal confirmation from the both of you that you are willing participants in this Arbiter Training-Sim or the software won't let me initiate it."

"I'm ready and willing," says Hank.

"Me too," says Jimmy.

"Alright then, hold onto your butts." says Cerulean. She starts typing into her console which Hank and Jimmy can't see from their perspective since they only have a view of the back of her monitors. Their chairs recline a bit more and the helmets above them automatically lower further on their heads. Hank and Jimmy can hear small servos articulating as the VR helms reconfigure to fit their heads perfectly. A small rubber seal extends out of the bottom of the helmet and adheres itself around their neck and shoulders which feels slightly claustrophobic since it is pitch black inside of the helmets now.

"Can you guys hear me?" asks Cerulean.

Jimmy and Hank both respond that they can. Without further warning Cerulean starts counting backwards from ten. As soon as she hits one the helmets rip off of Jimmy and Hank's heads and their chairs fall out from under them. They are falling through man-sized leaves, different sized branches, and dense vines. Jimmy's stomach lands on a branch at some speed which immediately causes all of the air to leave his chest. Hank hits a similar branch a few feet lower but his weight is too much so the branch snaps and he keeps falling. Their eyes that were just starting to adjust to the dark helmet interiors are now being assaulted as the light slanting through the leaves hits their pupils. Hank is grasping at everything he can, leaves, vines, branches, but everything is snapping with the combination of his momentum and weight.

"Fuck!" shouts Hank as his hands slip from yet another vine and he continues to tumble and fall. His rapid descent takes him past the lowest level of branches and he knows the inevitable time to hit the ground has come. The last branch he hit snapped him around so he is falling back first now. He can see Jimmy above him jumping from branch to branch and swinging from vines like a spider-monkey trying to get to him. That's when he hits something with some give, but the fall is still hard enough to almost knock him out and then he falls again another ten feet or so landing face first on the ground. One of his wrists took the brunt of the fall and Hank can already tell it is broken.

Hank rolls over and is surprised to see something that looks vaguely like a Woolly Mammoth. He doesn't remember them being so muscular with three trunks and six eyes though. The mammoth is fucking pissed that it just took a Hank missile to the spine. It's snorting hard and starts stomping its front two feet like it plans to charge Hank's position. Hank flips over onto his back and starts pushing away with his feet slowly to slide his body backwards through the dirt and strange undergrowth that he doesn't recognize around him. As he is about to hop up and run he sees Jimmy swinging from a vine Tarzan style straight at the Mammoth…

"Take this fucker!" Jimmy shouts before impacting with the thing's skull, feet first. The mammoth's head visible rocks to the side.

Jimmy bounces off and lands in a heap, the Mammoth is staggered. He pops back up faster than a crackhead looking for a score and is running towards Hank. Jimmy reaches down with one hand for Hank to grab.

"Come with me if you want to live," he says with a smirk. Hank reaches up to grab Jimmy's hand still shell-shocked from all of his injuries and other strange on-goings. As soon as their hands touch a mammoth's tusk erupts through Jimmy's chest and his blood sprays Hank's face.

"NOOOO" Hank shouts. The Mammoth rears up taking Jimmy's body with it then it lifts its front legs and brings them down onto Hank's chest, instantly killing him.

Chapter 10

"Hank!... Hank!... Hank wake up you son of a bitch!" Hank could hear shouting and the clashing of steel. He felt sun on his face and idly wondered if he had passed out from heat exhaustion working in the gravel yard.

"HANK MOVE!" Hank's eyes snapped open just in time to see a boot coming down towards his face. The memories flew through him, particularly the one where he had just died this same way to a mammoth's foot. *Not Again*. He rolled to the side and the foot hit the rocky sand where he had just been. He looks up at what can only be described as a gladiator. It's a man about five feet tall covered in random pieces of leather armor. In one hand he idly spins a net and in the other he has a short sword. On his head he wears a helmet that reminds Hank of the Crusaders back on earth.

Earth… He was clearly not there now. Jimmy was next to him swinging a short sword himself as two gladiators took random swings at him and pushed him backwards. Jimmy was also dressed as a gladiator... The man, well creature, alien maybe, who had tried to smash Hank's face in threw his net. Hank grabbed it out of the air and it wrapped around his arm a bit. The net was obviously built for smaller opponents. Hank shook the net off and walked towards the thing in the gladiator armor. He had to finish this quickly, Jimmy needed his help. Looking at the creature now reminded Hank of a zombie from earth folklore. It had mottled and wrinkly green skin, and black eyes below its helmet. As Hank got closer the gladiator took a few probing swings at him. The sword looked extremely sharp and Hank made sure to step back as it swung.

It was a dirty move that Hank had in mind, but he didn't really have many other options. He reached down and grabbed a handful of the loose rocky grit below him and threw it into the gladiator's face. The gladiator spun his head to stop it from entering his eyes but that was the only opening Hank needed. He stepped in and grabbed the creatures sword-bearing arm with one hand and the straps running across the creature's chest with his other hand. Using the strength of his neck and arms he pulled the creature towards him and unleashed a head-butt with the desperation someone can only have when a friend or loved one is in trouble. Despite the gladiator being helmeted the blow still dazed him and dented his helmet in, locking it into place at an angle where his eyes wouldn't line up with the viewing slot. His vision was now obscured. Hank dropped the man into the sand and pried his short sword out of his hands.

Hank being awesome at throwing stuff decided his best course of action was probably to throw stuff. He picked the gladiator attacking Jimmy that looked the most energetic and threw the short sword. The sword glanced off of the gladiator's upper thigh scoring a light gouge. Hank started running straight at him. This gladiator was also in the five-foot range height wise, and seeing Hank the giant rushing at him like a charging bull was all the incentive he needed to retreat. The other gladiator still attacking Jimmy hadn't turned around to see Hank yet. So Hank held his arm out like a clothesline from hell and clipped his neck in his sprinting pursuit for the one still retreating. The clothesline technique flipped the gladiator attacking Jimmy straight onto his back and Jimmy took the opportunity to stab downwards into the alien's abdomen.

Hank continued to chase the fleeing gladiator, but he was just a bit too quick for Hank to catch up. So Hank let him run and returned to Jimmy. Hank had a minute to check out his surroundings. He was in a giant circular pit with walls that were at least twenty feet tall of smooth stone, with the occasional portcullis to let in more gladiators here and there. Above the pit was a roaring crowd sitting in stands, drinking alien drinks and eating alien foods. One of the men in the stands was holding a small wriggling purple creature that reminded Hank of a gerbil. He ripped it in half, blue blood squirted in his face and he handed each half to kids on the left and right of him. The two kids greedily ate the small creature. *Where the hell are we?* Hank looked down at his own attire and realized he was wearing a leather skirt of some type and he had two leather pieces mounted on each of his forearms and shins. Besides that he was naked. The draft coming up the bottom of the skirt was quite alarming.

"What now Hank?" asked Jimmy as they went back to back.

"I don't know man, I'm still trying to cope with the fact that I was killed by a mutant Woolly Mammoth."

"Yeah, sorry about that, I tried to stop it."

"Are we in the game, this looks real as shit."

"We are in the game, or maybe this is hell," said Jimmy who was eyeballing the alien Hank had chased off. He was digging around in the sand and scavenging weapons.

"Hank, grab a weapon out of the sand!"

Hank took Jimmy's advice and snatched up a shield and a spear. They both turned their attention on the gladiator who had ran. He was yelling into the crowd, specifically in the direction of a shaded box that held aliens in fine looking robes.

"I wish I knew what he was saying," said Jimmy.

"He is telling them to grant him mercy by balancing the odds. He says it's not fair that I am so big and have a partner, it would be like him versus three," said Hank.

"How in the hell do you know what he is saying?"

"Oh, you know I just realized that wasn't English. It's an Arbiter thing, we can speak any language. I'm not even sure how that works yet."

They didn't have time to talk more because one of the large metal portcullis gates started to open. The loud clanking of the internal mechanism and chains that were lifting it drew everyone's attention, even those in the crowd. The archway went almost pitch black about ten feet in so no one could see what was coming. The crowd quieted waiting to see how many warriors would come out, and what kind of armaments they might bring. Hank heard someone in the crowd shout that they wanted to see a chariot. Loud screeching started echoing out of the archway, then many someone's shouting in a harsh language. It wasn't a language even Hank could make out it was more guttural authoritative noises like "YA, YA!" it reminded Hank of cattle herders back on earth.

Then everyone present saw the surprise that the aristocrats ruling the gladiatorial games had lined up. Three disturbing and raucous creatures that looked like a mutant wolf and a mutant lizard had had a one night stand were being prodded forward by a team of zombie-men-aliens bearing spears. As soon as they crested the edge of the archway entering the arena the portcullis slammed down separating the prodders from the creatures. They sniffed around and locked eyes on Hank, Jimmy, and the remaining zombie-man gladiator. The last gladiator started sprinting towards Hank and Jimmy at top speed while yelling something, this prompted the creatures to pursue.
"What's he yelling?" asked Jimmy.
"He is saying team up, he is cool, he has a neutral aura," said Hank.

The gladiator arrived a few seconds before the creatures. He spun and jumped and landed in line with Jimmy and Hank. He planted the butt of his spear in the sand and angled it downwards towards the creatures, this wasn't his first rodeo. Hank emulated him, but had to crouch a bit due to his superior height. The creatures were too smart for that old trick though. They slowed down instead of impaling themselves on the impromptu spear blockade. They began to circle the three competitors. All three of them pointed their weapons outward each focusing on a beast and they all moved as the creatures stalked.

"Someone's going to have to make a move or the leaders up there are going to try to spice things up again," said Jimmy.

"I think I could snap one's neck pretty quickly. We had an old junkyard dog when I was a kid who had free reign of the gravel yard. He was a mean son of a bitch and I wrestled him often," said Hank.

"Let our friend here know when you move, I'll keep the others off of you the best I can," said Jimmy.

Hank barked the word *ATTACK* in the gladiator's language and rushed the first wolf-lizard mutant. Hank hadn't been lying, he had some serious dog wrestling skills. He quickly locked onto the thing's neck narrowly dodging its teeth, and then made a jump for it's back using the strength of his arms and the creature's neck as a pivot device. The other two wolf-lizards tried to rush Hank to help their comrade, that was Jimmy's cue. He rushed one himself, which was the only thing he could really do since the other creature was on the other side of Hank's wrestling match. Jimmy started taking swipes at the beast hoping the last gladiator was handling the remaining creature. A loud cracking noise emanated off of Jimmy's side along with a creature's yelp, *Hank had done it*. Jimmy not wanting to be shown up threw himself into the fray even harder. Swiping and etching ever closer, the creature made many attempts to nip his arms, but Jimmy's tall and skinny frame worked to his advantage as he shimmied and dodged.

Finally the creature Jimmy was whittling away at decided it had enough. It backed away from Jimmy and stopped trying to engage. Around this time Hank hopped on the last creatures back that was being kept busy by the gladiator trying to spear it. Hank ripped its head back which let loose a sickening crunch, and the beast with Hank still on its back fell into the dirt. Hank hopped off to rejoin his compatriots. The last wolf creature was at the far end of the arena yelping and licking its wounds. All three knew where to look next to get an idea of their fate. Their eyes turned towards the leader's box.

"Fuck this noise, let's end this spectacle," said Hank who picked up one of the discarded spears. Hank looked to their new alien partner and barked something in his language, the alien let out a terse reply. Jimmy was confused until Hank filled him in.

"He is a slave, he will work with us if it means he has a chance at freedom. Follow my lead," said Hank. Without further warning Hank lobbed the spear directly at the leader's box pinning one of the aristocrats to his chair as the spear had flown directly through the alien's chest. One of the other leaders stood up, an alien with blue skin, four arms, and tentacles for a beard. He shouted into the stadium. Hank was on it with his translation duties.

"He said *kill them*."

Hank took the spear from the gladiator's hand next to him and threw it as well killing the tentacle bearded alien.

"Dude, you have to teach me that," said Jimmy. The gladiator next to Hank spoke in his native tongue again and Hank nodded at him. They walked over to the wall of the arena pit. Hank put his back against the wall and crouched a bit and then cupped his hands in front of him. The gladiator ran straight at Hank and jumped into Hank's hands. Simultaneously Hank shoved and threw his hands up as hard as he could. He propelled the gladiator straight up into the arena stands.

"You next bud," said Hank.

"But you will be trapped down here," said Jimmy.

"Then the lesson we learned here is to always bring a ladder, this has been great Arbiter training. Are you going or what?" asked Hank.

"I'll go, I'll try to find a way to get you out of here."

Hank crouched down a bit and cupped his hands once more. Jimmy did his best to copy the gladiator's style and ran right for Hank's cupped hands. He landed on them and jumped as hard as he could as Hank pushed upwards. He might have weighed more than the alien or he screwed the maneuver up because he only made it to the lip of the arena wall which he grabbed and held onto. Memories of his youth spent jumping walls flashed through him as he pulled his body up and over the rest of the way landing on his back in a puddle of someone's spilled drink, well he hoped it was a spilled drink.

As soon as Hank had finished getting Jimmy over the wall, the sand and grit of the arena below him started to tremble. "Fuck, what now..." The sand below him shifted and then it started to sink in a wide radius around him. Hank tried to run out of the area but the faster he ran the faster the sand below him began to fall away. The whole floor of the arena below him finally gave out. Hank jumped in a desperate attempt to hit the ledge of the area that was giving away. He landed on a semi-solid area that was still crumbling and tried to scrape his way upward. Everything he grabbed also broke away until finally there was nothing left to grab and he fell backwards. Gravity took him on an insanely long fall, he expected to land and die at any moment. Except he never landed, he just kept falling as the just before dusk light of the arena above him faded until he was falling through pitch black nothingness.

His fear of dying faded and gravity's pull lessened until he stopped falling. The strange thing was, he was still in a pitch black area, and he was floating...

"What kind of metaphorical bullshit is this, am I supposed to be scared without a nightlight?" He lost track of time in the nothingness and went into introspection. His thoughts spiraled to Suzie, to Eugene, the man and woman he had almost accidentally killed at Town Hall. To some of the good times he had with his father. A memory he thought long lost and forgotten came slamming back into the forefront of his mind. He was 6 years old sitting in the passenger side of his dad's old truck. He was so short he could barely see out of the window, and he had to push off with his hands to get the added height he needed to see the town flash by, but his little muscles couldn't hold out for long so he had to repeat the process often. His dad wouldn't let him kneel or take his seat-belt off in case of an accident.

His father had just made a very lucrative gravel deal and he was rife with extra cash that wouldn't last long once he paid some bills and had some of their equipment serviced. That didn't dampen his mood though. Life is fleeting and you best take the small wins when you can, and you celebrate the fuck out of them! *I Love Rock and Roll* by The Arrows came on the radio and his dad goofily played the air drums next to Hank as they drove, this made Hank laugh. His father pulled into a new burger joint in town that was rumored to have the best shakes for 300 miles. He bought them both the largest size in chocolate. A pretty girl came out to their car and delivered the shakes to them through the truck's window. Hank dug in with a spoon because the shake was too thick to drink through a straw. He was absolutely ruining his face with chocolate and getting it all over the interior of the car. Sitting there next to his dad with this awesome dessert and the neon of the restaurant's flashy signs shining into the car was just about the best thing Hank had ever done he figured.

When he looked up at his father, he noticed his dad was crying. "Dad don't be sad, I'm sorry about getting chocolate everywhere."

"I'm not sad you big goof. I'm just happy," said Hank's father as he reached over and tussled Hank's hair. Hank wasn't sure what to say and his father could tell. His father always took advantage of teachable moments and never left Hank confused for long.

"When I was slogging through the muddy fields in Vietnam killing the bad guys I never imagined my life would turn out like this. Look at me now Hank. I'm a business owner with a wonderful son who also happens to be my best friend. I can provide for you like my father never provided for me. I can make you better than I ever was." His father's eyes turned serious for a second and he gently stopped Hank from digging the spoon into the shake again.

"Listen Hank, and listen good. I need you to be better than me, I've seen your potential. You are capable of great things. My time is over, I'm past my prime. I'm here to steward in the next generation and leave the world better off than how I found it. You have a good heart, don't let it go to waste. Help those in need when you can. Stop those who would do harm to others. Be humble and don't take advantage of others. The world has enough shitheads, be better.

"Dad you said shitheads."

"I know son, don't copy me. Now give your dad a hug."

"But dad I'll get chocolate on you."

"I don't care," said Hank's father. He took the shake from 6-year old Hank and put it up on the dash. Then he unbuckled him and pulled him into a giant hug. Hank could smell the cigar his father had smoked earlier and the old spice his dad was wearing. The combined scent was a smell he thought of as *the dad smell*. He could feel his father's tears on his cheek.

His father whispered the reminder once more in softer yet more serious tone. "Be better than me. Take care of people. Never stop fighting for what's right."

Hank came back to reality, *well virtual reality*... He was still floating in the black. "Yes father," he said to the universe. He hoped his dad was out there somewhere listening. Hank wasn't sure if he had somehow triggered what happened next or if enough time had gone by that the next simulation just auto-triggered. Either way, things started happening. A light began in the distance in front of Hank, at first just a pinprick, but it became ever larger. It was red... A red piece of metal large and flat and curvy, and it was flying straight at Hank. He tried to swim or move out of its path but nothing he did made any difference, so he stopped and waited for the metal to hit him. When it arrived it didn't hit. It stopped just a few feet out from him abruptly. Hank was trying to figure out what its purpose was, it seemed to glow with an inner light. Then more pinpricks of light appeared in all directions and the cycle repeated.

They were mostly red metal pieces but some were gray, some were dull metal, some were complex mechanical components. The all flew directly at Hank and stopped just

172

short of hitting him. As they continued to fly in from all directions the ones already floating in front of him began connecting themselves to their neighbors. Screws, pins, bolts, and rods flew into place in record time further connecting the pieces. It was quite amazing to watch. Some of the pieces welded themselves together. Hank could see the heat in the perfect welded seams being created out of thin air, but even that died off and disappeared just as quickly as it had arrived. Something large, grey, and soft looking flew straight at Hank, stopped, and spun directly behind him. It conformed itself to his backside. It was a seat. As the rest of the pieces continued to snap together Hank realized it was going to be a vehicle of some sort, and he was already sitting inside of it. The more it came together it became ever more apparent that it was some kind of futuristic or alien sports car. The dead giveaway for Hank that the vehicle's origins were not of earth was that a lot of the metal components inside of the sports car had the same purple metal coating that Cerulean had in her ship. So this car was from one of her worlds.

The second the final components were installed the darkness around Hank began to brighten. Slowly at first, but then the brightening began to speed up. A bright star grew in the void somewhere below the position of Hank's feet. It grew in intensity and size as it rose over Hank's current position. Then some form of ground rose out of the blackness and continued to rise until it met the bottom of Hank's car. Buildings sprouted like trees around him. Holograms appeared on the buildings advertising things

Hank had never heard of, in languages he had never seen before. Superstructures began to grow out of the buildings crisscrossing across the sky, bridges, walkways, and something that looked like giant gerbil tubes. Cars that looked similar to Hanks emerged out of the street. Whatever material the street was made of sealed up cleanly behind the cars as if it had never happened. Strange aliens came into focus behind the controls of the cars, they were all frozen in place.

The last of the features of this strange new world popped into place. Suspended gardens hung from every building and below every bridge. Trees grew in the most interesting places, glass spires that were twisted and curved grew between the buildings. Hank wasn't sure what their purpose was, but it looked as if they had been dancing and then had frozen in place. Hank could see cars in the sky flying on perfect invisible roads above him… Before Hank could finish taking in the minute details the scene came to life, including Hank's car which was seemingly traveling at over 100mph down the road he was on.

"OH SHIT!" he shouted as he cranked the wheel to one side narrowly avoiding a car. His vehicle was traveling at least twice as fast as the cars around him and he was dodging left and right as fast as he could to not rear end them. He was driving on what appeared to be an eight lane superhighway. Strange horns were being sounded by the offended drivers who had seen Hank almost run them off the road. Hank studied the vehicle's controls, everything had strange labels in a different language with symbols he had never seen before. Some were easy to make out, but others were completely foreign. Whatever Arbiter mechanism allowed him to understand different languages kicked in and Hank was able to read a few of the labels, but not before his eyes would be jerked back to the road in order to avoid more obstacles.

No matter how hard he tried he couldn't seem to study the controls at the same time as directing the car. If he studied the controls too long he would crash and die. If all he did was dodge he would eventually die anyway, this was an unsustainable situation. He was going to have to take a chance if he wanted to get out of this alive. The controls of the car were very similar to that of an earth car. At first this confused Hank, but he came to the conclusion that it made sense. It was a pretty basic set up for anything with a few legs, a butt, and some arms. Definitely an *if it's not broken don't fix it* type situation. There was only two pedals, Hank wasn't pressing either of them currently. He tested one slightly and it did nothing. So he tested the other and felt some small resistance, *this must be the breaks*.

He applied steady pressure to the brake pedal and the car started to let out a high pitched squeal. Then the noise stopped all of a sudden and a few of the temperature gauges in the car spiked. All of the tension in the brake pedal went out. Words started flashing across the inside of the windshield. It must have had a built-in digital display. It read "Malfunction, critical error!" There was so many buttons in front of him he wasn't sure what to do next. He took another guess, doing something was always better than doing nothing in situations like this.

"ACTIVE VOICE COMMANDS!" he shouted in English. Nothing happened, so he shouted it again in the language the gladiators spoke in the last simulation. This time the car replied in the same language.

"Voice command mode activated. How can I help you?"

"Fix the brakes!" Hank shouted as he narrowly dodged by a truck hauling at least three forty-foot long box cargo trailers.

"Running mechanical diagnostic…. One moment please…. Diagnostic complete. A small incendiary device has disabled all function in the brakes and the accelerator. You are locked in at this speed, this appears to be intentional. The only thing working properly in the vehicle are the engines and the steering column."

"What are my options?"

"I have already alerted authorities, they are en-route to rescue you, but at your current speed I only calculate a 6% chance of success for them."

"Are you allowed to tell me that?"

"No, it goes against the calming protocol for customers who are on the brink of impending death. It appears some of my systems must have been damaged as well."

"Maybe I could jump to another vehicle."

"I calculate your chances of surviving such a maneuver at 2.6%, but that is just an estimate. I would need more data to get a more accurate calculation to ascertain-"

"Fuck you car. You don't know me."

"Very rude sir, very rude indeed."

"You got any tools in this shitbucket."

"Not familiar with the term *SHIT BUCKET*, but this vehicle has no onboard lavatory. We do however have a small suite of tools for emergency situations."

"GET ME THE TOOLS!"

"The tools are only meant to be recovered while the vehicle is parked. There may be a way but it is a non-regulation maneuver against safety protocols. Do you consent?"

"Just get me the damn tools!"

The backseat in the car flew forward violently and random tools shot into the car cracking the front windshield. Something banged hard into the back of Hank's head and his right elbow.

"God damn, what did you do!"

"I lowered the backseat and inflated a small flotation device at a rapid pace. This maneuver ejected the tool container into the passenger compartment."

"You really fuckin suck at your job."

"Oh, I'm sorry I have failed you sir. Maybe I should commit suicide and end my miserable existence."

"Hold that thought. Does this sucker have autopilot?"

"Yes sir, but it is not recommended at these speeds."

"Turn it on."

"But sir, at these speeds there is no way the autopilot will be able to accurately compute weather conditions, the actions of other manual drivers, vehicles that aren't plugged into the grid, dust that has built up on the sensors and cameras of this vehicle, temperature variations that impa-"

"JUST FUCKING TURN ON THE AUTOPILOT!"

"Yes sir!"

Giant red words blinked across the windshield "AUTOPILOT ENGAGED," and Hank hesitantly let go of the wheel. He was coming up on another vehicle fast and if he didn't crank the wheel he would rear end it so hard he would most likely kill himself. He waited and held his breath. The seconds ticked by as he approached and at the last possible moment the wheel turned on its own accord and his vehicle transitioned safely into the next lane over.

"Damn, did you wait long enough? You could have changed lanes long before that you asshole."

"Sir, I am the onboard A.I. for a Revulon 5000 model roadster. I am not an orifice that spits out excrement. And I told you that the autopilot-"

"SHUT UP!"

Hank started digging around the interior of the car looking for the tools the thing had spit out. He found one that looked suspiciously like a claw toothed hammer, that would work. He kept digging until he found the final tool he was looking for, a crowbar with a big hook on one end. No matter how futuristic and automated things got a crowbar would always have its uses. With the crowbar in one hand and the hammer in his opposite hand he yelled:

"Is there anything at all you can do to get this thing to slow down?"

"The only viable option would be to destroy the engine further using the already damaged self-repair mechanisms. This could have disastrous effects. Many parts of this vehicle are highly combustible. I suspect a 3.9% chance of instant immolation if I even attempted this maneuver. Furthermore-"

"Stop, I've heard enough. If I stay here I'm dead either way. Get me close to a big vehicle and try to slow us. And open these windows up right now!"

The vehicle complied and the windows rolled down. Hank pulled himself up to a sitting position on the window sill which wasn't an easy thing to do for a man his size. Next he swung the claw hammer, claw first, into the top of the car. It pierced right through. He let out a sigh of relief. He had been worried a futuristic car like this would be super durable. Instead it was similar to earth cars, in the way that parts of the structure were super durable and some parts were meant to break. He pulled the hammer out and ran the hooked end of the crowbar through the hole he had made. Now he had a good hand hold. Using the crowbar as leverage he climbed onto the roof as the wind tried to suck him off the top of the vehicle. Hank passed an alien version of a minivan and had just enough time to see a handful of blue kids from Cerulean's race sitting aghast with mouths open at the sight of him crawling around on the roof. Hank saw another one of the super diesels ahead hauling three storage compartments that were all about forty feet long, just like the last one. He bent over and yelled into the cabin of his car while making sure to not let go of the crowbar.

"That truck there, as soon as we are about halfway past it do whatever you have to do to slow the vehicle down. If you can alert the other drivers to clear out of the way as well, that would be great. Sorry for being cranky earlier we got off to a bad start, but I believe in you."

It was too windy for him to hear a response but he hoped the car had heard him, and he hoped the car wouldn't screw him over for being terse earlier. He wasn't sure if being polite would help, but it couldn't hurt. It was so windy and the car was moving so fast it was hard to even keep his eyes open. The car did its job, as soon as he was just passing the middle storage trailer on the diesel something in the car below him jerked hard and he almost lost grip on the crowbar. Something under the hood caught fire and flames shout of the seams around the engine compartment. A slew of vehicle parts shot out of the bottom of the car and sprayed the traffic behind him. It was now or never.

Hank yanked the crowbar out and jumped. He smacked into the side panel of the box trailer that had to have been moving at least one hundred miles an hour. He would have bounced off and became a smear but he sunk his claw hammer in deep and tried to find somewhere to hook his crowbar as well. His weight was too much for the thin-skinned storage compartment wall and with all of his mass hanging on the hammer it began to rip down the side of the car dragging hank lower with it. He stopped when the claw on his hammer snagged a support beam near the bottom of the trailer. Hank's feet were dangling mere inches from the road and he had to tuck his legs up to even get that much clearance.

Hank could see some of the contents of the truck now that he had made a tear in the other wall. It was some kind of sealed crates made out of a material he didn't recognize. What he did recognize were the tamper proof security bands around them. These were common on earth for different types of cargo and each security band had a serial number on it to ensure that if someone snipped one it would be hard to replace. Hank swung his crowbar hook up to the highest crate he could reach and ran the hook through some of the security bands and prayed they would hold his weight. He pulled the claw hammer off of the support beam transferring all of his weight to the crowbar for a second and jammed the edge of the claw hammer behind a different security band as well. He repeated the process, climbing the side of the trailer until he crested the lip. Once on the top he carefully moved forward. He got to the front end of the storage trailer and had to jump to the next one. He could see the cab of the truck pulling the whole thing.

He got to the cab and carefully lowered himself using the crowbar as a handhold again until he was dangling in front of the windshield.

"DAMN IT!" he shouted when he looked inside. The driver's seat was empty. This thing was fully automated.

Either way the truck must have gotten the message because it started slowing down and it took the next exit off of the highway. "About damn time!" Hank shouted into the wind that was dying off as the truck further slowed. He hoped whatever came next would be less of a pain in the ass.

Chapter 11

Hank rode on the top of the truck in a crouch with one hand on his crowbar which was latched to the lip of the truck's cab. He was headed down the exit ramp on the highway and he could see the truck was headed for a police blockade. There were at least 20 police cars and six ambulances, he only knew what they were because his Arbiter translation ability was letting him read the words on the side of the vehicles. Half of the cars hovered in place, and half had wheels. A few of them had officers popping out of the roof manning deadly looking turrets. These guys weren't fucking around. The diesel stopped about a hundred feet out from them. Some of the officers were at ease but others had guns drawn pointed not quite at Hank, but close enough to make any sane man nervous.

Hank figured he needed to take charge of this situation quickly. He hopped off of the diesel and fell the 13 feet or so to the ground. Pain shot through his knees but he couldn't let the assorted alien police officers see that he felt it. So he stood up quickly and proudly marched over to their barricade. Once he got within earshot he shouted:

"Hi there! I'm Arbiter Hank, thanks for the quick response time. Do you have any directions for my next mission?"

A distinguished looking older fellow marched over. Well Hank assumed he was older, it's hard to tell with aliens. He was about the same height as Hank, so tall, but less broad across the chest. His skin was a light green, and his eyes were a dull red. He was completely hairless, but Hank couldn't tell if that was a feature of his race or if he had just chosen that look. He had crow's feet in the corners of his eyes, which Hank associated with age, but again maybe all of his people had those. He was the only one of his kind around so there was no one else to compare him to. He wore a spiffy dress uniform which also said police on each arm. His chest read Lieutenant Commander Hampton. The other police officers in attendance were a myriad of different races. Hank even recognized a couple of their races from memory, including one Noxian, the same race as Dractus.

The Lieutenant Commander in front of him had a gentle look on his face, not quite a smile but almost there. Hank could tell without even using his intuition that this was a good dude. The type of man who is followed out of mutual respect not fear. Hank ran a scan with his Intuition and his suspicions were confirmed doubly so, the lieutenant commander's aura was calm, happy, and good.

"Hello there!" Hank said with a smile.

"We will get this sorted out in short order Arbiter, no worries."

"That's great to hear," said Hank.

Two aliens in dull gray coveralls ran over carrying some equipment and dragging thick cables. They laid the equipment out, and started connecting power lines to it. Hank didn't recognize any of it. The situation was so surreal watching all of the cops and the techs work. One of the cops in a turret seemed to notice the situation was low priority so he leaned back and pulled out what looked like a cigarette and started casually smoking. This was too much for Hank, he had to ask some questions.

"Sir, I don't mean to offend, but can I ask you what could be a personal question?"

"Go ahead."

"Are you real? I mean, I'm in a computer game still I think."

The older alien police commander seemed to ponder the question before answering. "What is real? This morning I woke up with my wife and we enjoyed an amazing breakfast together. I kissed my kids goodbye before they went to school, and then I went to work. Now I'm here talking with you. My life is good, fulfilled. You say I'm in a computer simulation, that's fine with me. Maybe you are right, or maybe you are just crazy. Either way tonight I'm going to go home to my loving family and enjoy myself. Did that answer your question?"

"Not in the slightest, but I like your style," Hank said with a grin.

"Well it was nice to speak with you, but the technicians are ready. Please step through and good luck."

The two technicians had set up what looked like a circle of steel on the ground with a large box connected to it and power cables heading in and out of the box. They both had tablets hardwired into the box and they were manipulating the fuck out of them. One of them yelled "Stand back!" all of the officers nearby complied and he pressed a few more

185

buttons on his tablet. The ring shot blue light skyward about twenty feet. At first the light was hazy and thin but it soon solidified into a non-transparent field. It reminded Hank of lava, only blue. Jumping into it didn't seem all that appealing, even though he felt no heat coming from it. He looked at the kind police commander once more, the man only gave him a nod and a small smile. *Fuck it.* Hank jumped through.

Hank landed in a crouch, and he threw his fist out to stop his forward momentum. He had landed on something soft, carpet… The next thing he noticed was his arm, he pulled his fist up and turned his hand palm up. His arm was covered in a silver garment of some kind. He stood up and took in his surroundings. He was in an extremely plush office. The walls were lined in extremely nice shelves made of some kind of material that Hank didn't recognize. The shelves were covered in books, and knickknacks, and other strange objects. Dented in helmets, broken guns, twisted swords, spheres made of different materials, these were just some of the things Hank saw.

There was a large futuristic bulkhead style door and a smaller door near the back of the office. Hank headed for the smaller door, it slid open automatically before he got to it. Inside was a small bathroom with a closet. Hank went to the mirror. He was wearing a long silver trench coat that went all the way down to his ankles. It fit loosely over his large frame, but comfortably. The shoulders of the coat had very finely detailed epaulets on them which made Hank's

186

already large frame look larger. Underneath the coat he was wearing the same silver armor that Cerulean and Dractus wore. Slim fitting, but armored in vital areas and areas that might take damage more often. On his feet he wore heavy duty combat boots that were also silver. The strangest part of the whole situation was that he looked older, and his hair was down to his shoulders. He also had decorative silver dye in different parts of his hair, and a wedding ring on… He had a patch on his upper left shoulder that showed two bipedal figures shaking hands, under it were the words *Arbiter Diplomatic Corps*.

This was a lot to take in. Hank gripped the sides of the sink in front of him and took a few deep breaths. A voice called out from the office behind him, "Sir?" Hank walked back into the office to find a young human woman with shoulder-length brown hair in some form of futuristic office attire.

"Sir the diplomats from BG-49 and RS-13 are here, they are waiting for you."

"What? Me?"

"Sir, don't tell me you didn't prepare again... Here take this," she said as she handed him a thick dossier.

"Let's walk and talk sir," she says as she pulls Hank gently by his upper arm. He follows her out into the hallway.

"Open the dossier sir, you browse while I talk. The first thing you have to remember is that the diplomat from RS-13 just had a granddaughter. If you don't mention that you heard about her and how cute she is, he will be upset. Make sure you bow when you meet him, and grip his elbow, he will also grip yours. You don't let go of your grip until he lets go of his. The diplomat from BG-49 is a technophobe so he won't be using a rebreather. His planet's air composition is slightly different than what we keep in this building so expect him to be slightly winded. I've had the air in the conference room slightly adjusted to make him a bit more comfortable, but if I adjust it too much he will notice and think we are catering to him with technology, and that will anger him.

Don't ask me how a race that hates technology is okay with space travel, because it doesn't make sense to me either. Tracy, who is the secretary to do D'jan Mirot told me that they basically traveled here in a giant flying box full of trees and animals. They literally hunt the animals through the trees and cook the meat on campfires in the spaceship! isn't that radical!? Sorry I'm off track, when you meet him he is going to want to wrap one of his tentacles around your neck to check if you are strong enough for him to deem you worthy, whatever that means. After that-"

Hank listened to the woman, who was apparently his secretary, carry on about the small nuances between the two diplomats and the manner in which he should broach each subject. Apparently the planets they were representing had a hostile enemy in common who had broken the laws of the Arbiter Core. So this common enemy was now "free game" as far as the rest of the governed universe was concerned. They hadn't been openly hostile enough to warrant intervention from the Arbiter Core itself or the coalition of planets, but they had been picking off lone ships and stealing from targets of opportunity without fear of reprisal, that had to change. Getting these two planets to openly declare a united front against the hostile planet might be enough to get the hostiles to calm down. What would happen in the room Hank was headed to, what seemingly appeared to be a small talk between three beings, could potentially save millions of lives and stop a major conflict. This all gave Hank a renewed outlook on negotiations, and made him realize just how damn important they really were.

His secretary stopped in front of a glass lined room that was beautifully and lavishly decorated. One section of the room rested against a dark rock wall that had a small waterfall coming out of a crevice. The crevice had a decorative metal grate over it. The water fell into a small rut in the floor that actually cut through the entire room and went under the conference table and ultimately out of the room.

"Any last second questions sir?"

Hank had a million questions, but none of that mattered. He knew what needed to be accomplished and he understood how important this was. This particular task was WAY outside of Hank's wheelhouse, but Hank wasn't a quitter. This may not be a test of brawn or endurance, but by God, Hank was going to give it his best.

Hank looked at his secretary one last time. "They are about to get the fuck negotiated out of them," he said before he threw the glass door open and marched into the room.

***

Jimmy flew through the portal, hit the ground and rolled to distribute his momentum before finally popping up to his feet on high alert. He had just been murdered trying to escape some sabotaged car scenario. It had not been pleasant. He was in an office with plush carpet. The walls were lined in extremely nice shelves made of some kind of material that Jimmy didn't recognize. The shelves were covered in books, and knickknacks, and other strange objects. Dented in helmets, broken guns, twisted swords, spheres made of different materials, these were just some of the things Jimmy saw. He felt heavier, he looked down and noticed he was wearing some kind of silver outfit. He ran to the smaller door in the room because he guessed it was a bathroom, he was right. He went straight to the mirror.

He was wearing the same style armor that Cerulean and Dractus had.... Arbiter armor. On top of the armor he wore a decorative silver trench coat with stylized epaulets on each shoulder. He looked a little older. His face had some age lines on it that it didn't have before, but he was clearly in better shape. His metabolism and lifestyle that had held him up from ever putting on some serious mass apparently didn't exist in whatever new world he was in now because he felt and looked ripped. His hair was pulled back into a tight ponytail and someone had strategically added silver dye to it in neat patterns that made him look fierce. There

190

was strange writing on different parts of his clothing, it was a language he had never seen before. All of a sudden he could read it. It declared him as an Arbiter diplomat. Not only was he an Arbiter now, he was some kind of big shot with a nice office to boot.

"Sir?" he heard from somewhere behind him back in the office. He bolted out to see a hot looking human secretary. Before she could say anything else he blurted out:

"Please tell me we are boning."

The secretary blushed profusely before replying "Oh Jimmy we don't have time for that right now. The diplomats have arrived and they are waiting to speak with you."

"One moment," he told her before heading back to the bathroom mirror. He looked at himself again. Tall, proud, muscular, banging the hot secretary, a highly decorated Arbiter to boot... He wanted this life. He knew he was still in the virtual simulation, but this wonderful place had just shown him a vision of his future. He swore to himself then and there that he would become an Arbiter. Jimmy didn't regret or despise his position in the FBI, and he knew that the few people in the FBI who knew what he was doing in his undercover capacity considered him to be a brave hero. This was different though. From what he understood Arbiters were one part superhero, and one part celebrity. Judge, Jury, and executioner to the entire universe. No hiding, no scheming, you find the enemy and chop his nuts off. Compared to Jimmy's dark and dirty work it seemed like a paradise.

***

Hank landed on a wooden platform and stumbled precariously close to an edge before catching himself. The few seconds he had looked over the edge had shown him that he was at minimum hundreds of feet up. He stood up and backed as far away from the edge as he could until his back bumped into something. He spun around and was surprised to see it was the trunk of an enormous tree. He was in a tree, a tree city to be more specific. All around him trees were ringed with wooden platforms just like the one he was on. Some even had full on houses built into them. Among the trees were millions of vines of various lengths coming down from the rich canopy above him. Most were thicker than Hank's wrist and hundreds of feet long. It looked like some of them even went all the way to the ground.

The confusing part was that there were no bridges connecting the tree platforms. *How are you supposed to cross?* In the distance Hank could see a few little hairy alien kids playing what looked like a game of tag on one of the platforms, they hadn't spotted him yet. Hank crouched down not wanting to spook them. After a while he noticed they even had tails like monkeys. *Was this the planet of the apes?* He continued to watch them play and laugh for a bit, but something was nagging at him. *Shouldn't there be protective railings?*

192

He understood and liked the idea of a culture living up here. Ample protection from the elements and natural predators, easy place to collect water, etc. *Aren't the parents afraid the children might fall though?* Or maybe they do fall often and that's just a part of the life here. Some cultures have strange customs, and accepting the morbid as common is a regular phenomenon in secluded areas. As Hank continued to watch the kids and ponder his questions he noticed one of the bigger kids became a little overzealous and shoved one of the others kids close to the edge. Hank held in his breath as the kid near the edge tottered and almost fell before regaining his balance. Before he could step away from the edge another kid shoved him off completely. "NO!" Hank shouted.

Instead of falling, something amazing happened. The kid opened his arms wide exposing thin flaps of skin that ran from his forearms to his sides just below where a human's rib-cage would start. They worked like inefficient wings and the kid glided right to the nearest vine which he grabbed like a pro and used to quickly ascend. Once he was slightly higher than the platform he had started on he jumped again and glided back to where the other kids were and rejoined the game of tag like nothing had happened.

"A world of gliding monkey people! COOL!" Hank shouted with boy-like wonder. He wasn't sure why this concept interested him so much, but he was really happy to be here.

Something loud landed on the wooden platform that Hank was on vibrating the whole thing. The impact had happened just around the bend of the tree trunk out of Hank's vision so he couldn't see what it was, but loud and fast footsteps started up immediately. The tell-tale sign of someone running on a wood floor, Hank knew the sound well. The person came into view, it was a blue male with short little horns on his forehead, the same race as Cerulean. With no hesitation the blue man ran to the end of Hank's platform and jumped. The blue man grabbed a vine and his momentum swung him forward a bit. He let go and flew to the next vine. *What the hell?* Before Hank could think too much about it, large red letters popped up in his vision that read: "PURSUE THE CRIMINAL!"

Hank wasn't particularly afraid of heights, but the idea of jumping didn't look appealing. Then he noticed the criminal was headed towards the kids… Maybe he was heading there because that was the next solid platform, or maybe it was something nefarious… Either way Hank knew he couldn't risk the safety of the kids. He ran and jumped.

Hank and Jimmy went through scenario after scenario. They faced things as simple as gunfights with unruly criminals, to scenarios as complex as defusing a bomb. Hank had a particularly fun scenario where he got to attack an enemy missile silo using his Killdozer. It was great for leveling the first floor, but once he had to descend into its

194

depths he unfortunately had to leave the Killdozer behind. After a few more solo scenarios Hank and Jimmy got to link back up to work in a civil unrest situation.

That one was particularly confusing for Hank. His Arbiter Intuition was making every decision twice as hard for him. A father guarding his children throwing off a positive aura might flare evil for a second when he tries to rip bread away from someone else in the hopes of feeding his children. An evil deed for a good cause, *kind of*, ensuring his kids could eat would mean other kids would starve. Jimmy who wasn't weighed down with Arbiter abilities treated the scenario as a black and white situation. If someone was breaking the law they got shot with the less than lethal weapons that Hank and Jimmy had been provided with for this scenario. The weapons let out some kind of strange energy blast leaving the victim convulsing on the ground for a few minutes.

Hank couldn't really tell if he had won or lost that scenario since the whole thing had left a bad taste in his mouth. There had been too many factors to consider, too many moving parts. Shit like that was why Hank preferred to just find the bad guy and smash 'em. On the other hand, Jimmy had seemed nonplussed by the situation. Which again made Hank wonder why he had been chosen to be an Arbiter over Jimmy. As soon as that scenario was over a single glowing blue portal had opened up in the intersection they had been working in. Jimmy and Hank knew the routine by now and jumped through. They arrived to weightlessness, wearing some kind of spacesuits floating among the stars.

They were about ten feet apart with a tether connecting them. In the distance, maybe 600 meters or so they could see a space station. A mechanical voice came from inside of Hank's suit.

"Only 13 minutes of oxygen remaining."

Before Hank had more time to ponder his current predicament large wording started flashing across his vision.

"EMERGENCY SIMULATION SHUT DOWN, EXITING IN 3 SECONDS!" Sure enough a few seconds later Hank's view of space went black and then his VR helmet recessed up above his head giving him a view of Suzie and Cerulean sitting behind the monitor bank. Jimmy was skeptical at first, he had digested enough science fictions books and shows to know the classic trope of putting the characters into a simulation that looks exactly like their own reality. His fears were assuaged once his helmet came up. Reality was... *cleaner* than the VR, the edges were harder, the smells were realer. When you are actually in the situation and surrounded by it, it's hard to tell the difference, but actually coming back to reality left no question in his mind that this was the real world.

"Why did we get pulled out," asked Jimmy as he jumped out of the VR chair and began to stretch.

"We got a possible lead on the whereabouts of the demons," Cerulean replied.

"Why am I not hungry? Why don't I have to pee? How long were we in? Why am I not tired?" Jimmy blurted out.

Cerulean just knowingly smiled before replying. Your first Arbiter VR session can be intense, I understand. I grew up on a planet with full immersion VR, but it's nothing like Arbiter tech. And most of the stuff we do in the Arbiter VR is super illegal under universal law. Plus the stress of it would kill most regular folks. To answer your questions though in no particular order; you were in for 17 hours, we all had a good night sleep while you two trained. You aren't tired because the VR actually put your body into what you humans would call REM sleep. So on the contrary you should be extremely well rested. You did pee multiple times, the chairs you were in took care of that. The chair you were in also had a basic intravenous nutrient drip to keep your energy up, but I suspect you will be starving soon. We are in route to the demons suspected location now. Let's head to the chow hall and I'll get you two something to munch on and give you the rest of the details."

Cerulean's ship wasn't very big so they only had to go a few doors down to get to the small room designated for eating. They all sat down around a small table, except for Cerulean. She was at some kind of touchscreen embedded in the wall next to a recessed area that reminded Hank of a soda fountain. She clicked a few more things, but Hank couldn't see what she was doing fully since her body was blocking the view. Suzie scooted closer to Hank, uncomfortably so. Hank still needed to break it off with her. He knew his future was going to be tumultuous at best and he only needed those he could trust implicitly around him. He knew Suzie was infatuated with him, but that didn't mean he could trust her. She had already burned him once. Cerulean finished up whatever she was doing at the strange machine and brought over some small gray and dull looking cubes on plates. They were about the size of a human fist. She set one down each in front of Hank and Jimmy.

"What the fuck is that?" asked Hank. Jimmy didn't add an additional comment but you could tell by his face that he was equally as appalled at their *dining selection*...

"It's a nutrient cube, basic space food meant to be non-poisonous to as many species as possible. Not that it would matter to you Hank. An Arbiter's stomach can filter out toxins and poisons."

Hank considered it for a minute, before deciding that he was hungry and his combat experience in the military had ingrained in him the fact that being fed and urinating before battle was key. He picked up the cube and roughly shoved the whole thing in his mouth. It was already pretty gelatinous to begin with so he only chewed it a bit before consuming it entirely with just a few swallows. It had tasted like white rice and stale green beans, so overall not so bad.

"It's edible," declared Hank.

"I got through about half of one this morning and gave up," said Suzie.

Jimmy hesitantly took a bite, and then finished his as well in short order. "I pretend to be a crime-lord 7-days a week.

I've eaten some interesting things in my time, overall that wasn't terrible in comparison.

"Dractus will eat 10 of those things mushed into a ball and slathered in the blood of a Kalrothian Sandworm," said Cerulean. Jimmy raises his eyebrows at this comment, but decides he ultimately doesn't want to know.

"Right, the intel," says Cerulean as she points at a wall that a recessed screen slides out of before continuing. "This is a small town in Washington called Winthrop. We believe it to be the demon's current location. We are en route now."

The screen shows a satellite view of a small town basically surrounded by hills and trees in all directions. "Winthrop only has a population of four-hundred, and it's over one-hundred miles from the nearest airport, so it's very secluded. All communication with the town ceased about 6 hours ago, and all internet and phone lines in and out of the area have been cut or destroyed. A delivery driver that was dropping off food and supplies mysteriously disappeared as well after a scheduled drop-off there. He never checked in or returned from his run. His cell phone's last ping showed him entering the town, but now that can't be tracked since the area is in essentially a digital blackout. We hijacked a few satellites and took some photos, here," she says as she pressed a few buttons on her tablet which causes the screen to show new images.

The new pictures clearly show scattered fires and bodies laying in the streets.

"Some of the residents appear to be holed up in their homes shooting at anything that even comes remotely close to their A.O., but the bulk appear to be dead or missing. We are assuming that this is the work of our demons, but even if it isn't they need an Arbiter up there ASAP. Human authorities haven't gotten wind of this yet so we will be the only ones responding. We are going to drop Suzie off here in about five minutes near a major airport in Idaho. Then you two need to get suited up in some armor we worked up for you on our 3D printers when you were in sim-training.

"Hank, can I have a word in private with you?" asked Suzie. Hank knew this moment was coming.

"Sure, let's head out to the hall."

Once they were out in the hall they could both tell that there was an air of awkwardness between them, Suzie was the one to break the ice.

"So you are walking better, those aliens sure know their stuff."

Hank hadn't even noticed until she mentioned it that he basically felt fully healed. "You're right."

"Listen Hank, I want this to-"

"I think you should go home Suzie."

Suzie got quiet and didn't speak for a minute. "Can I ask why, we just made love yesterday. I just thought... I don't know, I thought I meant something to you."

"You did, you meant everything to me. Then a small mix up happened, Eugene cut you, your father turned on me, and you abandoned me. I needed you, I needed your support and you threw me away like garbage. I need someone who will stick with me when the going gets tough and you have a track record of doing the opposite of that. My life is about to get really complicated, hell it already is really complicated. I'm not dragging you with me out of respect for you, but I can't be with you because I don't trust you..."

Suzie was openly crying now, but Hank wasn't done yet. "You think I don't want to take you with me? You are beautiful, hell you are stunning. You got your face cut up and somehow that only made you better looking. You are an animal in the sack. Hell, I like everything about you, but I don't know you beyond the hyped up image I have of you back from high school. I'm about to leave the planet for a long time if I don't die hunting these demons. You think it wouldn't comfort me to have your beautiful face nearby? I'm doing what is best for both of us..."

Suzie had turned her back on him, and she said one thing before storming away. "You are a bastard Hank." Hank didn't disagree with her, but he was the bastard he had to be.

Chapter 12

"How did the drop off go?" asked Hank.

"She was pissed and it was awkward," replied Jimmy

"To be expected."

"If you say so, It's none of my business. Too bad she didn't get to see you in your pimp suit before she left."

"Hardy har har."

Jimmy had just walked Suzie a few miles through a wooded area to the nearest road so she could catch a taxi to the airport. He had also given her a few tips on how to stay off of the radar with her digitally counterfeited 2-million dollars. Now Hank, Jimmy, Cerulean, and Dractus were en route to Washington to see if the small town really had been taken over by demons. If that wasn't the case they intended to help anyway in whatever capacity was needed. Hank and Jimmy had just finished putting on the 3D printed armor that Cerulean had provided them. Which ended up being a goldish or brass color. Jimmy had immediately christened them "pimp suits." Cerulean had said that the color was just happenstance because it was one of the strongest lightweight alloys that her onboard 3D printer could work with.

Their "pimp suits" were skin tight layered scales that had a surprisingly comfortable under layer that rested against the bare skin and helped to wick moisture. The armor also had raised plates over the knees, shins, elbows, spine, pectorals, shoulders, forearms, and genitals. Which gave the pimp suit the general vibe of a futuristic motorcycle outfit. Or maybe the suit of a backup dancer in a music video. Dractus had been at the front of the ship monitoring the evolving situation in Washington, but he had stopped by shortly to give Jimmy and Hank tips on getting in and out of the Arbiter armor, before adding: "It's just like ours, except shittier."

Dractus… always the wordsmith… Jimmy spun around in a mirror a few times before decided he was tired of looking insane. So he threw his old jeans on over the armor. He tried to get his t-shirt on as well, but it wouldn't fit over the shoulder plates without the bottom hem being higher than his belly button. So he settled on his thin bulletproof vest and his FBI windbreaker. He almost looked normal now except for the gold dragon-scaled shirt sticking up from under his vest. Hank followed his lead since he also didn't want to look like the newest breed of Power Ranger. Some Jeans, work boots, and one of his yellow "Steel Gravel" tank tops and he almost looked normal. Since the tank top was sleeveless it fit nicely over the suit and shoulder armor.

Dractus' voice blared through some kind of on-board intercom, "Alright puny humans, we are landing. Meet us at the back ramp."
"Well, it's showtime," said Jimmy who was stuffing his last few magazines for his pistol and rifle into different pockets all over his person. "I'm a little light on ammo. I hope they have a gun store in this one-horse town."

"Of course they do, every rural town has a gun store. Why don't you just ask Cerulean for a weapon. I'm sure she has an armory somewhere on board."

"Good point."

"Jimmy I have to ask. Why are you wearing the bulletproof vest? Dractus said this stuff is already strong enough to stop a bullet."

"I'm not going to be riding in a bulletproof bulldozer. I'll take all the protection I can get," said Jimmy before he zipped up his windbreaker completely hiding the golden armor.

Cerulean had thought ahead because when they met her at the back ramp she had two weapons cases sitting open on top of some cargo boxes. Inside each case was an enormous looking pistol which had five bulbous micro-cylinders hanging off of the bottom of the barrel diagonally in each direction. So five going down left, and five going down right. Hank realized if it wasn't for its size and the strange offshoots that the weapon would look eerily familiar to a Glock set up for competition use.

"Gentleman, welcome. I'd like you two to have these weapons, but not before I explain them," said Cerulean. "I confiscated these off of a Kalrothian arms dealer some time back. Before we parted ways I got him to explain them to me. These are highly experimental and highly illegal mass drivers with built-in gravatonics. They have a 1000-round built-in magazine. When the ammo is gone the gun is done for, unless you return it to the manufacturer for reload. The heat meter is on the back portion here. That should be facing you at all times if you have the barrel pointed down range, keep an eye on it.

The heat produced from the amperage and electromagnetic fields on this weapon are extraordinary. Luckily, the manufacturer thought of this so the bulk of the heat is vented forward and up. Having said that, you should understand that only so much heat can be vented at once and the weapon is always riding a precarious and dangerous line. So pay attention to the heat meter on the back. If you don't, the gun will explode which will surely kill you and everyone around you. The weapon is also set up with a magnetic holster and your armor has a few magnetic holster receivers. I'll show you, watch me."

Cerulean took one of the weapons out of the box. Then indicated an out of the way button on the side by pointing at it. "This turns on the magnet," she said as she pressed it and then placed the weapon against her outer upper-thigh. When she removed her hand the weapon stayed in place.
"Here, you try," she said as she handed it to Jimmy. Jimmy replicated what she had done and sure enough it stuck to his upper thigh, right on top of his jeans, just the same as it had for her.
"Cool," he said.
"Cool indeed, but that's not all," said Cerulean who lifted the other weapon out of the box. "When you put your finger on the trigger, this happens," she said as she aimed the weapon away from everyone and placed her finger on the trigger. Two small metal bars flipped up near the back of

the weapon and a small hologram appeared between them of a red cross.

"It's a holographic reticle which is automatically zeroed-in based on the planet's gravity and weather conditions. If it fails the weapon still has iron-sights."

Hank looked confused before piping up. "Can someone explain this weapon with less nerdy terms?"

"It's a really small rail-gun Hank," said Jimmy before continuing. "It fires really tiny pieces of dense metal, really super fast. Like so fast that it will probably fly through a lot of buildings before stopping."

"Which is why it is so illegal, so watch your backdrop," Cerulean added.

"I don't need this. I'll be in the bulldozer, and I have my own weapons," said Hank.

"Keep it anyway. You never know," replied Cerulean.

"Stop all this standing around, there are demons to kill!" shouts Dractus.

"I'm with Dractus, let's do this," says Hank.

"Wait," said Jimmy. "If we are taking these badass railguns, what about you two?"

"Dractus has his ax, and I have a few weapons on me as well. If it gets too bad though I thoroughly intend on retreating back to my ship and having it do a few strafing runs over the area. I have enough ordinance on this ship to glass half the planet."

"Dractus what the hell are you going to do with an ax if a gunfight takes place?" asked Jimmy.

"It has been my experience that people can not fire a gun when you chop their hands off," replied Dractus.

"Right… Well, I'll trust you know what you are doing. I'm ready," says Jimmy who slings his AR15 over his back.

As they descend down the ramp and hit the ground Hank sees a beautiful sight. Hanging below the ship suspended by cables as thick as one of his arms is his Killdozer. The ship itself is parked on uneven ground in a clearing in a dense forest. There is a light dusting of snow on the ground and the air is chilly. The ship is supported by multiple telescopic legs that are all extended to the exact length to not only keep the ship level, but also to keep it taller than the height of the bulldozer that is tied up below it.

"Well that is a fucking cool design," says Hank.

"They are Smart Cables, normally only top of the line tow rigs have these but I had my baby here retrofitted," says Cerulean as she pulls out her tablet.

She presses a few things on her device and the cables start unwinding from around the bulldozer until only a few remain which gently lower it the ground. The second it hits Hank is up and running to it. He hops up to the cab and rips open his door. The inside of the cab is still covered in dried blood and littered in his firearms.

"I'm sorry for leaving you. It's been too long."

As soon as Hank sits in the seat something strange happens. The soul that he absorbed into his body, the man he had killed in the bank, it starts slowly peeling out of him and flying towards his engine compartment. He can see the screaming face of the man as it flies away from him. *Had his body acted as some kind of temporary storage device until he could get back to the dozer?* Hank cranks over the bulldozer and it starts on the first try. He still can't tell if it's running so smoothly because of the Arbiter upgrade or the due diligence of his father's meticulous maintenance. Either way he says a silent prayer to the universe above, whatever deity might be listening, and his father in heaven.

Jimmy appears at his open cab door. "Dude it smells like death and old blood in here."

"Yeah, sorry I forgot my little pine tree air freshener."

"Well I'm pretty sure I'm riding with you. Cerulean and Drac-man went to get their bikes, and I don't feel like riding back-bitch behind Dractus."

"Bikes?"

"Oh yeah, you haven't seen them yet. They are fucking cool. Arbiters get all the cool toys. Uh, how am I going to fit in here?"

"You probably won't, it's pretty stuffed with all the weapons and whatnot. You might want to ride on the hood and I'll slow roll it. Or maybe I can add a crew compartment or something, hang on." To Jimmy's credit he doesn't even comment on how Hank is planning to magically add a passenger seat.

Hank remembered he had 4 upgrade points earlier after he had fuckin trounced Eugene's goons and killed the corrupt bureaucrats at town hall. And he had only spent 3 of the 4 points.

"You'll want to see this," said Hank to Jimmy indicating the screen that was recessed into the dash of the Bulldozer. Hank brought up his upgrade menu and it looked just like last time.

"You have two upgrades available, please choose where to invest your souls:
Speed + (1)
Armor + (1)
Offense +
Defense + (1)
U.I. +
Efficiency +
Advanced Upgrades (Click for more options)"

Hank was surprised to see that he had two upgrades available. Maybe he had accidentally killed some evil cops or something with his ripper stunt, he was throwing a lot of asphalt in the air. Or maybe the bank robber he had killed had thrown him over the edge into his next level. Oh well, he wasn't going to look a gift horse in the mouth. He also noticed right away that the options he had picked last time had a little number next to them denoting how many upgrades he had given each one, which was nice. Pretty easy to remember your prior choices when you had only picked three, but if Hank was going to do this for a living it would be nice to have a visual reminder once the upgrades started stacking up.

Jimmy interrupted his line of thought by asking, "Why are Armor and Defense listed separately? Aren't they essentially the same thing?"

"Looking at this now I can see why you would wonder that. Last time I worked with this menu I was being chased by hundreds of police officers and being shot at so I didn't have time to worry. To answer your question though, no they are not the same. *Armor* seems to be the raw efficiency of my armor plating. On the other hand *Defense* is somewhat of a misnomer, really it seems to be defensive measures. When I put a point into that one it gave the dozer the ability to let out an electrical pulse to fry critters crawling on her beautiful hull."

"Misnomer? Listen to you Hank, you are starting to sound like you actually graduated the 5th grade."

"Oh fuck off. Seriously though I would love to know what this *U.I.* option is?"

"U.I. stands for user interface. I'm not the biggest gamer, but I've played enough to know that one. That would actually probably be a good upgrade for you. So you wouldn't have to use this shitty old TV anymore."

"Hey, it's not shitty. It works just fine, and be quiet, she can hear you." said Hank as he gently rubbed the bulldozer's dash. "The bad man didn't mean it little Killdozie."

"You Arbiter fuckers are weird."

"It's good having you here Jimmy."

"Ditto. Now make my ass a passenger seat."

Hank selected "Advanced Upgrades" hoping there was a passenger seat or passenger compartment option. Instead he got an unpleasant surprise.

"*ADVANCED UPGRADES* LOCKED UNTIL YOU TURN IN YOUR CANISTER" flashed across Hank's screen.

"Well what the shit does that mean?" asked Jimmy.

"Cerulean mentioned this. If an Arbiter dies his or her canister melts. So over at Arbiter HQ they've jury-rigged a system to check on Arbiters. They hold onto your canister and if it melts they know you're worm-dinner. She didn't mention anything about my upgrades being dependent upon it though. The more I learn about this stuff the more it seems like every Arbiter and their abilities are vastly different than their peers," said Hank.

"Speaking of that. Cerulean told me that what you did at the bank, using your Arbiter power through the solid wall to be able to tell where the bank robbers were. She says that is basically impossible by Arbiter standards."

"Well I always did like being stronger than the rest."

That answer didn't really sit well with Jimmy, but they had more pressing matters at hand.

"So I guess I'm riding on the running board," said Jimmy. Cerulean and Dractus took that moment to come roaring out of the ship on their auto-cannon laden motorcycles. Cerulean took the ramp, but Dractus didn't even bother. He jetted off the top of the ramp at an angle immediately going airborne and laughing his lizard laugh like a madman all the way to the ground. Hank didn't have a good view of it, but Jimmy saw the whole thing.

"I'm glad that crazy fuck is on our side," Jimmy remarked.

Cerulean pulled up alongside the dozer wearing a slim fitting helmet. Dractus pulled up next to her of course not wearing a helmet.

"Do your best to keep up puny humans! HA HA HA!" said Dractus before throttling his bike so hard that his back tire shoots a giant arc of dirt into the air.

"It's on LIZARD BOY!" yelled Hank as he slammed the bulldozer through the gears as quickly as possible up the slight incline they were on. Dractus hit the top of the ridge narrowly steering the bike between two trees and went airborne as he crested the lip and disappeared from view.

"Shit, you are going to have to squeeze in!" Hank shouted to Jimmy as they were quickly approaching the same trees and Jimmy was still standing in the open door on the running board. Jimmy hopped in and crouched the best he could in the confined space with one of his hands on Hank's shoulder, and Hank slammed the armored door shut.

"Shit, Hank you are about to hit the trees!"

"That's the plan. Why do you think I wanted you inside?"

Hank crested the top of the hill much faster than should be possible in a machine like this, and his dozer's blade pushed the trees over easily. Large snaps filled the air, as loud as gun shots as branches snapped and tore.

"Jesus! This thing is powerful," shouted Jimmy.

"Somewhere a hippy is crying over those trees," replied Hank.

They barreled on through the forest chasing after Cerulean and Dractus who were treating the dense forest like a dirt bike track. It was obvious that they were both letting off steam, and that they were both very proficient riders. Hank on the other hand was forced to repeatedly smash down trees. There just wasn't a route anywhere close by large enough for the bulldozer to take. Hank noticed he also had to keep repeatedly shifting his blade higher and lower so he could run over his own giant pile that he would always inevitably end up pushing around while driving through the underbrush. This made him wonder if he could upgrade his dozer's blade.

Hank slowed the dozer a bit so he could focus on his upgrade menu. There was really nothing glaringly obvious that would make it better. Unless the upgrade he needed was under the *Advanced Upgrades* tab which he couldn't access for now. He decided to try the very nebulous *Offense* upgrade and he also took Jimmy's advice and put a point into the *U.I.* upgrade. A large shearing metal noise accompanied with a crack like Hephaestus hitting his anvil emanated throughout the bulldozer. Simultaneously the old T.V. that was once a dust covered relic in his workshop but was now embedded cleanly into the dash of the bulldozer, began to widen.

It grew until it was about twice the width as it was before. Now there was a partition down the middle of it. On the right side of the partition was the current view from his rear-facing camera. On the left side was a small menu that had only two options with space for more, it currently looked like this:

"+Oscillate Blades

+Electric Pulse"

Hank pressed the Oscillate Blades button and was pleasantly surprised with the result. His bulldozer's solid pushing blade was now jointed in about 20 different places and every piece started spinning in opposite directions. It basically created the world's largest shredding machine right on the front of the Killdozer. All of the bushes and downed trees he was pushing were instantly shredded into fine mulch. The sound was a combination of pleasantly pleasing and absolutely terrifying. Hank noticed the oscillate option now read "End Oscillation" so he pressed it to stop the spinning. The separated pieces of the bulldozers blade all spun soundly back into place to make a solid front once more.

"BITCHIN!" shouted Hank.

"That was fuckin cool," Jimmy agreed.

"I just wish my backpack was in here. I left it up in Cerulean's ship. This would be an opportune time for a celebratory cigar."

"Well are you going to let those aliens beat us there or are you going to stop pussy-footing it?"

Hank happily accepted the challenge and shifted into the highest gear possible. Some of the uneven terrain was pretty jarring but the wide base of the treads helped a lot with that. They repeated the strangely satisfying pattern of bursting through trees at top speed and oscillating the frontal blades whenever the pile they were pushing got so heavy that it would bog them down. If Hank wasn't leaving the planet he could probably start a booming business creating firebreaks for the forestry service at previously unheard of speeds. The pattern became cathartic for Jimmy and Hank. Watching Dractus and Cerulean pull stunts that would put the X-Games to shame in between shredding seemingly immovable objects. It felt good to be out here, as a team.

Soon enough the fun ended or lessened really since their spirits were all high, when they cleared the last bit of dense woods and came out on a hill with a good view of the town below them. At first glance it was much like the satellite images, but upon closer inspection the town was alive. It was too far to tell what was going on but people were everywhere, carrying things, moving from place to place. Something looked off about their movement, it just seemed a little too jerky. Hank had a bad feeling about this. Cerulean popped her helmet off and pulled out a telescope from some kind of hidden compartment on her motorcycle, or awesome-cycle, or whatever she called it. She scanned around for a bit before saying:

"Shit, something is wrong with the town's folk."

She handed her telescope to Dractus. Jimmy hopped out of the Killdozer and Hank left the door open so he could hear the conversation better. Dractus threw the telescope over to Jimmy right after he shouted "Catch." Jimmy caught it out of the air as well before looking for a bit and throwing it to Hank. Hank stood on his running board and looked over the edge of his door with the telescope. The townspeople were all moving with a purpose, their faces neutral. Their skin has weird black stains on it. Some of them were feeding wood to the many fires around town. Others were all carrying bits of something in one general direction. Hank kept scanning until he saw something truly disturbing. A few of the townsfolk were meticulously dissecting a human body with different sized kitchen knives. Hank watched as they carried a few of the pieces over to one of the fires to be cooked.

"We have to get down there. Figure out what's causing this."

Cerulean nodded and put her helmet back on before roaring off down the hill towards the town.

"You can close the door up Hank. I'm going to ride on the running board. I don't want to be stuck inside in case we have to help someone in a hurry," said Jimmy.

Hank complied and Jimmy hopped up on the running board. Jimmy drew the mass-driver pistol and put it into his left hand so he could hold on with his right. Dractus and Cerulean were already far ahead of them and moving at a slow roll through the main drag of the town, the stained people seemed to be ignoring them. Hank sped up to catch up to them and was soon only a few hundred feet behind them.

The town was quaint and rustic in a well-kept sort of way. All of the buildings looked like they were from the 1800's. it was hard to tell if they were designed to look that way or if they really were that old. A nice covered boardwalk stretched in front of the storefronts offering people a nice place to stay out of the sun as they browsed. Overall Winthrop looked like a classic little slice of America, or it would if it wasn't half burnt down with stupefied humans butchering and cooking each other. Drac and Cerulean rolled to a stop so Hank stopped too. Hank's cell phone started to ring in his pocket and cerulean put her hand to her ear with her thumb and pinky extended, the hand symbol of *answer your damn phone*. Hank noticed Jimmy set his alien gun down on his hood and pulled out his own cellphone as well.

Hank answered the call from "Unknown Number," it was Cerulean. "Yes, this is a group call. Don't look so surprised that I can access your primitive tech. Me and Drac are going to grab one of these fools to take some samples, cover us. Also I know you, Jimmy, have some law enforcement experience, and I know Hank has military experience. So this should go without saying but watch where you are aiming. Friendly fire is a very real threat with those mass drivers. Use your human guns if it makes you feel more comfortable, just don't shoot me or Dractus. I'll leave this line open while we collect samples so you two can listen in if you want. Last thing, Hank, try your Intuition. Cerulean out."

Hank put the phone on speaker and set it on his dash. He did as Cerulean suggested and looked at the nearest jerky town's person and pushed his intuition. It was a shirtless man in his 30's covered in blood encrusted jeans and limping. He was carrying something wrapped in a dirty blanket. He was moving in the same general direction of the rest of the people carrying, well something. The ones that weren't carrying stuff were moving the opposite direction as him. Hank suspected based on the smell and general size that the man was probably carrying some cooked human in that blanket, but he didn't want to focus on that too much. He couldn't get a solid reading off of the shirtless man so he used the same trick that he had used at the bank, imagining his power as a weight that had to be lifted. He pushed harder and still didn't get a reading.

His door was still closed, but he remembered Jimmy had answered his phone as well.

"Jimmy you still on the line?"

"Yeah Hank."

"I can't get a read on these people. They aren't good or bad. Think they're zombies?"

"I don't know. I'll go check."

Jimmy hopped off the bulldozer and walked over to the same dude Hank had tried to get a reading on. He pushed two of his fingers against the guy's neck and walked beside him. Then he grabbed the guy's shoulders and tried to stop his forward momentum. The guy flipped and started screaming like Jimmy was burning him. Hank couldn't hear

218

the conversation from inside the dozer, but he did recognize Jimmy's placating gesture of raising both of his hands into the air showing that he meant no threat. The guy kept walking as soon as Jimmy let him go. Jimmy jogged back over to the dozer and knocked on the door so Hank cracked it open.

"Well they are alive, but its like they are in some kind of a trance or something. His skin also has strange black stains all over it. It's clear he is on some kind of mission. We should see where he is headed."

"We will as soon as Dractus and Cerulean get their sample. Enjoy the show," said Hank as he pointed to Dractus.

Dractus had just grabbed a random woman in a stained floral dress and bear-hugged her from behind. The woman started having the same fit that the man Jimmy had grabbed had. It seemed the longer Dractus held her the worse her fit got. She started kicking and trying to bite. Cerulean jammed her with some kind of needle that had a tether leading back to her tablet. Dractus continued to hold onto her while Cerulean typed away at the tablet.

"Hey guys you there?" asked Cerulean over the speaker phone.

"Yeah we can hear you," replied Hank.

"Preliminary findings are showing me that these folk are tainted with bits and pieces of Bertha's DNA. I've never seen anything like it before. If I had to make an educated guess, and please understand that I'm not a doctor I'm just reading information off of a screen here. Bertha has tainted these people somehow and they are following her orders."

"Is there a cure?" asked Jimmy.

"Not in that context. I can't rewrite DNA on the fly. Again, my best guess is that we need to kill Bertha to snap these folks out of whatever trance they are in. I know you guys think I'm the tech-nerd in this group, but I'm not. I'm a space tow-truck driver with a nice ass, who likes to kill bad guys as a side hobby."

"Concur on the nice ass part," said Hank.

All chatter over the speaker phone ceased as every person mindlessly going about their tasks in a 500-foot radius stopped what they were doing and stared at Dractus still holding the struggling woman.

"Let her go Dractus!" Jimmy shouted at the phone. Cerulean relayed the order and Dractus dropped her. She immediately scurried off to do whatever she had been doing before, and all of the town's people also resumed their previous tasks.

"Well this is definitely some kind of hive mind," said Cerulean.

"Let's follow the ones carrying shit," said Hank.

"That was my next move as well," replied Cerulean.

"We are about to walk into some crazy shit aren't we?" asked Jimmy.

"Probably," said Cerulean before hopping back onto her bike and trailing the procession of people carrying *stuff*.

"Guess that means we are rolling," said Hank who then popped the dozer into gear. Jimmy was already on the running board so all he had to do was hang on. They trailed the procession of stained-people until they found out where they were headed. A large stone building a few stories tall with four circular stone columns in the front of it. The building reminded Hank and Jimmy of the town hall from the movie *Back To the Future*.

"Is that the town hall?" asked Jimmy.

"I don't see what else it could be." replied Hank.

Cerulean and Dractus backed their bikes up to the building, probably a good idea if they had to leave in a hurry. Hank contemplated doing the same but decided to leave it facing forward. They could run if they wanted to, he would smash the whole fucking building down if there was an issue.

"I wish there was some way to set the Killdozer to shock anything that climbs on it or in it in my absence. I would hate for one of those creepy ass stained people to get in here," said Hank. A strange mechanical voice came out of the speakers on the television in the bulldozer.

"The vehicle will shock all uninvited passengers in your absence."

"What the hell. Who are you?" asked Hank.

"I'm the Killdozer U.I. Mark 2. The Killdozer now accepts limited voice commands and requests."

"Why didn't you announce yourself earlier?"

"The system needed time to initialize and you didn't make any requests."

"Fair enough. Don't shock Jimmy or the Arbiters."

"Jimmy, and the other two with you have been set as friendlies."

"Uh okay, I'm going to leave now."

"Yes, sir."

Hank looked over at Jimmy who just shrugged his shoulders as if it say: *yeah weird shit happens to us*. They met up with Dractus and Cerulean and circled up. Cerulean seemed to take charge like always.

"Alright, the most likely scenario is that Bertha is in there and these folks are bringing her food to lay eggs and further develop her spawning ground. So expect to get swarmed by hatchlings. If it is too thick in there with enemies we back out and retreat back to my ship. Any suggestions or complaints?"

"I'm going to guess the reason we aren't just letting Hank knock the building down is because of the innocent bystanders?" asked Jimmy.

"Yep, like I said earlier I'm hoping that once Bertha is dead that these folks will snap out of it. Having said that, I'm not dying today, neither is Drac or either of you." If that place is too dangerous we will be destroying that building. Either Hank will run it over or I'll drop a bunker buster on it that will level this whole area. Killing a few innocents to save thousands or more is a dark reality that we face sometimes as Arbiters. If anyone here isn't okay with that you can and should leave now."

No one left.

Chapter 13

"Everyone good with the plan?" asked Cerulean. The team nodded in response. Hank double checked the magazine on his 1911, and then made sure he had one in the chamber before re-holstering it in his concealed carry crossbreed holster. He drew the rail-pistol, ready to fight. There was still a large line of people carefully shuffling into the large stone building carrying their bundles of *something* wrapped in different types of cloth. Dractus walked up to one of them and yanked the bundle away and shook it out onto the lawn. A perfectly grilled human arm rolled out… Grill marks and all on it, it looked like it might even be slathered in some kind of grill sauce. *What the fuck is going on here?* The person who was carrying the arm quickly collected it and re-wrapped it before getting back into the line to go inside. Dractus looked back at the remaining team, no words needed to be exchanged.

Dractus took lead which on some primal level upset Hank, but he had to admit as far as Arbiters went this was a veteran crew and he was the low man on the totem pole. He may have lots of experience shutting down evil humans, but he had exactly zero experience fighting space-faring demons. Hank felt slightly unsure about the rail-gun which was why he had brought the 1911 as well. In the military, before each mission you test fire your weapons. They had just rushed the entire way here leaving Hank no opportunity for a test fire of the rail-gun. As an Arbiter though his

Intuition told him a lot. It wasn't exactly a lie detector, but he got the strong feeling that Dractus and Cerulean would never give him a non-functioning weapon. So in this instance, he decided to roll on faith.

Dractus was marching ahead, only a few steps from the door now which was still congested with humans who were seemingly waiting for their turn to feed this Bertha alien. Even in their addled state of mind they seemed to know to move when Dractus walked near them. Apparently getting stepped on by a giant lizard man didn't sound appealing, Hank couldn't blame them. The rest of the team was hot on his tail. The inside was only semi-lit. The electricity in the building was out, but someone had dragged in some kind of metal stands that all had a large flattish bowl on the top. In each bowl rested a small fire. The inside of the building opened up into a large room with stairs at the back that led to the next story up, but the stairs had a landing before they split like a t-Intersection.

On the landing were three different sized thrones constructed of random materials and coated in some kind of black sludge. Hank thought he noticed a few human bones among the eclectic mix. The team spread out a bit and scanned the walls, ceiling, and every nook or cranny they could see. Jimmy was hyper alert after having the space-demon-monkey thing jump on him in the warehouse, he wouldn't be gotten twice. At the edges of the firelight off of the main path to the thrones Hank thought he could see giant translucent eggs, like the ones Jimmy had told him about. He cleared his throat to get everyone's attention and pointed them out.

"Yep, this is one of her nests," said Cerulean quietly.

The stained-humans were still coming in behind the team carrying their bundles of cooked flesh, seemingly unaware of the Arbiter team's presence. They were carefully unwrapping their *gifts* and setting them in a large pile at the base of the stairs. The whole place reeked of evil, even Jimmy with no Arbiter abilities could feel it in the air. The team was beyond tense and ready to open fire on the first hostile they could find. *Why were the thrones empty?*

Dractus pulled his giant ax off of his back and held it in front of him in a fighting stance. "COME OUT COWARDS, FACE MIGHTY DRACTUS!"

"Oh yeah, I should have warned you about that. That's like uh… his thing," Jimmy said to Hank followed by a short giggle.

Cerulean patted Dractus on his back, "Don't worry big buddy. We'll get you someone to chop."

"Well can we at least burn some of these eggs while we wait?" asked Hank. "Anyone got an incendiary device?"

"I do, but we will have to get the civilians out of here first," said Cerulean.

Dractus saw his time to shine so he grabbed a few humans under each arm and started stomping around near the stragglers until they had to back up to avoid him, like a sheepdog moving its herd.

"GET OUT PUNY HUMANS!" Dractus shouted as he threw the arm fulls of people out the front doors and then slammed them shut. Stained-people immediately started banging on the doors, upset that they couldn't fulfill their task. Dractus grabbed a nearby bench and threw it in front of the doors then ripped one of the legs off and shoved it through the looped door handles. Hank had to admit that Dractus was quick and efficient. That whole affair had taken less than a minute. Cerulean pulled something off of her belt that looked like a Tic Tac box with a metal prong on one side. She jammed the prong into the side of her tablet and started typing.

"What are we thinking, two minute timer?" she asked the room.

A strange and deep voice answered her before any of her friends could. "I wouldn't do that if I were you."

Weapons snapped to shoulders in the blink of an eye as the Arbiter team looked for the source of the voice. It came again from somewhere on the second floor.

"I'm sorry I wasn't here to greet you. I was reading, I do enjoy this planet's literature."

The voice was bouncing around on the marble floor and walls of this place, but then its owner came into view. He was a giant of a man, smaller than Dractus but bigger than Hank by a little, and entirely covered in a shiny black rock. His eyes were like bright embers, burning red. He was slowly marching down the staircase until he got to the landing. At which point he sat in the second biggest throne. Hank tried to probe his aura with his Intuition. It came up neutral. It wasn't like the stained-people where the aura just didn't exist, it was there. It was just such a perfect shade of grey. Extremely neutral and unwavering, too neutral... Something wasn't passing the smell test.

"Well, welcome to my temporary home. You may call be Obsidian. As I was saying I wouldn't recommend lighting off that firework you have there. If my associate Bertha feels her nest burning she will get quite angry."

"DEMON!" shouted Dractus.

"Stand down Dractus," Cerulean quickly adds. "Obsidian, I am the Arbiter Cerulean. I carry the highest authority of the law. If you are allied with Bertha of your own free will, I am afraid that I will have to arrest you and transport you to the nearest suitable prison."

"I don't recognize your authority Arbiter. I am a free person on a free planet and I am allowed to associate with who I wish. If you chose to arrest me that would be kidnapping and false imprisonment. I thought you Arbiters were supposed to be the good guys?"

"You don't have to recognize my authority, for God does."

"Ah, therein lies the conundrum. For isn't it also true that God chooses your opposite, those you call Demons?"

Hank could tell Cerulean was stymied for a second. She had come in here guns blazing, not expecting a philosophical debate.

"No one knows how demons are chosen. Everyone knows how Arbiters are chosen. Demons chose to hide from God's light and the righteous path of the Arbiter," Cerulean replied with more confidence than Hank thought possible.

"What if these so-called 'Demons' are only hiding to avoid being unfairly prosecuted by the Arbiters. Did you know that those you call Demons, call themselves The Balance. For they are the ones who cut the cancer out. They are the ones who kill the plague bearers so that the healthy may live. They are the ones who reduce the population when people are starving, leaving ample food behind. Are these not good deeds? Evil at face value, yes, but ultimately saving more people than the short-sighted actions of the Arbiter. If a forest becomes too dense, does it not burn down? Who are you to decide that these people are demons?"

"Enough!" snapped Cerulean. "I have no time for blasphemy. You have admitted in front of witnesses that you are allied with the demon known as Bertha. You sit on a throne in front of her thralls and the cooked corpses of innocent sentients. Sing whatever marry tune you want, you are evil. Submit to capture or die at the hands of God's chosen!"

A chill ran down Hank's spine. He felt the power in Cerulean's words and he knew them to be true. Never had he felt words have that much meaning and strength behind them before. The only thing that had ever come close to stirring that much raw emotion in Hank was his oath of enlistment he had taken to join the military. The creature known as Obsidian interrupted Hank's line of thought.

"Well that is unfortunate. I do love a good debate and I hate that you ended ours prematurely. I do consider myself somewhat of an honorable man so I feel it is only fair to warn you that any attempt to harm me in any way, or even so much as touch me, will anger my friends."

Another voice came from up the stairs in one of the offices that had a door open. "What's all that commotion down there?" the voice shouted. Hank couldn't quite place it, but it sounded so very familiar. A naked man walked down the stairs with a barely clad teenager under each of his arms, one male and one female. The teenagers were thralls, that was clear to Hank. Their skin had the stains on it, the sign of Bertha's influence, and their eyes were glazed over.

"Ah my good friend Eugene," said Obsidian. "Greet our guests, the Arbiters."

Eugene? It only took Hank a second to take in every detail of the man. He was fit, and hairless, nothing like the Eugene he knew, but the face... That face was burned into Hank's memory. It looked just like the Eugene that Hank knew from high school. Without even realizing it he tapped into his Arbiter Intuition and took a read. It was the same aura that Eugene had before, and it was oozing pure evil. That was all the evidence he needed. In less than half of a second he aimed the rail pistol and fired; he had to aim low to avoid hitting either of the teenagers. Hank was unfamiliar with this weapon, but not unfamiliar with weapons in general. In fact he was quite proficient with firearms. So his shot ended up taking Eugene in the thigh. Eugene screamed and fell over, his two thralls stared stupidly not knowing what to do and the room froze in a tense Mexican stand-off. Everyone waited to see who would make the next move.

"Fine fine," said Obsidian. "If you would like to dispense with the pleasantries and skip right to the part where I murder you, we can do that. It's time for you to meet the rest of my friends." Obsidian calmly started descending down the stairs. From the second story came the screech of hundreds of creatures. Cerulean didn't wait, she started the two minute timer on her incendiary device and threw it into one of the spawning grounds off to the side and then drew a small pistol from somewhere on her lower back and fired it at Obsidian. A thin blue line of light bounced off of his chest and he smiled. Hank and Jimmy went next and started hosing him down with the rail-guns. Visible chunks of his body started chipping off. Before they could finish their barrage creatures started crawling out of the second story, down the stairs, across the ceiling, along the walls. Gravity seemed to be little more than a side note to these new contenders.

Hank and Jimmy shifted focus and started trying to thin their numbers. The main horde seemed to be coming down the stairs. Dractus jumped ahead of Jimmy and Hank and they had to cut their fire to avoid hitting him. He began to swing his mighty ax in great giant circles. As he spun it began to glow. At the end of his next rotation he stopped in place with unheard of grace. The second he stopped his momentum somehow bled off into deadly arcs of electricity that sprayed outward from his ax's blade into the evil horde of demon spawn. Obsidian and Eugene were also in the blast radius. Obsidian was unaffected and casually walked back to his throne to enjoy the show. Eugene however who was already whimpering began to scream in pain. Unfortunately the blast also partially hit the two teenaged thralls who were knocked unconscious. It was an impressive display of raw power and Hank had to remind himself that the ax Dractus was carrying was more than just a cutting instrument. It was an Arbiter's weapon probably filled to the brim with evil souls and abilities.

The creatures that had been crawling on the ceiling and walls had avoided Dractus' blast. They began to jump or let go of their handholds to try and land on Team Arbiter. Jimmy was ready for this and was already firing. Hank wasn't ready. Two landed on Hank's massive shoulders and tried to scratch his face and bite his neck. Everyone else was to busy shooting or cutting into the hoard to help him. He swung his railgun upward and started taking pot shots, that's when he felt the intense heat coming out of the end of it. This gave him an idea. Instead of shooting wildly he just started pressing the end of the barrel of the railgun into the creature's legs and arms. It instantly seared their flesh and sent them screeching. One of them jumped off of Hank and ran back up the wall. Now that he wasn't overwhelmed Hank was able to grab the last one who was still trying to bite him, and throw it onto the floor, where he promptly stomped its head in. Viscous black sludge erupted from the thing's skull.

"IF IT BLEEDS I CAN KILL IT," shouted Hank.

He went back to helping his friends. Dractus was like a whirlwind with his axe which now had a thin glowing red energy that extended about two feet out from its outward facing blade. As Dractus spun through the enemies, anything the red energy touched sizzled and burst into flames. His movements were hectic and angry. Cerulean on the other hand was the picture of calm. She had her micro-pistol in her left hand that was still shooting some kind of blue beams that would sear flesh. In her right hand was a thin Katana she had pulled out of somewhere. Her face was passive and her movements mechanical as she carefully shot anything that approached her. Those that jumped from the ceilings or walls at her were sundered in half by her razor-sharp katana. Jimmy was wild eyed and blasting creatures as fast as he saw them. Despite his haunted expression he was holding his own and killing or disabling just as many if not more than the two veteran Arbiters and Hank.

"Jimmy! Check your heat meter!" Hank shouted when he noticed two forward facing fins at the front of Jimmy's weapon that were letting out great gouts of heat that were warping the very air in front of his weapon.

Jimmy's eyes went wide at whatever he had seen on his heat meter and he immediately threw his gun into the approaching horde on the stairs and yelled "RUN!" before bolting towards the doors they had entered through. Cerulean followed suit knowing her incendiary was set to go off any second. Dractus let off a quicker and smaller blast of electrical arcs, just enough to stun their pursuers and provide cover before retreating himself. Hank stayed focused on shooting anything that twitched or looked their way. Dractus ran ahead of Jimmy and smacked the barricaded doors with his entire body at a run. They exploded outwards sending wood shards everywhere. The people who were on the other side of the door got sent spinning like bowling pins. Hank turned to leave when he heard and saw Cerulean's incendiary device half buried in the sludge and biomass of a spawning nest start letting out a loud hiss and strobing red. He knew it was time to move like his life depended on it, because it probably did.

As Hank crossed the threshhold at a full run he felt a heat flash at his back. He spun around to see most of the interior of the building on fire. *Well that wasn't so bad*, was his last thought before the tolerances and safeguards on Jimmy's discarded rail driver, sitting among the now abandoned thrones, finally melted, causing the weapon's unstable power source to detonate. Hank was blown backwards and sent rolling across the asphalt of the street. He woke up a short time later to the feeling of rain. He opened his eyes, it wasn't rain… It was raining sludge and bits and pieces of the alien spawning grounds… The street was shaking and his friends were yelling. He looked up to see the biggest fucking alien-gorilla-thing being trailed by hundreds more of the small-monkey-creature-man-things.

His friends were firing uselessly at the giant alien and her hoard. He noticed that his friends were also now painted and smeared in the raining black sludge as well. The familiar and pleasing sound of an AR15 firing made Hank glance at Jimmy who was firing his now that his railgun was gone.

"Holy shit, she got bigger!" Jimmy shouted.

Hank didn't have time to lay around in pain, he knew this was an ideal situation for his Arbiter's weapon: The Killdozer. He did a quick self assessment looking for injuries. Surprisingly he felt alright, the knock-off Arbiter armor under his clothes had done its job. And with the exception of the large growing lump on the back of his head he felt alright. He hopped up and ran to his bulldozer. As soon as he hit the seat it was running without him having to trigger the ignition.

"Thanks!" he shouted at his vehicle.

He carefully backed up trying to avoid the scattered stained-humans who were now standing around dumbly trying to figure out how to bring their 'food' into the burning building. As soon as he was aimed at the approaching hoard and the giant monster alien known as Bertha he started shifting through the gears as fast as he could. He hit the *Oscillate Blades* option on his weapons menu, and again watched in amazement as his solid blade segregated into more than twenty individual pieces and started to spin. When he was headed through the woods before he had left the front of his bulldozer as the solid blade. He had been afraid to jam the individual ones against the ancient trees and break them or get them stuck. He didn't have that fear now, these demon-monkeys were mere flesh and blood.

He aimed directly at Bertha's ankles, her hoard noticed his intent and jumped in front of her defensively. The first thirty or forty were instantly turned into a dark mist as Hank impacted their front ranks. The mist sprayed Hank's windshield and obscured his vision. He spun the dozer out of the path of Bertha's ankles at the last second and aimed the dozer at the rest of her hoard that were behind her in mass.

An inhuman scream came from Bertha's throat "NOOOO, MY CHILDREN!!!!" it had sounded like 10 or 20 women were screaming all at once, but the sound had only come from her. Hank fed another twenty or so to his blades, but these ones knew to fear the infernal machine that had shredded their brothers and sisters. Some of them jumped out of the path of the Killdozer at the last second and others jumped clear directly over the spinning blades landing along the hull of the machine. Hank stopped the spinning blades and let more and more climb onto his vehicle. Once he thought he was basically at critical mass and there wasn't enough room for more, he hit the electrical pulse button. More inhuman screams came from the demon-spawn as he shocked them with deadly amounts of amperage. It was hard to tell if they were actually dying or if he was just knocking them out, but if they weren't attacking his friends he didn't care.

Bertha was furious at the violent machine that had cut up her wonderful children. It was shocking some of them now as she chased it. The stinging wounds of the other Arbiter's weapons kept pelting her back which only angered her further. She grabbed a small car and threw it at the reptilian Arbiter who was cutting more of her children with his angry ax. The car landed on top of him and a few of her children, she mourned their loss, but smiled at the Arbiter's pain and possible death. She ordered the rest of her children to swarm the remaining two Arbiters now that they didn't have the big ax man covering them. She would deal with the one in the angry bladed metal vehicle.

She leapt on top of the aggravating machine and was surprised that it didn't shudder or tip over. This vehicle was dense. She felt electricity surge through her, but it did little more than tickle her giant frame. This town had fed her well and her size and birthing abilities had grown. After her successful healing of the human demon Eugene she had decided to try and alter the method to see what else she could do to these humans. She was delighted to find out that she could make them into thralls once encasing them in her larval sacks and tweaking a few of her chemical emitters. Maybe once she peeled this little Arbiter out of his vehicle she would enthrall him as well.

She yanked on different pieces of the vehicle but none of them budged. So she started punching the compartment where the driver would sit, this part looked the weakest.

She started to feel give as she rained down more and more blows. The metal was hard and unforgiving against her organic fists, but this man had hurt her brood, she wouldn't stop.

"That's enough Bertha, I've brought a can opener and help," said Obsidian who had finally decided to show up. He carried a giant pry bar that was at least as tall as he was. Down the street Bertha could see the human they had recruited to join The Balance in his own infernal machine. His Balancer weapon had evolved again since the last time she had seen it. It stood on two feet and had grown two arms, it looked like a giant metal man now.

Obsidian climbed onto the machine and eventually got up to the roof before jamming the pry bar into the seam of the door. He used his mighty strength to shove until the pointed tip screeched inside of the vehicle a bit. Obsidian leaned back and yanked trying to use his momentum and weight to get the door to pop open. Bertha smiled in pure glee exposing her many rows of teeth. With Obsidian's help it wouldn't be long now until she got her revenge. Eugene arrived and bent his own machine over to grab the front of the bulldozer and hold it into place and stop its forward movement so that Obsidian could work more efficiently.

PAIN, BURNING PAIN! Bertha felt her broodlings dying back where she had left the other Arbiter's. Her psychic link to them told her they were burning.

"MY CHILDREN!!!" she yelled as she left Obsidian and Eugene to go see what had caused this new loss of life.

Hank was in a tough spot. His windshield was entirely covered in demon blood and he had disabled his windshield wipers ages ago back in his shed to install the added armor. He was pretty sure Bertha was going to crush his cab in at any moment and kill him. He had no idea how his friends were faring. He was stuck on something in front of him and couldn't pull the vehicle forward to escape this onslaught. And now some asshole with a pry bar was trying to crack open the Killdozer like a sardine can. He was out of options and he could hear the joints on his door groaning as the asshole pried. Hank made a note to himself to bring dynamite or grenades or something in the future. Man he would love to shove a stick of dynamite out of the bent portion of his door right now.

He looked around his cab and eyes landed on his pile of weapons stacked in the back corner. He grabbed the Remington 870 and shoved a few slugs into it and set it on the dash, he had a feeling he would need it soon. Then his eyes landed on his screen and the small blinking upgrade button in the corner of it. He pressed it.

"You have seven upgrades available, please choose where to invest your souls:
Speed + (1)
Armor + (1)
Offense + (1)
Defense + (1)

U.I. + (1)

Efficiency +

Advanced Upgrades (Click for more options)"

SWEET FUCK, SEVEN UPGRADES! This could be the edge he needed to get out of this mess! He quickly pressed *Speed, Armor, Offense, Defense, U.I.*, and lastly the elusive *Efficiency,* which he pressed twice. All seven upgrades spent. Deep in his body his Arbiter Intuition was screaming that he should focus on his engine compartment. Whatever mechanism was deep inside of his Killdozer was burning and using the evil souls to power the upgrade process. Hank made a mental note to look under the hood soon and see what kind of engine was running this beast now.

Hank noticed even his dash was changing. A small metal circle about three inches in diameter was pushing itself out of the top of it, and the area that had cracked to allow its passage was healing itself and adhering perfectly to the sides of the small circular metal pedestal. Whoever was working the pry bar got his door to crack open another inch. Hank looked up out through the crack into glowing red eyes, it was the rock man. He grabbed the Remington 870 and shoved it up through the top of the bent door and rapid fired off three slugs into Obsidian's face. Obsidian jumped off of the vehicle with his prybar to avoid further punishment, *no one likes a lead facial.* The metal circle on Hank's dash started producing a strange light that blinked a few times before sputtering forth a small hologram into existence. It was a miniature version of is Killdozer about 2 inches tall with a large smiling mouth on the front grill of it behind the bulldozer blade. The headlights had been made to look like friendly eyes to complete a smiling happy face on the front of the vehicle. The mouth started to actuate and the thing began speaking in a friendly and cartoonish manner.

"Well hello there. I'm the Killdozer Mark 3 User Interface. You seem to be in a spot of trouble here. I'd like to activate the windshield wipers now if you'll allow it."

"Do it!" Hank shouted, realizing he was positive that he didn't have windshield wipers before his latest set of upgrades.

The wipers cleared off the black sludge and what Hank saw actually surprised him, which was saying a lot since Hank assumed he was immune to surprised after his Arbiter VR training. It looked like a goddamn Transformer straight from his childhood was attacking him. It was as if someone had built a mech-suit while only using parts from old cars, and sitting in the chest cavity of the mech behind a pane of transparent material, clear as day, was Eugene with a sadistic smile on his face. He had the entire mech suit bent over with both of the mech's hands on his hood holding Hank's dozer into place.

"Sir we are taking damage to our treads, let me show you." The small hologram's friendly appearance shifted into a more realistic one for a second, and then the whole thing spun to a side profile and zoomed in on one side of his treads. Obsidian was there using the pry bar where he could bending things out of place and breaking things.

"That dick."

"I concur sir. We need to leave this area as soon as possible, which we can't do while the mech suit is holding you into place. May I recommend the Ripper Cannon?"

"What the fuck is a Ripper Cannon?"

"The ripper on the back of the vehicle has been upgraded sir, due to the point you put into offense. Additional joints were added to it as well as other useful features, well like the cannon. Use the ripper control like normally, but pull it hard in the opposite direction and the ripper will swing over the top of the cab."

Hank did as the little hologram asked and noticed the ripper on the small hologram swung over the cab as well and was now pointed forward. He also noticed the ripper spike had two long tubes running along each side of it a few feet back from the spike aimed forward, *they almost looked like gun barrels*. A floating red reticle appeared on his front windshield. Hank felt the ripper control handle had a little bit of play in it. He moved it around a bit and the reticle moved with it corresponding to his movements.

"Yes sir. I see you've gotten the hang of it quickly. Now you can use your weapon's screen or a voice command to fire the ripper cannon."

Hank centered the reticle right on Eugene's face. "FIRE IT," he shouted. A large swath of projectiles impacted on the front of Eugene's mech and threw it backwards while cracking the glass. Hank shifted the dozer into gear and immediately drove forward. Eugene noticed what was happening too late. He tried to crawl his new mech suit out of the way, but Hank's Bulldozer was too fast and it entirely ran over the legs on his mech suit, crushing them mostly flat.

"God damn, what did we just fire?" Hank shouted in happiness.

"Gravel sir. Your armor no longer needed it, so it was repurposed into ammunition. It is finite and will have to be reloaded, but-"

"I get it, we fired a cubic fuck-ton gravel. Fucking awesome."

Chapter 14

Dractus lay below the crumpled car having what the humans might call a 'Fuck My Life' moment. One second he was happily carving up demon spawn, the next second he was laying on his back below a tiny human electric car. This turn of events did not make Dractus happy. On top of the rest of this shittiness his tail was crushed at an extremely painful angle beneath him. Dractus knew one thing for sure, whoever had done this to him was going to pay. He wasn't sure what the extent of his injuries were, but he was glad that it was a small car and not a large one. His ax was pinned to his chest otherwise he would have activated his laser blade skill and cut this thing off of him. Unfortunately because of the close proximity of the weapon to his body he didn't have a lot of options and he couldn't get any leverage to lift the car with his arms pinned to his chest.

Dractus wondered who would help him out of his current predicament. Hank was probably strong enough to move the car off of him, definitely not Jimmy or Cerulean. Hix ax had a concussive blast skill that he could use but in this confined space he might liquefy his internal organs with a stunt like that. As he continued to ponder different avenues of escape and forms of retribution for the one who had done this to him he noticed a few of the demon-spawn were getting closer to his position. He could see their clawed feet from his limited view under the deformed vehicle, and he could hear them skittering about. Surely they were looking for a way to get at him and eat his corpse, only he wasn't dead.

All of a sudden the weight of the car was ripped off of him. Dractus looked up to find his savior… It was the smart cables from Cerulean's ship. He had forgot all about that. To be fair a car had just landed on him so a lapse of critical thinking was understandable. Before the demons could descend upon him a few of the smart cables wrapped around their torsos and ripped them up into the air towards the hovering ship. Dractus watched and laughed as the smart cables dropped the creatures once they were about a 150 feet up. *Enough messing around, time to see if I can move*, thought Dractus. He fought through the aches and pains of moving and got to his feet. He tried to get to his feet quicker by pushing off with his tail but a great pain shot through it all the way up to his spine. He swung his tail around into his view and he notices a large piece of metal is embedded in it which he painfully dragged out.

"SOMEONE WILL PAY FOR THIS!" he shouted.

Above him he heard a large **WHOOMPH** noise. He recognized that sound. It was Cerulean's ship firing a special type of ammunition. What ammunition was yet to be seen. Dractus' eyes caught sight of a large black flying projectile about the size of a football. It had two stubby wings on the sides of it, meant to stabilize its descent. It flew until it landed among a pack of 30 some odd demon-spawn who had been headed his direction. A second later a great spout of fire flew into the air where the specialty ammunition had landed instantly killing most of the demon-spawn. The ones that remained alive were running around on fire trying to put themselves out.

In the distance Bertha's haunted cry called out "MY CHILDREN!" Surely she would be headed this way to investigate. She had to have been the one who threw the car at Dractus. He would head to where her children had died and wait for her.

***

Jimmy and Cerulean were fighting back to back, picking off Bertha's broodlings as they tried to rush them over and over again. Hank was still down the street causing hell. Jimmy was sending potshots Hank's way when he could in a futile attempt to keep Bertha off of his bulldozer. Earlier he had seen her beating on it and he had done his best to provide cover fire, but Bertha's hide was so thick that his rounds weren't having much effect. Sure if there were ten of him focusing fire she could probably eventually be brought down, but not by a lone human firing and one rifle.

Cerulean was only half paying attention to the battle, her attention was split with flying her ship remotely via her tablet. She was currently using it to lift a car off of Dractus. The headstrong asshole had been so busy cutting apart these spawnlings that he hadn't noticed a flying car... It wasn't that she didn't appreciate Dractus' battle tenacity, she just wished there was a little more critical thinking and less bloodlust every once in a while. Occasionally she

245

would take a reprieve from directing her ship with her tablet and fire off a beam of searing laser from her micro pistol.

That was a stop-gap though, she knew the only way to win this battle was with her ship. It was well past time to bring in the big guns. Luckily Hank's antics had drawn Bertha away from the town hall where most of the humans were. So if she lit Bertha up now there might be no casualties. She just had to get Hank out of there so she could drop some serious ordinance. *SHIT*, she could see a large hoard heading towards Dractus, *an incendiary shell should fix that*. Normally she would let him handle that kind of thing, but he had just been hit with a car...

Bertha let out one of her haunting screams when the shell landed and ignited, "MY CHILDREN!" She hoped Dractus was smart enough to get out of dodge if Bertha was headed his way.

She started directing her ship over to Hank's position, but she noticed her ship's cameras showed a dire situation. Some kind of giant robot was holding Hank's vehicle in place as Obsidian attempted to pry it open. She was readying some specialized ordinance when she saw Obsidian fall off the vehicle holding his face. What had Hank done to him? In her peripheral vision she saw three demon-spawn jump off of the nearest building and began heading her way. She drew her pistol and shot two of them in their disfigured faces, the third one scrambled away in fear. Once she brought her tablet back up she was just in time to see Hank's vehicle start to subtly shift. Its entire form began to look sleeker and stronger, then the tail on the back of the vehicle spun upward and released some kind of explosive shot into the robot's face. *GET EM HANK!*

She continued to watch in pure enjoyment as Hank ran over the retreating robot's legs. She saw Obsidian was trailing Hank's vehicle at a run, moving way faster than a rock man should be able to. He had something in his hands and he slapped it onto the back of Hank's bulldozer and then ran off the road into the nearest building. A second later the back of the bulldozer exploded into green flames, *NO!* Cerulean decided to do something she had never done before, she instructed the smart cables to grab Dractus, Jimmy, and herself. Quickly enough she was being pulled hundreds of feet into the air. She then instructed her ship to launch a specialty round of fire suppression foam at Hank's vehicle. Lastly she launched the smallest bunker buster in her arsenal at the building that Obsidian was taking cover in. She was delighted when she saw Obsidian's limp form thrown threw the street on fire as her ordinance went off and the building exploded, *asshole deserved it.* The smart cables set Dractus, Cerulean, and Jimmy down close to the smoking bulldozer.

"You robbed me of my revenge!" Dractus shouted.

Jimmy looked a little green, "Need more of a warning before you do that."

"Look," she said as she pointed at the bulldozer that was now partially a smoking ruin. The whole back end was melted, but the cab and front end looked intact.

"This is why you don't bring initiates to hunt demons for their first mission," said Dractus as he ran over to the bulldozer.

He tried to grab the door but it was so hot that is burned his hand, "Cerulean can you open this door?"

Before she could respond the door popped itself open. "That won't be necessary," said a small voice from somewhere inside the vehicle. Dractus was surprised to see a small holographic version of the Killdozer with a little smiling face.

"You have been marked a *friendly* in this vehicle's database. If you would please remove Hank from this vehicle quickly. It lacks the appropriate climate control to keep someone like him alive, and I had to keep the door locked to stop his enemies from killing him in his diminished state. Dractus grabbed Hank and unceremoniously dumped unconscious and overheated form on the ground a few feet away from the bulldozer which was still putting out so much heat that it was uncomfortable to be around.

"Get up lazy human," he said to Hank's unconscious form. Dractus felt something metal push up against the back of his neck. Out of the corner of his eye he could see it was Jimmy with his human weapon.

"If you drop my friend like that again I'll put a bullet in you," said Jimmy. Dractus casually smacked the barrel away.

"Don't be so melodramatic, he is alive."

Cerulean ran up and pulled out a tether out with a large bore needle on one end of it. She plugged one end of the tether into her tablet and jammed the other end into Hank's neck.

"GOD DAMN! Have you rude fuckers never heard of bedside manner? The man is obviously injured. Can we stop throwing him on the ground and jabbing him with needles?" shouted Jimmy.

Cerulean didn't reply immediately. Jimmy could see all kinds of data scrolling across her tablet in a language he didn't recognize.

"Well, what's the prognosis doc?" asked Jimmy.

"It's looking like extreme overheating, and the percussion from the blast did some damage to his soft tissues. He will recover, but he is going to be in an extreme amount of pain when he wakes up.

"We have a problem," said Dractus. Jimmy and Cerulean turned to see what he was talking about. Bertha was walking up the street towards them absolutely surrounded by the stained-humans. Her black oily skin was leaking sludge from a hundred wounds.

"ARBITERSSSS!!!!!!" she screamed, again it sounded like the voices of twenty or thirty women cranked up to decibels so loud that it actually shattered nearby car windows.

"That has to be every living human left in town that she has at her feet," said Jimmy.

"It's a smart move, she is stopping me from just blowing her up with my ship. She knows we won't kill the civilians," said Cerulean.

"YOU HAVE KILLED ENOUGH OF MY CHILDREN!" screamed Bertha. Then she grabbed one of the stained-humans and threw him into the air. She opened her maw and swallowed him whole on his downward arc. The Arbiter team watched in sick fascination as she chewed. The lump of the human she had eaten moved down her throat. Bertha's many wounds started closing in seconds right in front of the Arbiter team.

"She used his soul to power her own regeneration," said Dractus.

"I'll evacuate the humans using the smart cables," said Cerulean. "You two have to kill her or at least keep her busy while I clear them. Once they are all clear we will blow this entire town to hell."

"Easy enough, just delay a thirty-foot tall super-demon," Jimmy said sarcastically.

"Don't worry, I'll give you an unfair advantage," said Cerulean.

She went into deep concentration manipulating her tablet, before finally saying, "watch this." Every smart cable on Cerulean's ship jetted down at once grabbing all of the humans closest to Bertha. Simultaneously a specialty round of ammunition was fired that smacked Bertha directly in one of her armpits and detonated. There was no fire or explosion, not this time, just a massively expanding blue blob. It completely encompassed Bertha's right arm and began to harden. Bertha began to beat on it with her left arm to try to remove or break it up, but it was still sticky and drying in places and mostly she was just making a mess and degrading her situation.

"GO NOW," Cerulean shouted as she worked to clear as many civilians as she could with her smart cables.

Dractus ran off first, Jimmy on the other hand calmly walked forward twenty feet and went to a kneeling position and began trying to shoot out Bertha's eyes. Every shot he landed on Bertha's face made the stained-humans spasm. Dractus who had just ran past the first line of stained-humans smacked the flat side of his axe against the roof of a car and let out a concussive blast. The blast wave washed over the thralls who were trying to block his path and knocked them over like so many dominoes. He rushed through the gap he had made and took a running leap at Bertha. She raised her hand to swat him away, but he executed a perfect front flip and rolled into a ball, which reduced his size enough to avoid her swat. As soon as he was just past her arm still in mid-air he stretched his body back out. With his axe in both of his hands still flying forward he activated the laser edge and scored a deep gash on her underarm before finally landing on his feet. Jimmy had watched the entire maneuver and had to admit that Dractus was a first class badass.

As soon as Jimmy was sure Dractus was clear he opened fire on Bertha's face again. The same pattern repeated, every shot he landed caused the stained-humans to have a spasm. Then finally he did it, he landed a shot right in one of her eyes. While Dractus was dancing around her taking shallow cuts with his ax and avoiding the blows from her one free arm. Bertha roared in defiance and held her gushing and split eye that was shooting out a jet of black sludge thanks to Jimmy. All of the stained-humans went into a continuous spasm and then immediately stopped. The stained humans all turned in one direction, their eyes were focused on one point: Jimmy.

"Oh farts..." said Jimmy.

Half of the remaining stained-humans left the protective perimeter around Bertha to chase Jimmy. His first thought was to take cover at the bulldozer, but Hank and Cerulean were still there and he didn't want to drag danger their way. So instead he took off down an alley between two buildings. Once he was about 100 feet down it he turned around to check if he was being followed... A tidal wave of stained-humans fought to get into the alley entrance. All of them had pure hatred on their faces, and they were all trying to get to Jimmy.

"DOUBLE SHIT!" he shouted before running again. He saw a large building in the distance so he headed towards it. He glanced once behind himself to see at least 35 adults running like Kenyan sprinters to get after him. These weren't George Romero style shamblers, the fuckers could run. Jimmy ran towards the two plane double doors on the front of the plane brick building and threw them open. He headed inside, into darkness, he had to crack a door back open when it closed behind him to get enough light to see his surroundings. One thing he saw was a blue plastic chair with metal legs resting against the nearest wall, the kind they keep in schools. He grabbed it and ran it through the handles of the door. He wasn't sure if that would hold so he took his belt off and ran it through the handles as well cinching it tight. The second he was finished fists started pounding on the door.

He had to put some space between him and this angry mob. He turned around and looked down the dark hallway. There was an open door somewhere down the corridor with sunshine coming through it. He headed that way at a jog. He ripped around the corner and ran into the room. It was a sunlit classroom complete with children's drawings hanging everywhere and the alphabet painted at the top of every wall. There was 16 school desks in four rows of four and the standard teacher's desk and chalkboard at the front of the classroom. He went and sat at the teacher's desk to catch his breath. The chair should have been a dead give away that he was in some kind of school.

He was exhausted after the whole ordeal, and being chased through town. He leaned back and laid down on top of the desk and closed his eyes for just a second to collect his thoughts. That was when he heard the very distinctive sound of a basketball being dribbled from inside the room he was in. He shot up lightning quick and brought the AR15 to shoulder. There was five kids in the classroom now, he hadn't ever heard them come in. One of them who looked about nine was wearing basketball shorts and a jersey, he was dribbling a basketball. The one next to him was a girl of about seven, she was expertly doing tricks with a yo-yo even though her eyes never left Jimmy's face. The next one in line was a 12-year-old girl in thick glasses. She had a meter long ruler that she began to smack against one of her hands. The last two were identical ten-year-old twin girls in stained floral dresses with long blonde pigtails. They both had a pencil and a pencil sharpener in each of their hands. They were meticulously sharpening the pencils until they were razor sharp.

"Oh you gotta be shitting me."

The twins were the ones who responded. In perfect unison of course, "You hurt Big Bertha mister, now you gotta pay."

All of the children wielding their impromptu weapons advanced on him at once.

***

Cerulean was hard at work directing her smart cables to grab the rest of the civilians when she saw the last half of them break off to chase Jimmy. *What had that man done?* Oh well, less for her to worry about. She was just about finished clearing the last of them. Dractus was still busy dodging and weaving. Scoring blow after blow on Bertha. Cerulean glanced up from her work to check on Hank. His body was gone… She looked around and couldn't find him, she was worried but her mission was to clear the civilians and she couldn't fail. Some of them she was setting on rooftops with no easy ways to get down. A few she had shoved in dumpsters and set heavy things on top of them to make it hard to get out. She was having to get really creative to keep these people back. They were dead set on protecting Bertha. The faster she secured this area the faster she could evacuate her people and launch a bunker buster right down Bertha's throat.

Dractus was running out of stamina. Even with one arm, Bertha was one of the most dangerous opponents he had ever faced. He was waiting for her to get sloppy so he could score a fatal wound, but it hadn't happened yet. He dodges in under one of her arms as she swung at him, but he didn't have time to swing his ax so he simply extended one arm mid-run and dragged it along her ankle opening a thin angry wound. Then he rolled out of her range as her giant fist flew forward to grab him. He had cut her more times then he could count but her body was massive and powerful now. If death by a thousand cuts was a real thing he still had about 900 more to go… Bertha roared directly at him knowing she wasn't quick enough to grab him. Dractus surprised her by roaring right back. Then she did something that Dractus wasn't expecting. She ripped a stop sign out of the ground and threw it at him.

It took all of his agility to avoid the missile with a mighty leap in which he had to twist his body in mid-air to fully avoid the projectile. As soon as he landed Bertha threw a loose handful of wood and brick at him that she had pulled off of the corner of a building. Dractus knew he didn't have time to run or dodge. So he centered himself and channeled his energy into his axe creating a temporary force-field. The debris bounced off of it, but visibly shoved him backwards. Bertha had a strategy that would keep him on the defense now, *SHIT!* All she had to do was keep throwing things at Dractus that were big enough to maim him and he couldn't attack.

All of a sudden fire sprung up along Bertha's shoulders. Then more fire exploded at her feet. A figure came running down the road. It was Hank! He had two black eyes and every inch of his exposed skin was beet red. He had a sledge hammer in one hand braced over his shoulder, and a bottle with a rag on fire in it in the other hand. He threw the bottle just as Bertha turned to assess the new threat. The bottle hit her squarely in the chest and exploded covering her in sticky flames. Dractus knew he wouldn't have another opportunity like this so he rushed in as Bertha tried to brush off the flames. Hank rushed in from the other side. She had to decide what the bigger threat was which was hard to do while on fire. She picked Dractus. She backhanded him so hard that he went flying through a glass storefront nearby. This meant the path was wide open for Hank who was running with a sledgehammer held high over head.

The only target on her that he could even come close to reaching was her knee. So that's what he went for. Hank had been breaking things with a sledgehammer his whole life. He used every ounce of strength he had and all of his years of experience. The sledgehammer connected with her knee and blew right through her skin and muscle, slamming dead on the bone. The shock of the hit reverberated up Hank's arms and he felt something crunch. Bertha screamed and fell over, parts of her still on fire. Hank has just enough time to yank his sledgehammer out and get out of the way of her fall. The sledgehammer made a very disturbing sucking sound when he pulled it out. As she screamed and thrashed Hank walked carefully up to her head. She was in a world of pain, so much so that she couldn't even focus on Hank's position. That didn't mean a flailing limb couldn't cripple him though, he knew that and was careful to avoid them.

Hank raised his sledgehammer high and waited for an opening. As soon as he saw one he ran forward and brought it down on Bertha's sizable head that was now as big as a large microwave. The sledgehammer landed squarely and punctured part of her skull, silencing her.

"Nice shot," said Cerulean who was standing about ten feet away.

Hank noticed that he hadn't felt or seen an evil soul leave her body, "I should hit her again, I think she is still breathing."

"Don't, we will take her alive. She will be questioned and disposed of at The Hall of Arbiters."

"Well should I put her out, she is still on fire," said Hank who pointed at a portion of Bertha's shoulder that was still burning.

"Give it a few minutes to burn, we don't want her getting unruly during the trip."

"Are Dractus and Jimmy alive?"

"Yep."

"How can you tell?"

"I've got their vitals here. I have transponders in both of their suits," she said as she held up her tablet.

"Of course you do."

"You did good here Hank. You helped save a lot of lives."

"Where are Eugene and Obsidian?"

"I've got a satellite tracking Eugene. You know I actually thought he was a robot at first. He is crawling his broke-ass mech a few miles from here through the woods. I have no idea where Obsidian is."

"Well let's collect our team and go hunt those fuckers down."

"That's what makes you a good Arbiter Hank. You are beat to shit, you just had your organs partially liquefied, and you still want to hunt demons."

An explosion in the forest behind town drew their attention. Some kind of giant rocky spear was flying straight up out of the atmosphere.

"Well, that's Obsidian's ship."

"Shit is Eugene with him?"

"No."

"I have one request, no, one demand. Eugene is mine."

***

As soon as Hank had gotten back up to the ship he limped over to med-bay and passed out. He woke up in the morning covered head to toe in the transparent medical wrap with the blue lines running through it. Literally even his face was covered in it. Cerulean had been kind of enough to cut holes for his eyes and mouth in it, which was thoughtful. Hank tested his feet and found that he could move with only minimal pain. Which was good since yesterday he had felt like he was a few minutes from death's door. Hank found Cerulean drinking coffee in her pilot's chair.

"Is that Earth coffee?"

"Yep, giving it a try. Want some?"

"Take me to Eugene. It's time to finish this."

This was a feud years in the making. Eugene had hurt too many people. He needed to pay. Cerulean understood without Hank having to say more. She flew the ship over Eugene's location and told Hank to meet her at the back ramp once he had pants on. He looked down and realized he was still only wearing the transparent medical wrap, *whoops*. Hank went back to the med-bay where his backpack full of clothes were. He threw on some pants and boots, he didn't even spend the time to find a shirt. He met Cerulean at the back ramp. They were hundreds of feet in the air. Cerulean tapped a few things on her tablet and a smart cable came up into the back ramp and hovered in the air a few inches off of the deck next to Hank. The end of the smart cable had a handle like device on it.

"Put your foot through there and hold on tight. It will lower you to the ground. When you are ready put your foot back through and it will pull you back up here a few seconds later. Make sure you have a good grip,"

Hank nodded and did as instructed. He soon found himself descending dozens of feet per second. He was too pissed off at Eugene to be afraid of the stunt he was pulling. Images of Eugene cutting Suzie flashed through his head as he headed towards the alpine forest below. Hank idly wondered how many people Eugene had hurt and murdered since then. The two teenagers from Winthrop town hall… Bile rose in Hank's throat he was so angry. The smart cable started slowing as it neared the ground. Hank could see Eugene's broken mech laying a few feet from a pond. He must have used the arms on it to drag it this far. Eugene was sitting on the shore with his feet in the water, he didn't know Hank was coming. Once the cable was about 12 feet up and still falling Hank jumped and landed hard.

"EUGENE!"

Eugene's head spun around and his eyes opened wide in fear.

"That's right Eugene, you should be afraid! I'm going to make you pay for everything!" Hank felt tears on his face and he wasn't sure why. His face felt hot and his body was shaking. Eugene got up and tried to limp away from Hank. Eugene's leg still had a hole through it from the rail gun so he couldn't move fast.

"YOU FUCKING COWARD," Hank yelled. Hank took off after Eugene with long strides and shoved him into the mud at the edge of the pond. Hank shoved Eugene's head into the water and held it there. Eugene struggled to breathe, but Hank wouldn't let him up. When Eugene's struggles begin to feel weaker Hank pulled him out and threw him onto the pond's shore. Eugene sputtered and rolled onto his side, coughing up water. Hank only gave him enough time to take ten good breaths and then he was on him again, hitting him. He broke his nose first, then a few of his fingers, before he gave Eugene another minute to rest.

"Those kids in the town hall, WHAT WERE YOU DOING TO THEM?" Hank shouted.

Eugene's eyes were wild, looking around for some way to get himself out of this situation. Hank smacked him across the face a couple of times.

"YOU TELL ME OR I'LL KILL YOU!"

"I raped them, I raped them Hank. I'm a sick man, I need help. I-" Eugene sputtered out.

Teenagers… Kids… he had raped them.. Hank got up and kicked Eugene a few times until blood shot out of Eugene's mouth. Hank walked away crying. He had done *that*… to kids…. Hank knew he should take Eugene alive to face whatever brand of justice the Arbiter's practiced. He knew the Arbiters were straight shooters, he knew there would be a fair trial. Fuck that. He had hurt kids. Hank stormed back over to Eugene who was trying to crawl away.

"I can't give all of the people you hurt justice, but I can make you pay."

"No Hank don't. You are an Arbiter, Obsidian told me about your kind. Arrest me! ARREST ME!!! PLEASEE!!!"

"No."

Hank grabbed one of Eugene's arms and put one of his feet on Eugene's chest, and then began pulling and pulling. Eugene's screams only got louder and more feral the longer Hank pulled, but Hank never stopped pulling. Hank felt several pops and a crack, he was sure he had ripped the arm out of its socket. Hank walked off and sat on a large rock as Eugene continued to scream. When Eugene finally stopped screaming and was just gently crying Hank walked back over to him.

"Time for the other one."

***

Cerulean was waiting at the back ramp when Hank came back. Hank had jumped in the lake to get the copious amounts of blood and mud off of him so he was soaking wet. Cerulean surprised him by wrapping him up in a giant hug that he didn't realize he needed. She pulled his head close and whispered in his ear.

"Justice isn't always pretty. If you ever need to talk, I'm here."

He nodded and left her to go get dry clothes and to visit his friends. Dractus and Jimmy were laying in med-bay beds a few feet from each other talking and laughing about something when Hank came into the room.

"God damn it's good to see you guys," said Hank. "Even you, you french-kissin son of a bitch," he said to Dractus. Drac of course just smiled and sent his lizard tongue flying around a few times. Everyone in the room laughed.

"So I know what happened to him," said Hank pointing at Dractus. "But what happened to you?" he said while pointing at Jimmy.

Jimmy looked around a bit and seemed nervous to answer, "Oh you know, I fought off twenty of those enthralled humans. Big ones, they were lumberjacks complete with axes and saws."

"Don't believe this lying bastard," Dractus said while laughing. "Cerulean told me she found him in a school surrounded by beat up children."

"Oh it wasn't like that! Those fuckers stabbed me with pencils and tried to choke me out with a yo-yo string. What was I supposed to do, they were kids!"

Hank couldn't respond for a while because he was laughing so hard. "A yo-yo string? What other weapons of mass destruction did they use on you, a kazoo?" Dractus and Hank erupted into a new round of laughter.

"Oh fuck you guys," said Jimmy.

Epilogue

"How's Bertha?" asked Hank.

"Extremely secured, and connected to an IV bag full of enough tranquilizers to put something twice her size down. Speaking of that, I'll have to monitor her situation. She seems to be shrinking without any new food to eat. I've only heard of a couple of species in the known universes that can change their body mass like that, and I don't recognize whatever she is. My scans are coming up inconclusive as well... She is in smart cables so they will keep contracting as she shrinks. That in itself is redundant anyway with how drugged and injured she is," Cerulean replied.

"And the people in Winthrop?" asked Hank

"It seems as long as Bertha is deeply unconscious they are free of her influence. I would bet her control has a pretty short range as well. So once we fly out of here they will continue to be fine. Speaking of that, I'm ready to leave as soon as we pick up Dractus. He should be done firebombing the rest of Bertha's nest any time now. Got any last minute things you need to do before we leave?"

"I wouldn't mind loading up a crate full of bacon, cigars, and good whiskey before."

"We have variants of all of that on Prime. That's what we call the planet that the Hall of Arbiters is on."

"I figured as much. You still going to give me that personal tour?"

"Hank, let's skip the foreplay. We are Arbiters, we could die any second. Kiss me you big dumb lug."

Hank wrapped his large muscular arms around Cerulean and reached down to grab her well defined butt. He lifted her up and she wrapped her legs around his waist. They stared deeply into each others eyes. Jimmy chose that moment to walk into the room.

"Hey listen, I was thinking- Shit, y'all should lock the door if you are trying to play hide the weasel!" said Jimmy.

"Jimmy we are leaving the planet soon. If you got anything to do, now is the time before it's too late," said Hank before he sealed and locked the door.

Jimmy did have something to do. He popped open his phone and sent an email to a freelance hacker who was on his payroll. The email had four words in it: Burn it all down. The hacker received the email and sent out a series of emails thick with attachments to news and law enforcement agencies all over the country. The emails included up to date reports on everything Jimmy was working on and all of the suspicions he had about who was taking payoffs from whom. The information he had would lead the police to serious evidence of government corruption.

Some of it would even point to congressmen and senators taking payoffs from organized crime. A second set of emails was sent off to different criminal organizations. This set had the new aliases of every hardcore criminal who had turned on their own people and testified in exchange for immunity and entrance into the Witsec program. Jimmy never did understand letting a criminal go in order to punish other criminals.

The final set of emails went out to everyone in organized crime who Jimmy figured had a chance at redemption. People who were born into it criminal organizations, or who got into it out of necessity. People who only stayed in because their families would be in danger if they left. These emails had directions to run, with banking information for overseas accounts that they could use to establish new lives, and directions on how to get a new identity.

Jimmy had been holding onto this information for a long time now, and adding to it regularly. He always figured when this day came he would be hiding out on a beach somewhere. This information is going to rock the world and people all over the planet are going to be hunting the man who released it. To bad he won't be on the planet.

End of book 1

If you want to keep reading more Gamelit books from Cory Gaffner, try out his Oliver's Universe series. Book one for it is out now and it's called:

Oliver's Wishes

The first chaper for it is at the end of this book if you would like a sample.

A note from the author:

Hi all, thank you so much for reading my book, it means so much to me! If you want to talk to me about the book please do! Join my facebook group at the link below and we can discuss your likes and dislikes about it, or things you would like to see happen in the series.

https://www.facebook.com/groups/CoryGaffnerBooks

If you noticed a typo or something that needed to be grammatically fixed in this book PLEASE post about it in my facebook group OR shoot me an email at CoryGaffner@yahoo.com

Please Please Please leave me a written review on Amazon, it would really help me out! I can't explain how very important that is. Until a book gets 50 mostly positive reviews on Amazon (meaning 4 and 5 stars), Amazon basically hides it from most searches. Also if you have the time, head over to my author page on Amazon.com and Press the little "+Follow" button below my picture. If you don't press the Follow button then Amazon won't tell you when my next books are coming out. Including the sequel to this one.

If you enjoyed this book at all, I highly recommend you check out my other books as well.

The next page starts the sample for Oliver's Wishes.

Sample of Oliver's Wishes
Chapter 1
The Old Man

Gotta find the boy before I bleed out. For 50 years I've been trying to pass on this burden, to find the right person to protect it. I've failed that mission. My time is up, I have to give it to someone else before the Cabal gets me, and they will get me. The Cabal has killed everyone I have ever called brother. I don't know how they found me this time, but it doesn't matter. They underestimated me. They underestimated the *old man*. I may look old, but I stay in good shape and I have a few tricks up my sleeve that they aren't expecting. The pain in my side just flared up, ow. I'm using my hand to try to stop the light but steady blood flow. *It would be nice to pull over and pressure wrap it*, I think as I feel the precious blood seeping between my fingers, no time for that now though. I'm old enough to be honest with myself. Real self-honesty that can only come with age and hard-earned wisdom, and I can tell no amount of pressure is going to fix this wound. None of that matters now though, gotta find the boy.

I'm careening through traffic in a stolen Cabal truck trying to get to the grocery store where the boy works... The boy's name is Oliver. The only one to pass all of the tests... Well, all of the tests except for one. The test that some of my brothers considered the most important: The intelligence test. He truly failed that one, and then some. Oliver is as dumb as a bag of rocks, I'm not even sure why I screened him. Something about him just always felt *right*. He was old fashioned, sincere, and honest. He truly wanted to help people. The only thing holding him back from being amazing was his IQ, which was a very low 69. An IQ of 69 meant he had a mild mental disability. If he didn't have that disability this kid could have been a world leader. Instead he was a bagger at a grocery store. Cursed by some congenital mistake. Day in and day out helping people out to their car with their groceries, and all with a genuine smile on his face.

I had screened so many young men and women... So many... All of them, one by one, had failed. Petty, jealous, greedy, mean spirited, cracking easily under pressure, eventually they all showed their true face. The times are changing. It used to be easier to find candidates when things were simpler. People use to just be happy to have a home and a family, not anymore though. Now people can't even stand in line to buy a pair of sneakers without attacking each other like rabid beasts. Hell, I had seen people attack honored friends and family just for having different political beliefs. Don't get me wrong, greed and malice have always existed, they were just... *rarer*. If I couldn't have the perfect candidate, I would take the loyal one, the one that should he ever falter and use its twisted power... He would at least try to do something good with it, I doubt she would let that happen, but he would try. I could feel it in my own bones, he would try. Oliver is far from perfect, but he has a good heart, and that is what the world really needs, more people with good hearts.

The grocery store is coming up now and I can already tell I'm going way too fast. I yank the wheel to the side to try and avoid the curb and the stop sign in my path, but the blood on my fingers makes the wheel slip in the opposite direction, and inadvertently barrel through a few signs, some bushes, and finally into a parked car. I would be pissed if this truck was mine, ha ha oh well, the Cabal can afford a new one. *Gotta get to him,* it's 11am on a Thursday so I know he is working. I know his schedule like the back of my hand and the boy is like clockwork. The boy is a dam in a flash-flood of malfeasance, he would rather fall on his sword than miss a day of work, I know he is here. I have the *package* wrapped in a towel that is getting bloodier by the second under my arm. I need to make sure no cameras see it. I have to pretend the only reason for the towel is to stem the flow of blood. I can't leave any clues for the Cabal.

As I'm running across the parking lot I hear squealing tires behind me, damn the Cabal is fast and efficient, I'll give them that much. On the other hand they were just outsmarted and defeated by one wily old man, HAHA! As I enter the grocery store and look around for Oliver people start screaming. Probably because I'm leaking blood all over the place and I have a 1911 combat pistol dangling from my right hand. My left arm and hand are busy holding the towel to my wound, the towel with the package tucked neatly inside of it.

I spot Oliver on his usual lane, bagging groceries like any other day. That boy is a sentinel. No, that's not right. Oliver is 25 now, he is no mere boy. He is a man. A man of honor, and soon the man who will defend the most dangerous item in the world. Everyone starts screaming and running as I head towards Oliver. Not Oliver though, he keeps doing his job, bagging the groceries that come down the conveyor belt. I don't know if he continues despite the screams because he is doggedly determined or just too stupid to notice. Either way it doesn't matter, he is the rock in the storm.

I jump on top of Oliver, my entire large frame knocking him to the ground. I may look like a feeble old man but I'm a warrior, *I'm dense.* I make sure to cup my hand behind his head as we fall so I don't accidentally give him a head injury. Once we both hit the ground I carefully unwrap the towel between us, wary of the cameras in the store. I know where every camera is because I have surveyed this store a thousand times. I carefully remove the lamp from inside the confines of the towel and tuck it into the pocket on the front of the boys apron. I have planned this maneuver hundreds of times, I was just praying and hoping I would have never have to use it. I was hoping to have died with my secret. I was hoping to be buried with the lamp so eventually it would be forgotten with the passing of time. The Cabal have forced my hand though.

Once I have the lamp inside of Oliver's apron, I look down at his fierce face. He is confused but not scared. My left hand is still cupped behind his head so I crank his face next to mine and whisper the most important thing he will ever hear.
"Keep it secret, Keep it safe. Tell no one, never use it." Now that my arm isn't holding the towel to my wound, my blood is flying all over Oliver. There is so much more I want to tell him... I wish I could tell him that I'm proud of him. That he is the son I never had. That he has impressed me every day. That despite his disability he is a beacon of the human spirit, but I don't have time for that. The cameras are watching me and they can't know that I have entrusted Oliver with this burden, they can't know what he means to me.

Strong hands grab my shoulders and lift me upwards, and a second pair of hands rip the pistol away from me. When they lift me up, I close my eyes and play dead. I barely crack my eyes open enough to see two members of the Cabal wearing black suits and I'm sure they have fake law enforcement credentials on them. I let my legs out a little bit on purpose and they have to both grab me before I hit the floor, amateurs... They've just made a fatal mistake, you never grab a rattlesnake by its tail. I grab the closest ones bicep gently and pretend I'm barely coming into consciousness, and that I'm just grabbing him for support. I push the sleeve of his suit up and expose the flesh of his forearm and then I do something they don't expect. My body comes alive, straining every muscle I have I yank my body towards him, his body towards me, and I take a bite. My teeth shred the man's skin like so much paper and his blood rushes into my mouth.

A tiger is always most vicious in his death throes and I know I don't have a lot of time left. The other agent grabs my head to try to dislodge me so I turn my face towards him and spit out the blood and chunks of flesh from my mouth right into his face and eyes. I don't know if he is blinded or just disgusted but he fully lets go of me to try and wipe the gore away, another mistake. I feel my strength waning with the blood loss but I still have enough in me for a haymaker of epic proportions. I dump 50 years of hatred and fear into my punch and deliver it right to the bloody agent's face. He falls down and the his head bounces off of the tile floor of the grocery store making a sound like a gunshot. By god I may have killed him! I've still got it, *whew-hoo!*

Fighting isn't always about who the best fighter is, or who has the biggest muscles. Sometimes it's about who wants to win more, and who is willing to do the darkest things. Today, that man is me. Time to make a hasty escape, I have to lead the trail further away from Oliver. I look to the front of the store but there might be more Cabal agents out there, better take the back route. I glance at Oliver one more time as he is rising to his feet but I'm well past out of time, so I have to run. *I'll miss you*

Oliver. I make sure to grab my trusty old 1911 before moving on and head towards the back of the store. I have to enact the last part of my plan to throw off the Cabal. This plan should set them back years of searching, maybe forever.

I head to the back of the store and into the storage area, I'm passing by scared employees everywhere. Maybe they think I'm here to shoot the place up, I don't know, not my concern. Once I get to the very back of the store there is a box truck there that has just backed into one of the truck docks to unload produce. The driver is just getting out and sliding the rear storage door of the truck up. He doesn't know what's going on at the store yet. The unfortunate bugger turns around to find me, the bloody old man, pointing a 1911 combat pistol right at his face.

"Hand over the keys if you want to live," the truck driver is too stunned to move, "NOW!" I shout. He hands me the keys and I swish my gun to the side indicating that he should go and he takes off running.

I hop into the cab worried it might be a manual transmission, I haven't driven one of those for over 30 years but it's just an automatic. I slam the truck into gear and gas it, I feel weird movement and notice the back of the truck is spewing heads of lettuce and bundles of carrots everywhere. Whoops I forgot to close the back, haha, oh well. Maybe it's the blood loss but watching the vegetables fly all over the road as I swerve back and forth is really making me laugh. As I'm watching the vegetables in my rearview mirror I notice at least ten black SUV's following my trail, that has to be Cabal operatives. Fuck it, let's leave some more bread crumbs! I keep jerking the wheel back and forth to spew more vegetables all over the road. My destination is only a few miles away.

As I careen into the worst neighborhood in town, a hobo with a grocery cart is a little too slow to get out of my way. I try to jerk the wheel away from him but I wasn't quick enough to miss his cart which goes airborne. "HAHA, TWENTY POINTS!" I'm not sure where I got this point system from or why a hobo's grocery cart constitutes twenty, but I won't argue with myself. I have to do things to stop myself from passing out from blood loss, and playing a fun game might help. The house I'm looking for is just ahead so I swerve the truck hard and pull the emergency brake. The truck spins sideways and gets on two wheels for a moment before falling back down onto all four tires and finally stopping.

I reach into my jacket pocket for one of my final surprises that I can leave for the Cabal: a medium sized piece of Semtex, a plastic explosive. I've already jammed a pre-programmed five minute detonator into it. I stick it up under the console of the truck so it won't be visible upon a quick inspection and flip the switch to turn it on. All someone would have to do to turn it off would be to flip the same switch that I just used, but they will never find it in time, I hope. I left the truck parked right across the middle of the road horizontally so the Cabal following me will have a hard time getting around it, and I head towards the house, my future tomb.

The home is large and dilapidated, a two story home with many bedrooms. It hasn't looked good in over twenty years, and I've made sure of that. I own the home through a shell company that occasionally gets sued over the status of this very house, but greasing the right palms can make anything happen in the legal and political world. The house has peeling paint, broken and boarded up windows, and visible graffiti all over it, and the last I checked is an active drug den for crackheads and dealers. I'm really getting woozy now from the continued slow but steady blood loss but I don't have much further to go. As I walk up to the front door I notice the front yard is absolutely littered in cigarette butts, used syringes, and even the occasional brass casing from a fired round.

The front door is cracked open, the occupants don't even bother to lock it. Why would they though? No one in their right mind would enter this house uninvited. When I enter the dark house it takes a second for my eyes to adjust. There is minimal light in here, it's coming through in slants and shafts through some of the boarded up windows. The inside is much like the outside: disgusting. There are sleeping drug addicts everywhere curled up on dirty sleeping bags. I hear the sound of feet shuffling coming from the back of the house as one of the dealers comes to see who just opened the front door. I still have the 1911 in my right hand and I don't want to scare the young pup just yet so I put it slightly behind my back.

He comes barging into the entry room like he owns the place, I suppose in his mind he does. He is going for the imposing look. I guess that look helps him keep his usual customers in line, or maybe it just makes him feel good about himself. He looks like you would expect, covered in tattoos, white ball cap slightly slanted up, baggy pants, some stupid t-shirt with shit on it that I don't care to understand, and a track jacket with a hood which he has up, resting on top of his ball-cap.

"Nigga, you done walked into the wrong fuckin house. You don't look like you here to buy my shit, so you best get steppin," he says and sneers at me as he grips the handle of a cheap pistol that has been hastily stuffed into his waistband. I can't help but laugh at his pejorative, seeing as how this particular pretend tough guy is white.

"Actually young man, this is my house," I say calmly.

"Old man, you lost as fuck. This is Rooster's territory, and if he comes out here he is going to cap your ass." Young people give up information to freely. He just let me know there is at least one more drug dealer in the house and the second drug dealer is armed.

"Actually I'm going to cap him," I calmly say, and bring the 1911 out from behind my back.

When the drug dealer sees my pistol he starts to draw his but he isn't quick enough and I put a few rounds through his chest. The gunshots wake up some of the crackheads and they scramble out through the door behind me, but most of them are too high to notice or care. Maybe some of them are even hoping this is the time they get put out of their misery. I walk over to the downed drug dealer who is busy choking on his own blood "Young man, it isn't nice to deal drugs. Also FORTY POINTS!" I'm still confused as to where I'm getting these point values from, but if a hobo's grocery cart was twenty then a gangster drug dealer is at least forty. Time to clean up the rest of the riff-raff, the last thing I need is to get shot in the back by some drug dealer while I'm finishing up my life's work.

I head towards the back of the first floor and start hearing heavy rap music so I head towards the noise. The noise leads me to the farthest room from the front of the house. The door to the room is closed all the way and the music coming through it is still loud. I bet good ole Rooster didn't even hear me shoot his doorman. I try the handle but it's locked so I start banging on it. "GO AWAY" a female shouts through the door. I keep banging until I hear the music turn off.

"This better be good" the same female says. A young woman who looks maybe 18 but is probably younger opens the door which actually opens up into quite a nice little office. There are lavish rugs overlapping all over the ground, a pile of car stereos in the corner, a leather couch with a brand new gaming system in front of it, and a large cherry oak desk in the corner. Behind the desk sits an African American man dressed in what can only be called 'modern pimp clothes'. The young woman has gone back to stand by his side and by the look of her pupils she is high as hell.

"Hello there, are you Rooster?" I ask him in my most pretend fragile old man voice.

"Who da fuck is asking?" he says back in a deep voice.
"I'll take that as a yes," I say. I swing the gun around and Rooster's hands fly below the desk he is sitting behind, probably to try and retrieve his own firearm. I pull the trigger first, before he can grab whatever he is going for. His brains paint the young woman next to him and the wall behind him.
"ONE HUNDRED POINTS!" Minor drug lords are worth at least one hundred points, right? I look at the scared young woman covered in blood, and bits of skull and can't help but feel bad for her. My sympathy wins out and I go over to her and lift her chin up.

"Stop doing drugs and letting men like this use you. You are someone important. Go to school, get a job, raise children, and teach them to be good. Now run away or I'm going to shoot you in the head." The woman runs off, out of the house, good.

I reach under the desk to see what Rooster was looking for and come up with a sawed-off double barrel shotgun, sweet. I head back to the front of the house to peek out the front door and see exactly what I was expecting to see. The Cabal SUV's are all pulling around the truck I left in the middle of the road and starting to surround the house. I look down at my watch, *any second now.* The Semtex I left in the truck explodes and flips two of the Cabal SUVs over onto their sides, men get out screaming and on fire. The inside of one of the vehicles is painted in blood. "FIVE HUNDRED POINTS!" The rest of the vehicles in the Cabal convoy barrel through the downed cars and start spreading out, they won't bunch up again.

Next to the door frame I knock on the moldy drywall in a few places, slowly moving my hand back and forth as I continue knocking until I hear the hollow space that I had put there years before. Once I find it I lean back and shoot one of the barrels of Rooster's shotgun at the wall with my eyes closed. Sharp pieces of wood cut my face and chest but I'm too tired to care. I reach into the hole I just made and pull out a metal box. I pop the clasps on each side of it and reach inside to find my prize: An exact replica of the lamp I just gave to Oliver. Once the Cabal see this thing they are going to go crazy.

I get close to the door frame again, and lean my head slightly around the corner. The Cabal are out of their trucks now, taking cover and ready to fire on me. I push the nose of the shotgun around the corner and then pull the trigger, firing blindly. The barrel is probably too short to hurt them at this range but might as well keep them honest. Then I stick my hand out the door with the lamp in it and yell "HOLD YOUR FIRE!" I walk half my silhouette into the frame of the door and look out, with the lamp still held high in my hands.

"If you want it, come and get it!" Then I duck back inside and rounds pepper the door frame where I was just standing. Normally I would be dead in a situation like this, high velocity modern rounds would fly right through the low quality wood and drywall and shred me up something fierce, but when I had this house built I had a thick piece of steel embedded into the drywall that I'm currently standing behind right now. So instead of being shredded I hear the comforting sounds of bullets dinging off of steel.

Once the incoming fire stops I start walking towards the back of the house. As I walk I turn around and fire my 1911 through the open doorway to stop any Cabal agents that might be thinking of entering. At the back of the house, around a turn in the hall is a small closet for the water heater which hasn't worked in decades. I pull the panel off of the water heater which has a keypad underneath and I type in the password. The water heater starts making a strange noise and then it pulls itself back into the wall behind it and exposes a stairway that leads down into a hidden basement.

I march down into the room and lights automatically turn on, "Authorization Black Sky," I say out loud and a small pedestal in the center of the room starts rising from the floor. Once it rises about four feet up it stops, and a loud hiss emits from it as a small metal door opens on the front of it. I reach my hand inside and pull out the dead man detonator sitting on a charging station, and I clamp my hand over the trigger. All I have to do now is to let go of this trigger, and the whole house is going to blow. I'm going to wait though and take some Cabal bastards with me. On one of the sides of the room, a portion of the wall slides up exposing 8 older model televisions, they all have different views around the house from hidden cameras, and two of them are black. Some of the cameras must have gone out during the years since I had them installed.

I can see Cabal soldiers armoring up and preparing to raid the house. Some are heading to the back and side entrances and some are stacking up at the front door. They are communicating via radio to each other to synchronize their entry. I watch all three teams throw flashbangs into their respective entrances and wait for them to pop before rushing inside. On the front lawn four additional different Cabal teams begin to rush up to the house to join their cohorts already inside. At the back of their vehicle barricade I see a distinguished looking Japanese man, something about him gives me the creeps, and makes goosebumps form on my flesh. I look back to the screens and see one of the Cabal tactical entry teams has almost found the entrance to my hidden basement.

I back up a few steps and face the stairway as the heavily armored men come bursting into the room and surround me. I have the lamp in one hand now and the dead man switch in the other. "There are so many Cabal soldiers on this property right now, you guys are worth at least ten thousand points" I say as I show them the dead man switch. The lead Cabal operative notices what it is and tries to key his throat mic to warn the others "EVERYONE GET BAC------". Then the world went up in flames.

<u>END OF OLIVER'S WISHES SAMPLE</u>

About the Author

Cory Gaffner spends most of his days working with foster kids in a few different roles. He has been and sometimes is a full-time foster father. He is an honorably discharged combat veteran of the U.S. Army. His hobbies include throwing knives at stuff, competition shooting, and playing video games late into the night.

He currently lives in Arizona with his wife, sons, and two guard dogs. Cory is an independent author meaning he writes, edits, produces, pays for, and publishes his own books. That means he needs your help! The best way to help him is by leaving a constructive review that will help potential readers find his books!

Cory is a very laid back dude, so if you would like to get a hold of him join his facebook group "The Literary Works of Cory Gaffner."